THE TRIAD TREE

A NOVEL

By

Annette Cass-Landis

In the Brambles

Seeds of "we"

Grew roots of three

The Triad Tree

To Inge

This book is fiction. Although based on historical events, the places, incidents and geography are imagined or used fictitiously. My characters created in part on the lives of real people are fictional. They are the actors who persevered through five years of political and social upheaval under Nazi rule. Their stories disclose a history that speaks for itself

Annette Cass-Landis.

ISBN: 145360037X

ISBN-13: 9781453600375

ACKNOWLEDGMENTS

My deepest gratitude to Professor Emeritus, Patricia Hunt-Perry, Ph.D., whose steadfast support and assistance in every possible way and who guided this book to completion, has made her an invaluable companion in the preparation of this work.

For their contributions, many thanks to Judith Greber, Dennis Murphy, and Leo Maclaughlin, (now in Heaven). Each in their own way gave me the courage to write this book.

I would also like to thank Sam Morris for assisting in the research, Irene Alterman and Frank Welton for advice on German language and culture, and Nancy Oshinsky and Marylin Cioffi for reading and critiquing the manuscript.

I especially want to thank my editor, Alison Owings. Her knowledge of the political times, understanding of German ways, and fluency in the German language, broadened the dimensions of this book.

Most of all many thanks and unbounded appreciation to my two wonderful sons, Philip and Russell, who attended to my numerous computer emergencies and kept the beast purring. Without their expertise and their unfailing willingness to fix it, I would not yet have reached this day.

CHAPTER ONE

The Legacy

" Melly... Mellee....come to the window. It's me Melly, open up"

Melly Goldschmidt Wallerstein opened the window two inches, just enough to keep out the cold yet enough to be heard when she called to the street below. She pulled aside one corner of the shade to see if she could, who was calling and ringing the bell so stubbornly, which she, just as stubbornly, was trying to ignore. Usually she sent Kurt to investigate these mid-day intrusions. But from two rooms away, she could hear the record player and the haunting soprano of LaBoheme's Mimi, as she lay dying in her lover's garret. Melly knew there was another ten minutes before the opera ended and that until the final sound was sung and the last note of the orchestra rendered, Kurt would not hear, or pretend not to hear, either the bell or her calling him to take care of whoever was ringing it. When he was with his music he was completely into himself.

"*Ja*, who is down there?" Melly called to the street below, the insistent bell setting her nerves on edge. "Who is ringing?" She had lifted one year old Inge onto her shoulder, rubbing her small back in light circular motions, as if to make up for the interruption of her baby's lunch.

"It's me Melly... Hildy....Hildy Frankel....your best customer.... open up."

"Not now. I'm feeding Inge. Besides I'm closed. It's Mothers day. Come back tomorrow."

" I just need a piece of blue lace for a collar. Do you have?"

Melly searched her memory. Blue lace...blue lace..."*Ja, yes* I do." Then with an excited change of mind she called to the voice below, "Wait, right away, yes, I open up."

How different from just a few months ago, before the Nazis broke into the store below her home and slashed the dressmaker dummies and destroyed the glass showcase and screamed at the customers, "To hell with the Jews. Never buy from Jews. You have already been warned not to go to Jew stores."

Despite Melly's resolve to keep that memory from surfacing her thoughts uncontrollably flew there. Even now, safe in her home over the store, the faces of those Nazis and of her cringing, terrified customers flashed in her mind, as she recalled the horror of that episode.

It was even more horrific than that one day boycott of Jewish stores weeks before. Then the Nazis had stormed into the streets and held signs and shouted warnings not to buy "in Jew stores." Holding night sticks, two of them blocked the entrance to GOLDSCHMIDTS and turned people away. But in a few days customers returned, and within a week or two business was as brisk as it had always been. Even a bit better, it seemed to Melly.

But now, except for a few loyal patrons who occasionally came by, her frightened customers stayed away. These days every customer was important. Every sale crucial.

"Wait, just a minute. I come right down." she called again from the window.

Melly took a deep breath then made her way through the rooms: through the living room with its worn overstuffed crimson velvet sofa and chairs, their arms wearing white crocheted doilies now yellowing with age; through the dining room containing great grandfather Alonzo's massive mahogany furniture bearing ornately carved scrolls and serpents heads and tendrils of leaves with finely chiseled veins. She brushed past the cathedral-like clock with its man-in-the-moon face, its etched and filigreed brass pendulums pulling the time forward, its chimes now announcing the hour of noon. Passing the bedrooms through a narrow passageway, she proceeded to the stairway behind the kitchen. Holding Inge in one arm and her baby's blue lunch bowl in the other, Melly climbed down, one step at a time, feeling her way against the staircase wall with one side of her body and using her elbow to steady her descent. Just like a rat, she thought. Then, *"Ach,"* she moaned to herself, what a stupid thing to think, as she walked through the small dark corridor at the bottom of the steps and into the store.

She snatched a brown woolen lap robe from an oak stool behind the counter, cleared a spot near the tiny foot stove, still warm from that morning when Melly had gone over the accounts. She spread the fringed robe over the floor. Sitting Inge in its center, Melly called over her shoulder, "I'm coming, I'm coming," to her customer on the street side of the door. She broke off a piece of bread and offered it to the hungry baby who greedily put it to her mouth. Then flushed and out of breath Melly hastened to open the door. *"Ja,* right away," she called, "I'm coming,*"* as she finally unlocked it and ushered in her shopper.

For a brief moment Melly sized up Hildy Frankel. A frequent patron, but particular, she thought. Even so, she usually finds something to buy. Melly tucked a strand of hair behind her ear and smoothed the front of her pink cabbage-rose print housedress with her palms as if the movements of her hands could somehow calm her insides.

"So," Melly began, "You're looking for lace. Well I have some beautiful lace. Imported. Exactly what you want." From where she stood in the center of the floor, Melly scanned the shelves. Her eyes traveled up and down the stacks, noting their untidiness and, these days, their sparseness. She tried to hide her embarrassment by humming a little tune while thoughtfully searching. Finally a piece of blue, peeking from under a box of loose trimmings on a top shelf, caught her eye.

Ach, up there, she thought, always at the top. First chance I move everything down. Plenty of room these days to move everything down. Plenty of time, too. She mounted the first step of the rolling ladder, guiding its wheels to a position underneath the piece of blue. Climbing to the top she extracted the bolt of lace, secured it under her arm, then balanced her descent as she grasped the rungs, one at a time with her free hand.

Unrolling a yard she drew her hand along the underside, showing off its delicate intricacies, feeling its crisp webbed design. "It's lovely, Frau Frankel," her voice was soft, "from Czechoslovakia. You'll never see finer than this."

Hildy Frankel studied the fabric. She bunched a corner, lifted it to her face then drew it under her chin as if it were already made into a collar. She held it at arms distance and rubbed it between her thumb and index finger and murmured that it felt starchy and scratchy. She flapped it from her wrist like a flag in the wind then tilted her head from left to right to observe its folds. She held it up to the transom over the door, squinting as if to better see the patterns of light through its lacy design. She sighed deeply, looked at Melly and let the lace drop to the counter where she flattened it with the tips of her fingers. Adjusting her handbag under her arm, she quickly scanned the shelves for one last look.

"*Nein,*" Hildy Frankel finally said, "No, this isn't what I had in mind. Is there something else to show me? Something heavier, softer maybe?"

Melly sighed and began rolling the lace back around its bolt.. Without looking up she offered, "I give you a good price."

"You have nothing else then?"

"Right now this is all I have." She glanced up and saw her shopper walk towards the door. "Maybe next week a shipment comes. Come next week," she shouted to the door as it closed behind Hildy Frankel.

From inside Melly could see her customer briefly peer into her recently repaired storefront window as if she expected to see a display. Melly watched her shake her head sadly at the undraped wire stands, now headless stick figures on a bare stage, then turn towards the direction of the open street market across the square and walk away

For the next few moments Melly stood with folded arms and studied the near empty store, feeling herself on the verge of tears. For three generations, from the time great grandfather, Alonzo , first settled in Dusseldorf, erected the three story red brick building across from the cobblestone town square, and established GOLDSCHMIDTS, the shelves were always stocked, sometimes even beyond their capacity with bundles of pastel colored silks, and the finest Forstmann wools in subdued shades of camel, grey and jade. Rolls of tartan plaids, shepherd checks, and pencil pin-striped worsted serges filled bins and boxes. Plush black, green and burgundy velvets; elegant, richly shining taffetas and satins; crisp gingham, chintz and toile, all stocked the shelves so tightly that often two people were needed to extract a bolt: one to pull, one to hold the others back.

On higher shelves were dozens of display boxes, their sides swollen with cards of buttons and snaps and beaded ornaments. Nearby streamers of ribbons, bindings and heavy upholsterer's cordings, caught in drafts from the opening door, swayed on rolling spools, a giddy, dizzying profusion of colors, bringing squeals of delight from children and shushes to be quiet from parents.

Buckles of bone and white metal, various sized thimbles by the gross, some made of ivory for a special price, fancifully decorated tin boxes of needles, cards of trimmings, laces, snaps, hooks and buttons and spools of threads of every quality and color, crammed the showcases for customers to look through.

On top the counters were piled high with remnants of anything less than a yard, folded and priced for a bargain. Boxes the size of cigarette packs holding hundreds of pins and upholstery hooks of all descriptions, in wobbly stacks from the floor, spilled over onto the already crowded counter competing with chattering, energetic shoppers for just a little space to put down their purses.

And the next day and often the day after that, shipments would arrive with more goods, some items the same, some novelties.

This was GOLDSCHMIDT'S. How it was meant to be. Indeed, how it had been for generations. Each generation from father to son, now to daughter, handed down as their legacy a healthy flourishing business, a prosperous way of life, and a deep love for, and rooted connection to, the land of their birth.

Melly turned her attention to Inge sitting cross-legged on the floor, watching her mother with large solemn eyes.

Always watching, thought Melly. She's all the time watching. She picked up Inge's feeding spoon and blue bowl before lifting and sitting Inge opposite her on the counter.

"Here, *essen, essen,*" Melly cooed as she held the spoon to Inge's lips. "First we finish eating. Then we think about what to do about the business. Now if only your papa were different. *Ach*, what's the good talking. Your papa is your papa. We figure things out by ourselves. *Ja*, that's what we do. We give it a good hard think until we figure out something we can do.".

Melly's thoughts drifted off searching in her mind for answers. There must be a way. Something that I can do, somewhere I can go for help. I can't sit back anymore waiting for a miracle. For a brief moment she was unaware that the feeding was finished; that the spoon scraping for the last morsels had come up empty, and that Inge's lips no longer opened wide.

All at once Kurt's footsteps overhead brought her back from her reveries. Lifting Inge from the counter, Melly placed her on her shoulder and carried her upstairs. She tucked Inge into her basket and brought her to Kurt, who had just settled himself into his favorite chair near the window with his newest book of poems.

"You watch her for a little while today, *ja*, while I visit with my sisters this afternoon?"

"Oh sure, she'll be fine with me." Kurt's wide, delighted smile brightened his entire face as Melly handed over the basket. He placed it on the floor close to his chair, peeked inside and pulled the covers a bit higher then turned the basket away from the afternoon sun. "She'll probably fall asleep. You go, go.".

"We'll have *mittagessen* for supper? *Ja?*"

"*Ach ja,* sure. Go, go," he said, as he waved Melly away

Melly kissed him on his cheek, stole one last quick glance at Inge, then called over her shoulder, "I won't be very long," as she hurried from the room.

CHAPTER TWO

A Wedding and Back to Business

The marriage of Melly Goldschmidt to Kurt Wallerstein surprised, even shocked, many of the Dusseldorf townspeople. A calamity, they said, doomed from the start. They won't be together long. How could they be? Never were two people more different. After all, here was Melly close to forty, an old maid, outspoken, confrontational and fiercely independent. "She'd even tell papa what to do," joked Sabine, her oldest sister, to Bella and Rosi, her siblings, as they had tea one afternoon. "And he would do it," they screamed with laughter, swaying and bumping shoulders and holding their sides to gain composure.

Melly, the family pet, was the fourth born into this family of three girls, ten years after Rosi, up to then the youngest. Hovered over, cared for and indulged by the older girls, Melly became her sisters' treasured little doll, to the relief of their mother who suffered from a variety of ailments, none of which the doctors could put a name to.

But unlike her sisters who, by good fortune, inherited their mother's slender attractiveness, Melly resembled the women on her father's side; short, stout, and heavy breasted, with broad feet and ankles that sometimes swelled over the tops of her shoes. Hips that wobbled when she walked forced her into hated lace-up corsets at the age of fourteen.

And oh, even more than slender feet and taller legs, Melly longed for a firm body that didn't need a corset.

Her face was also much different from her sisters: they with their fine features, even toned olive complexions and fashionably bobbed hair. While she with her fleshy nose and flushed face, began every mornng by piling her lanky hair onto her crown in a loose untidy knot. Her only true physical beauty, her thickly lashed, animated large black eyes, never stilled and danced the steps of her soul for all the world to see. "You can always tell when Melly is lying," her sisters joked as Melly was growing up. "*Ja*, someday we tell her why she never wins at cards."

But it wasn't so much her paucity of style that made it difficult for some to picture Melly married to Kurt. A little powder, the right clothes and she could be attractive enough, they conceded. No, it was more her vigorous stubborn personality that made it hard to imagine Melly married to anyone at all, but especially to Kurt, so different in background and attitudes. She with her domineering ways and blunt manner. He, a dreamer, always with his head in the clouds. They shook their heads these doubters, and lamented over Melly's future and about how differently things would have turned out if only her parents were still alive.

Melly was twelve when she lost her mother and only nineteen when her father died. He left the family business to her. While she was growing up, one by one, her sisters married and established homes of their own. They never had any interest in the store and were relieved when it was not left for them, but rather for Melly, to run. And Melly welcomed it. GOLDSCHMIDT'S was no stranger to her. After her mother died, just Melly and her father lived together over the store, working the business side by side. When she inherited it she worked it as successfully and with as much pride as did the three generations before.

"I work hard. I make money," she proudly asserted to Bella who had stopped by the store one afternoon.

"Maybe you should work a little less," suggested her sister.

"Work less?" Melly called over her shoulder, as she puffed to the top of the rolling ladder with two boxes of seam bindings precariously pitched, like a waiter with a tray.

"*Ja*, Get out more. Be with people. Maybe meet someone, a nice man. You're almost forty already."

"Work less?" Melly shouted even louder, as she shoved boxes aside on the shelf to make room for the incoming elastics, then climbed down and faced Bella. "Throw away business? Maybe you haven't heard the old saying that money buys honey."

Melly turned from her sister and began examining a carton of lace trimmings, newly arrived that morning. She thinks I don't know what she's doing. A little talk here, more talk later on and maybe I'll soften up. She shoved the carton under the counter and straightened up to face her sister. "The discussion is closed. I need a man like a toothache."

Anyone could see that a husband, but most especially Kurt Wallerstein, could not fit into Melly's life. Even though four years her senior, Kurt had never in his life earned even as much as a *pfennig*.

"Not even as much as a penny!" shouted Julius, to Dora, his wife, who was Kurt's sister.

"I wouldn't know what to do, where to start," Kurt had explained to him, after moving himself into their modest house in the summer of 1925. . "I never worked. I never had to. There were family investments. But now, the investments are not paying."

"But you can't be like this all your life," argued Julius, "Without funds, almost a pauper."

"But I won't be like this always. Things will turn around. Our investments will pay again. You'll see, the old days will come back."

"The old days! The old days will never be back. Germany is bankrupt. It will never be again for you or your family like it was."

Kurt's family, the Wallersteins, a once moneyed, long established prominent family in Frankfurt society, became impoverished as their stock holdings in American corporations bordered on worthless. Before his world disappeared, Kurt, soft spoken and introspective, maintained a life of gentle ways. He occupied his time reading the classics, listening to opera on the record player and riding horses while he could still afford to keep them. As his universe gradually changed and as his needs dictated, he sold off whatever he had of value. Finally, with the family's consent, he sold the family home, and existed off the proceeds until the last .

With nowhere else to go, he appeared one day at Dora's and Julius's threshold and moved in. And Julius, corpulent, bearded and red-faced, declared to the back of his wife's head as she creamed her bird-like face in the bathroom mirror before going to bed, that he would not indefinitely support her playboy brother. As the weeks became months and the months became more and more intolerable, Julius, desperate for a solution, finally found one.

"Marriage," he suddenly exploded at dinner one evening, "Is the solution. Kurt, you need to marry. And you need to marry someone well fixed. That is what you need and that is what we will find for you."

Melly, on the other hand, didn't think she needed anything at all, except a child. She did so yearn for a child of her
own. For a little girl to fold into her bosom and tell things
to and feel her soft face against her own and breathe in her
scent. Sometimes when thinking about it Melly could feel
the love welling up, and with everything inside of her adore
that baby who was just a wish. *Ja*, to have a child would be
wonderful. As far as anything else, well, what was missing?
She had a good life. Wasn't she part of her sisters' large and
robust families? Wasn't she included in everything they did,
especially when the holidays came and sometimes celebrated even beyond their dates, just to prolong the festivities?
"Who cares if New Years Eve is just one night," they often
exclaimed. "We make it three nights, have three parties." *Ja*,
thought Melly, life is good. Why change it?

Then Julius placed a marriage advertisement in the
newspaper. Then Sabine showed the paper to Melly. Then an
outraged Melly shouted "For the millionth time I don't want
a husband, so stop bothering me!"

To which Sabine responded, "A woman should be married. It's the way to live in this world."

"I don't need a husband telling me what to do."

"But you need to have your own life, make your own
family, have children."

Melly had been counting the day's receipts. She marked
the amounts in her ledger, divided the bills into separate
envelopes and placed the neatly stacked envelopes into the
cash drawer. "*Ja?* well maybe!" She slammed the drawer
shut, angry without understanding why. "I tell you what, if he
can make babies, well just maybe I'll think about it!"

Sometimes Melly would think back to that first meeting
when she stood in the restaurant doorway and saw Kurt for
the first time that warm spring day in 1927. He was fair

and slight with soft grey eyes and straight sharp features. He reminded her of a paper doll from a child's book of cut-outs, he appeared so precise: white suit, white gloves and white shoes with grey suede spats protecting the tops. He sat at a table, legs crossed, reading a newspaper, and the sun which beamed from behind surrounded him in a glowing, golden frame. She marveled to herself that he looked like a prince, so far above anything she had expected, that she put off asking him about making babies until the second meeting.

After several afternoons together and many letters back and forth, the two families tended to the business side of the prospective marriage. Most importantly was the researching of family trees to ascertain that there were no Russian, Polish or any other ancestors who were not German on that tree. Only German ancestors, only "pure German" lineage would be acceptable to the Goldschmidts and the Wallersteins. Once having cleared that hurdle both sides negotiated conditions so that Melly and Kurt would each benefit from the union in ways each wanted and needed.

Six months from that first meeting, after a visit to the town hall where they completed marriage formalities, Melly and Kurt were wed in Frankfurt, in Rabbi Weisengrund's front parlor. Then following a short, modest reception they left for Dusseldorf: Melly to her business, Kurt to settle himself in his new home above the business. To the marriage he brought a meager stipend from Julius, gifts from his sisters of several pieces of antique furniture, and treasured family heirlooms thought to be of some monetary worth. On rare occasions, when Melly asked, he helped in the store by unpacking newly arrived shipments and stocking the shelves. In the mornings, when the cold weather came, he started the stove downstairs. In the evenings, after banking it for the night, he made sure that the store was as it should be, ready for the next day. But except for riding horses he occupied himself in much the same way as always, convincing the doubters even more that it was only a matter of time before Melly would become fed up and show Kurt the door.

Nevertheless, despite their differences it was plainly apparent three years into the marriage that these differences strengthened their marriage. Melly and Kurt were devoted to each other.

"How could anyone not love this man," said Melly as she strolled with Rosi during during one of their Saturday walks. "He demands nothing. Whatever I do for him he's happy. Whatever food I cook he eats. Whatever I ask, he does. He never even comes downstairs into the store unless there's something I need from him. And he never interferes with me or tells me to do this, or I should try that. He finishes up, and without saying anything goes back upstairs. When we take our evening walks he tells me how he cares for me and how our life together is better than he ever imagined."

But if Melly were to evaluate her blessings, the birth of their child, five years after their wedding, an exquisite golden-haired infant they named Inge, brought the greatest joy. And from the moment Inge was brought to her breast, Melly could not bear, even for the shortest time, to be apart from her. "So where are you taking her now?" Kurt often teased.

So many times Melly heard these same words as she prepared to carry Inge off someplace. So many times Kurt would shake his head and playfully tell Melly how perplexed he was over Melly's need to take Inge with her everywhere, even into the next room. And Melly, who could not explain it herself, who only knew she felt uneasy if Inge was out of her sight, would laugh and then Kurt would laugh, and it became a joke between them.

That evening, back from the visit with her sisters at Sabine's house, Melly stood at the kitchen sink, her arms thrust into hot soapy water. They had just finished dinner and the smells of cabbage rolls and potatoes clung to the air. She went over the day's events in her mind. First, there was Hildy Frankel who didn't buy. Then the discussion with her sisters. "Maybe you should just close up the store for a while until things improve," suggested Sabine. "*Ja*," said Rosi, "Find work someplace else for the time being." "Maybe even lease out the store, " said Bella. "Live off the rent money for a while." "But what's the good if the business is lost?" Melly remembered saying. "There must be a way to save the business. All I need is merchandise, stock, something to sell when a customer walks in. These days I place orders but deliveries don't come."

"Well, what about Otto Hoffmann?" asked Bella. " He was always our biggest supplier. He's still sending-no?"

At that point Melly had jumped from her seat and slammed her hand on the table, rattling the tea cups and sending the sugar spoon flying. "No, he is not!" she shouted. " But Hoffmann will be the solution once I tell him... once I make him understand.... He probably doesn't realize how bad it has become for us." She retrieved the spoon from across the room, dropped it into the dishpan, and said her "goodbyes."

"*Ja*, Hoffmann," she now muttered to herself over the dinner dishes. "I think he's the answer."

Melly finished scrubbing the last of the pots. She raised her shoulder to wipe away a soapy splash from her face, then without turning to face Kurt, still seated and enjoying his cigarette, she said, "Kurt I'm going to Berlin, to see Otto Hoffmann."

"Oh, and why is this?" Kurt rose abruptly and carried his ashtray to be emptied. "For what reason?"

"I need help with the business, and Hoffmann is someone who can do it."

"What do you mean? Why can't I do it? Just tell me what you need. Don't I always help you when you ask?" He was standing near her side at the sink, tight-lipped, leaning forward slightly to catch her full face, which she kept averted.

She felt her temper rise as it always did when being questioned about her decisions. "But there is nothing anymore for you to do."

"So, and why not?"

"Because there is no more business," she retorted sharply. Then immediately contrite thought, *ach*, what's the matter with me talking to him that way. He has no understanding of what it takes to make a living. She dried her hands on her apron, and handed it over for him to hang behind the door on its customary hook. Then with a softened voice, she patiently began explaining the situation about the declining business, forcing him to face that which, she realized, he chose to forget. She reminded him again of the boycott and the demonstrations against Jewish businesses and the recent break in by the Brownshirts and the destruction....

As she spoke she turned toward him and seeing his normally pale face become even whiter, her voice trailed off. Pausing until he no longer looked ghostly and troubled, she continued.

"I've had some savings, but they're almost used up. There's a chance I can bring the business back to life if Hoffmann helps me."

Kurt sat back down at the table, crossed his legs and removed another cigarette from his silver case. Before lighting, up he snapped the case shut and tapped the unfiltered end against his engraved initials on the lid, deep in thought ,it seemed to Melly.

"So, Hoffmann is..."

"One of our wholesalers, also a family friend from years back, from when I was a child." She stood facing him now, leaning against the front of the sink. Her hands with interlocking fingers were clasped in front. " You have relatives in Berlin...yes?"

Kurt inhaled deeply, letting the smoke drift from his nostrils. "*Ja*, my cousins, Simon and Ilse Wallerstein. She, Ilse is a Steinhardt. Why do you ask?"

Melly's eyes widened, her excitement rose. Her hands dropped to her sides then cradled her face. "You have Steinhardts for relatives?"

"Only through marriage." He brushed ashes from his lap. "Not close relatives. Simon is my cousin. Our fathers were brothers. We were close as children, but the family grew apart somehow."

Melly fell silent, deep in thought. Finally, she cleared her throat. " Kurt, I tell you what your can do for me. Please send a letter to your cousins that I am coming to Berlin next week sometime to stay over one night." She glanced around the kitchen, gave a final tug to the corner of the newly laid tablecloth. Not waiting for his reaction she walked directly into the passageway leading to their bedroom, her heels making clopping sounds on the linoleum. She did not have to glance over her shoulder to know that his eyes were on her back. But when she heard his chair scrape against the floor she knew that he had mashed out his cigarette and was headed for his writing table in the alcove at the far end of the same passageway. "*Ja*," she whispered to herself. "Is good."

CHAPTER THREE

Just Send Goods

"I've come to see Herr Hoffmann, please," announced Melly.

The walk from the Berlin station had taken longer than she had anticipated.. At first she considered riding to her destination in one of the taxis waiting outside the station. But as she peered diagonally across the street toward the way she would be walking she thought better of it. It was only a few blocks, and short ones if she remembered right. Better to save the money. Along the way swastika flags draped over the entrance to a school for girls, and Nazi banners flying on poles higher than the trees, unnerved her. She quickly looked away and peered into Inge's basket which she had set down on the cobblestones near her feet. Tucking the covers tightly under the sleeping infant, Melly picked up the basket and, with quickened pace, strode off into the darkened streets. She never expected that Inge's basket would become weightier by the minute, or that she would need to stop frequently to shift it between her tired arms, or that the mounting ache in her cramped fingers would force her to set the basket down every few minutes and pause while she exercised her hand. This is so foolish, she thought. Such a trudge to save a few pennies. But I'm almost there it looks like.

The streets were also quieter than Melly remembered, unusual for Berlin. But it was already night, and her stomach reminded her that she hadn't eaten. She supposed that mostly everyone was home having the customary *Abendbrot,* a light super of cold meats, blackbread and pickles...

For as long as she remembered Melly never liked too much silence. Unwelcome things, sometimes even terrible things happened in the quiet. But as much as the silence had made her uncomfortable before her mother died, she feared it more and trusted it even less afterwards.

Sometimes in a rush of memory she was reminded of that very moment when she knew that her mother was dead, In the same way as then, she would be unable to move, suddenly cold all over, frozen with dread.

She had just set aside her book for the afternoon and had turned her thoughts to the preparation of the evening meal when a creeping, icy realization permeated her entire being. There was no mistaking it. That sounds of lingering illness which had emanated from her mother's bedroom over the last few months, the cough, the muted moans, the grinding bedsprings had stopped. And Melly knew. She had remained in her chair, her favorite reading chair, huddled into the comfort of its dark worn cushions, staring past the window straight ahead into the evening sky, hearing no sound but the rhythmical clicking of the brass pendulum in the next room.

Then sometime later she heard her father's footsteps as he climbed the stairs from the store below, and heard in his steps the weariness of his day's labors. Only then did she leave her chair to meet him at the top of the stairs, dreading to tell him, as she knew she must, that his wife, her mother, had died. But when she saw his stricken face, she saw that somehow he already knew. Tight-lipped he walked quietly into the bedroom he had shared with his wife of 27 years. From behind the closed door Melly could hear his cries, while she sank into a kitchen chair, buried her face into her lap, and wept.

As a child finding herself on quiet streets like these she would sometimes rap a stick along the stretches of wrought iron railings, hearing the wrackety-wracks, like small explosions crack open the silence. But now as she walked these still streets, stealing glances into the large windows that lighted her way, catching glimpses every so often of upper portions of bookcases or the tops of pictures as she walked, even the sounds of her shoes could not dispel her demons. She quickened her pace and filled her mind with thoughts of why she had come to Berlin.

Now, standing before the housekeeper at the open doorway of the Hoffmann home. the sounds of clinking tableware and chattering voices from inside the house, reminded Melly that at any moment Inge would waken needing to be fed.

Strands of hair blown free of her combs, a disheveled Melly could see past the shoulders of the housekeeper into the brightly lit hallway. Still there, as she remembered, lay the Persian rug, woven with wools the colors of jewels, running the length of the polished floor to the painted tapestry wall along the back corridor. Suspended over the mahogany staircase a glittering crystal chandelier welcomed Melly as it had in the past..

Opening the door wider the housekeeper stepped to the side, signaled Melly to enter, while reaching for the basket. "What is your name please.?"

Quickly Melly leaned down and grabbed the curved wicker handles, snatching the basket from the housekeeper's reach. "No, I can manage." With one smooth motion she stepped inside, placed the basket near her feet, then turned to the housekeeper. "Tell him Melly Goldschmidt Waller-stein would like to see him."

She followed the housekeeper to a small, rear sitting room, the receiving room, she supposed, for tradesmen and others of unexpected business. Wearing her coat and sitting stiffly at one end of the sofa Melly placed Inge's basket on the cushion beside her and scanned the room, remembering the only time she had been in this house before.

She was a child then and her father had brought her along on one of his business trips. She recalled being puzzled by her father's warnings as the train pulled into the Berlin station. "When we get there," he said, "touch nothing. Remember. Nothing!" But later, while the two men shuffled papers and talked over coffee, and boredom set her to exploring the house, she understood. So many rooms. So many collections of Venetian Glass and tiny porcelain figurines. So many china lamps with hundreds of shimmering glass beaded fringes. She had tried imagining what it would be like to live in such a fragile environment, especially the way she and her sisters fought and played and landed on, or crashed into whatever was nearby, But she could envision only the aftermath of shattered glass.

She recalled that she had suddenly missed the boisterousness of her family and the solid surroundings of her home over the store. She had only been away a few hours, but a restlessness swept over her. She wished that her father's business would end soon so that they could leave.

Now, so many years past that visit, sitting in Hoffmann's receiving room, she smiled thinking back to that evening walk with her father as they headed for the train station. "I'm glad we're going home, papa," she had said. Then not wanting to hurt his feelings in case she had, she slipped her hand into his coat pocket and finding his fingers said, "I had a nice time though."

"Melly Goldschmidt! It is really you?" Otto Hoffmann stood beaming in the doorway, a round, animated little man, wearing spectacles and rolled up shirt sleeves. Except for grey sideburns and, on his crown, a tuft of thin grey hair brushed over to one side, he was totally bald. He seemed unaware of his napkin still tucked under his chin, or of the sugar cube destined for his tea, still held between his fingers. He took long steps into the room. "This is such a wonderful surprise. You should have let us know. We would have waited with supper. What can I offer you? *Ja* I know, some tea," as he reached for the bell cord. Then noticing for the first time his napkin swaying like a surrendering flag across his chest, he fell into flutters and embarrassing giggles, finally snatching and stuffing it and the sugar cube into his pants pocket.

"Its been such a long time," he continued, "years since the last time I saw you. What was the occasion? Who can remember? But is was even before you were married. And your husband, it's Kurt, yes? I remember from your letter his name. And how is he?" Then as if suddenly struck with a memory his expression changed. He nodded solemnly and his voice became sing-song. "*Ach* my dear Melly, You must forgive us for not coming to your wedding. You simply must." He took her hand and held it against his chest, his eyes holding hers. "But you know how it was with Hilde. She had not been well for such a long time and the travel would have been too much for her. You must tell me that you understand."

But before Melly could utter a sound he sucked in his breath and emitted a small, delighted gasp at the contents of the basket. Bending over the sleeping baby, he lightly tapped Inge's cheek with his index finger. "So, who is this?" he crooned. "Who is this little one in the basket?"

Melly remained silent while his babbles faded into the dim recesses of her mind. He will help me. He must. He was one of my father's dearest friends. My father lent him money to start up again after he lost everything in that warehouse fire. Nothing was left. Nothing. The building, the inventory, everything destroyed. And on a handshake my father gave him money. They were like brothers. Everything was on a handshake.

Melly picked up Inge, now whimpering, while she unwrapped her blankets and removed her bulky pink hat and sweater. "This is my Inge," she said to him. "And right now a very hungry baby. Yes tea would be nice please, and also some milk for her." She sat Inge on her lap and murmured into the warm , damp folds of her neck. "Soon. soon, you will be getting. The nice lady will bring something for you. Ah, such a good little baby." She brought Inge up closer, settling the baby against her soft bosom, hearing Inge's soft sigh before her thumb went into her mouth.

Otto Hoffmann brought his chair closer to where Melly sat. "So, tell me, what brings you here? Our families should visit, you know, like we used to when your mama and papa were alive. Remember when you were all children and we would come, every spring like clockwork we would come, and your mama would cook for days the sauerbraten and the dumplings and we could smell it all the way coming on the train."

"Herr Hoffman," Melly began, "please understand that this is not a social visit. I would not have taken such a long trip like this with my baby, and show up just out of the blue if it wasn't important."

"Of course, I understand that...I only meant...."

"My situation is terrible," she interrupted, "and only you can help me. I'm desperate."

"So? Tell me. What is it?"

"It's the business. It's very bad. It's never been so bad. Never."

Hoffmann folded his hands behind his head and leaned back further in his chair. "Ah, but Melly, it's not only you. Everyone's business is suffering. People all over are complaining about it. But what can we do? We have to wait it out until things get better."

Just then the housekeeper carried in a large silver tray. Melly watched as she spread a crisp, white cloth over the small table near Melly's knees before laying out the tea things: the steaming cobalt pot and cups with gold bands circling the rims and matching gold spoons with mother of pearl handles; cakes, nuts and sugared figs on ruby glass plates arranged in wheel-like configurations ; pitchers of cream and milk and delicate porcelain pots filled with assorted preserves alongside a platter of miniature biscuits and rounds of blackbread.

Melly waited until the housekeeper left the room before speaking. She marveled at the abundant tea table and the still gracious ways. The hard times of which mostly everyone complained did not appear to have reached the Hoffmann home. That's good, she thought. Good for me. He'll have no reason to refuse me.

She prepared a small plate of biscuits and sugared figs for Inge, filled a plate for herself, then held a cup of milk to her baby's lips. For the moment she had forgotten how hungry she really was until the food was placed before her. Remembering her manners, she tried not to bolt down her food, but, between swallows, she continued explaining the reason for her visit.

"Herr Hoffman, I'm here because for me it's not a simple matter of just waiting until things get better. For others, maybe they can hold on. But for me...for me... they won't let me hold on. They're driving me out."

"Who won't let you?" What are you saying?"

Melly cleared her throat and helped herself to tea. She would have to talk about it after all, something she had managed so far to avoid. It would mean going through it again when all she wanted was to forget it, blot it out, erase it, if she could, from her memory. But if she wanted Hoffmann's help he would need to hear it, to make him understand. She took a deep breath and began, struggling to keep her voice steady.

"Six months ago I went downstairs to open the store, the way I always do every morning, and there was a sign pasted on the front window. It said in big black letters DO NOT BUY FROM JEWS."

"Ah," he breathed while pouring the tea. "*Ja*, I heard about incidents like that." especially in Dusseldorf."

"And when I looked down the street Vogel's Bakery had the same sign."

"*Ja*, ja" he sighed, "Even here in Berlin once in a while something like that happens. But what can we do? We have to wait it out. When the economy gets better, everything gets better. It will stop."

"So I started to walk towards Vogel's...I was carrying Inge...I can't begin to tell you how upset I was...when I heard all this commotion, hollering and shouting, coming from around the corner. There was this gang of boys, six or seven of them, little Brownshirts, children, no more than eight or nine years old. They were carrying sticks and waving them around and yelling and when they saw me they screamed Jew! Jew! and raced at me with their sticks and shrieking and hitting me over and over and hitting Inge, the both of us, with their fists and sticks. I screamed they should go away. 'Leave us alone! Leave us alone.' But they didn't stop and Inge was screaming. That poor, baby, how she screamed. I threw myself down on my knees to cover Inge with my body. And I tell you to this day I still walk with pain in my knees from that time. And they kept hitting me and calling names, but not anymore to Inge. I was able to protect Inge. Then Kurt ran out to help me, but they attacked him too and beat him the same way until he fell to the street and covered his head with his arms. That was all he could do. Finally some neighbors came and chased them away...and...."

Her voice ebbed. The room fell silent.

"So..." Hoffmann sank back in his chair, his voice barely audible.

With a deep sigh Melly shifted Inge on her lap and handed her a sugared fig to suck. Composed now, her voice calm and steady she told him about the Nazi rallies against the Jews in Dusseldorf and then about the break-in at her store smashing everything and terrifying her customers.

"They are just starting to come back, my customers, but I have hardly anything to sell."

Reaching over, Hoffmann handed Melly a napkin from the tea table. He moved his head from side to side and clicked his tongue in sympathy. Melly mopped her face, damp with perspiration, and patted her neck in small dabs before blowing her nose. She noticed the strain in Hoffmann's face, different from just a moment ago. His lips became taut and his eyes suddenly narrowed. There's something there, she thought, something he wants to say.

She sat quietly, patiently, her attention fully riveted on him. She watched him slump down in his seat, his eyes cast upward. He inserted his thumbs into the side pockets of his vest and drummed his fingers on his stomach, but said nothing.

Maybe, she thought, I imagine. I imagine too much. She took a deep breath feeling the air expand her tightened chest. She cleared her throat. "For months now my suppliers are not filling my orders for merchandise. They're afraid. I have no stock to speak of. When a customer comes in, and some still do in spite of everything, there's nothing for them to buy. Nothing! Even your company, Herr Hoffmann, has refused to ship."

"But that's impossible. That can't be," he exploded as he jumped to his feet. Then lowering himself into his chair, seeming to think better of it, he said, "But I suppose it is possible. You see, Hans, you remember my son Hans, well, he has been running the business now. It's been that way for a long time. I seldom go into the warehouse these days. To tell you the truth I don't know much about what is going on with the business anymore. But If what you say is so....?"

Melly removed the remains of the fig from Inge's fingers, then to quiet her protests handed her a biscuit along with the command to "shush."

"All I'm asking is that you send me goods, to continue doing business the way we always did." She was on the verge of reminding him that if it wasn't for her father...but thought, no, it's not good to push too much. He is a decent man. He remembers. He will help.

Hoffmann brushed the crumbs form his lap and stood. "I remember what your papa did for me. I never forget that. Tomorrow I promise I will speak to Hans. Surely it's a simple matter just to ship goods." Then in a lighter mood, "Now come inside for a visit and don't worry too much. You'll stay here the night and get a good rest. In the morning you'll see, everything will be better."

"*Danke,* but no, I can't stay. Kurt's cousins are expecting us, and the day for me has been long, and Inge must be settled for the night." She tied Inge's hat under her chin and wrapped her coverings snugly before placing her back into the basket. "I'm already late, and I don't want them to think I have no manners. Already they must think that Kurt had some come-down when he married me." She leaned towards him and whispered reverently, like a special secret, "his cousin Ilse, is a Steinhardt." For the first time that evening Melly's eyes shone with mischief. "Well, maybe I can get them to like me anyway."

She hoped her little joke would break the tension, but it seemed to Melly that Hoffmann was preoccupied and did not hear. Suddenly he took both her hands into his and tapped them against his chest. Their eyes locked. "It is such a sad time for all of us, so sad for all Germans," he said. " My heart is so heavy I can't begin to tell you... with everything that is happening. But normal times will come back. We must believe that."

There it is again, thought Melly, that something in his eyes. He is keeping something back. I'm sure of it. He has something to tell me, but he is not saying what it is.

They were in the hallway approaching the front door. A feeling of exhaustion swept over Melly. She tried to evaluate the success of her meeting, but the outcome eluded her. He sounded as though he would try to do something. But then he never said definitely that he could. And now there is Hans, who she barely knew. She was tired. Too tired to think about anything except her next destination. She lifted Inge's basket and felt the ache again in her fingers and arms. Suddenly she remembered the Nazi flags and banners outside. She turned to Hoffmann.

"Could I ask you to treat me to a taxi?"

"Of course, Melly anything. What address should I give.?"

"Tell him Steinstrasse-6, near Unter den Linden.'

From the rear window of the taxi Melly weakly waved goodbye to Otto Hoffmann. He was slumped against the door frame of his house, his face cradled between his hands, He seemed unaware of his napkin now dangling from the side pocket of his trousers, almost to his knees

CHAPTER FOUR

The House of Strangers

Melly stepped from the taxi and faced the doorway of Steinstrasse-6. For several moments she was uncertain if she had come to the right place. Except for a dim light over the doorway there were no signs of life about the place. She wondered if Kurt's letter to expect her visit had reached them, so unwelcoming was the house.

"The servants and the family have already retired for the night," explained Ilse. She stood before Melly in the opened doorway, a white chenille robe, wrapped around her ample form, suggesting by her tone that she wished to be done with the amenities so that she too could go to bed, But, nevertheless, she smiled weakly and offered Melly some supper.

"Oh, no, thank you, no," declared Melly, "We've already eaten" as she held Inge's basket higher to show the "we." Then she softly asked if she could be shown to where she and Inge would be for the night, she was so very tired.

Melly slept fitfully during the night, awaking suddenly from time to time to semi-consciousness, sinking back into a doze, but never deeper than the surface. Finally, her endurance spent, she thought it less wretched to finish the night in a chair, which she pulled over to the fireplace hoping for a bit of warmth. But its embers were out by then, and the stiff chair only added to her night's misery.

She glanced over to Inge, lost amid the rumpled bed-clothes, sucking her thumb, sleeping soundly. All this travel-ing around from place to place is hard on her, she thought. But no one can take care of my Inge the way I can, not even Kurt, not even my sisters. who pleaded with me to leave her with them while I was away. No! Inge stays with me! Anyway it's only one more day and we'll be home. A ticking clock across the room gently broke the silence. She wondered how much longer before daylight.

Becoming somewhat accustomed to the darkness, Melly studied the furniture in the room, and recalled, upon being shown to the room, Ilse's sweeping response to her startled exclamation that never in her whole life had she ever seen such a room, except maybe in a museum. "All Louis the XVI, quite rare, quite old, and now I must say goodnight," as she abruptly closed the door behind her. Melly smiled. Such a dolt I must seem to be in all this elegance.

She shivered slightly in the chilly room and drew her coat up over her shoulders like a blanket. She thought about the reasons that brought her to Berlin, to this home of strang-ers. She realized for the first time how little she really knew of Kurt's family. Except for Kurt's sister Dora and her hus-band Julius, who visited occasionally, and a rare visit from his sister Hanchen, who otherwise spent most of her time at the spas, Melly had almost no knowledge of Kurt's relations.

When they were first married Kurt had shown her a photograph of his cousin Simon with his wife, Ilse. He, portly, and nearly bald , wore a wide toothy smile as he held high a rabbit he had shot. At his side a stout Ilse, blond, tall and smartly styled, leaned against him and squinted into the sun. A smile barely touched the corners of her mouth, while one arm stretched across and hugged his middle. Just like her very own captured prize, Melly thought at the time.

There were, of course, a dozen or so of his relatives who introduced themselves at the wedding, but they were only faces that she never saw after that day; whose names she couldn't recall if asked. Yet she knew it was an incredible stroke of good fortune to be related, even remotely, to the prestigious Steinhardts with their rich, prominent connections.

She shifted in her chair and drew her legs under her as she huddled further into her coat and turned over in her mind the events of the day, First, the delay at the train station in Dusseldorf because the tracks were scheduled for inspection that morning, caused her to consider canceling the trip to Berlin for another day."It will be already dark outside when we get there," she had whispered to Inge, wide awake in her basket and sucking her thumb. Melly gently removed the thumb and continued. "So?.... But what difference does it make as long as we get there, *ja?*" Inge thrust her thumb back into her mouth. Melly sighed, sat back and offered her baby a piece of dried fruit, which Inge eagerly substituted for her thumb. *Ja,* thought Melly, we go to Berlin today, no matter what!

Then she turned over in her mind Hoffmann's words: I'll speak to Hans, he had said. And try not to worry, he had said. But worry is all I do these days, all the time worry. What will happen to us if the business fails? How will I manage? The business is all I know. She thought about Hans. She remembered a gangling youth, who went off by himself when the two families visited. Now he's a man, who, she felt certain, would barely remember her and upon whose decisions her livelihood depended. Everything will look brighter in the morning, Hoffmann had said. But when Melly recalled his eyes and the unspoken words behind them, a dark heaviness settled inside her.

She peered across the room. At last, early daylight peeked in where the drapery did not quite close. A stream of sun cast over Inge, who stirred slightly, blinked her eyes, then fell back to sleep as she resumed sucking her thumb.

Pretty soon, Melly thought, the household will be awake and then she will have her talk with Kurt's cousins. How she dreaded it. How she wished the day would be already over, that she was finished with everything that brought her to Berlin, that she was home in Dusseldorf with Kurt, in her own surroundings, her own life.

She wondered about these cousins of Kurt, the kind of people they were, what their lives were like. They were the last hope she had to save the business. They were rich. They had rich friends, who knew the right people. People like these had connections. People like these could get anything.

How should I approach them? she wondered. She knew she must somehow win them over, get them to like her. Then they would understand her desperate circumstances and offer to help. Yes. She'd get their help. It was simply a matter of how it was put to them.

She rose from her chair aware of voices floating through the floor from the room below. Clinking chinaware, the aroma of coffee and freshly baked yeasty breads stirred her hunger and reminded her that Inge, any minute would awaken and demand breakfast.

Suddenly energized and eager to begin the day, Melly flung aside the drapery and let the warm, bright sun pour over her as she hurried into her clothes. She ran a quick comb through her hair, swirling its lanky mass onto her crown. Noticing Inge, now wide awake, sitting upright in the center of the bed and blinking into the sun, Melly dressed her quickly and placed her into her basket. Proceeding toward the smells of food, she first stepped into the hallway bathroom, ran a quick washcloth over both their faces, then continued toward the smells of food. Amid Inge's clamoring for breakfast, "*essen Mutti essen,*" and her own persistent cooing, "*Ja, ja,* soon, soon you will get," Melly marveled at her baby. *Only one year old and she has the appetite of a lumberjack.*

She straddled the threshold between the hallway and the dining room and leaned against the doorway, uncertain how to proceed. No one from the family had yet come to breakfast, and except for the comings and goings of the maids, the room was empty. She stood transfixed in the doorway, fascinated by the activity before her, in awe of the most sumptuous morning buffet she had ever seen.

Platters of breads and doughy cakes, pots of fruit conserves and honey, hand painted pitchers brimming with cream and scalded milk were paraded from the kitchen. Steaming pots of coffee and tiny individual bowls with butter creamed into swirls, were carried on huge trays and placed at the far end near the stacked china and flatware arranged just so. Completing the spread was something Melly had never seen before: saw: a bowl of boiled eggs in their shells, keeping warm in special petit-point egg jackets.

All this was tended to by two serving girls, wearing blue starched uniforms with white collars and cuffs, both with hair sleekly pulled behind their ears in vertical rolls, both in sensible black shoes.

She noticed the room itself. How different from her own dining room in Dusseldorf. This room was airy, devoid of clutter. Chairs were upholstered in silk brocade and placed around the table comfortably distant from their neighbors. Family photographs, pictures of misty woodland scenes, and assorted graphic memorabilia in rococo frames hung symmetrically and uncrowded above the buffet against a red velvet wall. At the far end, above a fireplace inlaid with Italian marble and flanked with high-back chairs, a life size family portrait of the Steinhardts dominated the room. Awestruck with the richness and elegance around her, she reminded herself that this was the Steinhardt home, the home of one of the richest families in Germany...maybe even throughout all of Europe.

" You may start if you wish," said the maid to the visitor standing in the doorway.

Melly stepped into the room. "It's all right? Before any-one else comes down?" She held tightly to Inge who, aban-doned her thumb and fidgeted vigorously in Melly's arms, stretching and twistisng towards the buffet. By now Melly's hunger was acute, coming in waves.

"Oh yes, quite all right.. The family always comes down at different times. Would you like something special for the baby?"

Melly glanced over to the buffet. "Oh, no, no. there's plenty there."

"Well, if you should think of something, my name is Frau Miller." She turned crisply on her heel and disappeared behind the swinging door to the kitchen.

Melly placed a soft roll, drizzled with honey, and a cup of milk on a plate for Inge and settled her at the table. She had just begun to help herself when the rap-tap of high-heels and Ilse's voice came into the room..

"*Guten morgen,* Melly," Ilse's morning greeting sounded formal to Melly, not at all friendly or even interested in why this distant relative was in her home. "You slept well?" Ilse dutifully asked.

Melly whirled, nearly spilling the contents of her plate. "Oh *ja,* just like a top."

Now for the first time in the light of day Melly could clearly see her hostess. Stylishly stout, Ilse wore a wine colored hat, shaped like a cone; its black veil draped back; its crown stuck with a slanted foot-long quill. A fur piece, styled from a tiny fox head and silvery paws, dangled down one shoulder, its plump tail down the other. Her crepe dress, with voluminous leg-of-mutton sleeves, was fastened with pearl buttons from elbow to wrist.

Fascinated by Ilse's elegance, Melly watched Ilse place her slim, envelope purse on a nearby chair, remove her fur and brush it lightly but briskly with her hand, then blow the hairs into waves before letting it drop to the floor. Filling her coffee cup, Ilse walked to the opposite side of the table and sat down facing her guest "Now, Frau Wallerstein, what can I do for you?"

Melly studied Ilse's white powdered face, pencilled thin high arched brows, rouged cheeks and bright red mouth. Her blonde hair, swept into a bun at the nape of her neck, accentuated her lined forehead. A questioning frown between her eyebrows gave her a tired, and probably older look, thought Melly, who guessed her to be about fifty.

Feeling uncomfortable, put off by Ilse's queenly, polite correctness, Melly's thoughts raced. Maybe I won't be able to reach this woman so very different from me. All my planning and rehearsing in my mind the night before, first, I'd say this, then she'd answer that, might have been for nothing. But no matter, I came here for a reason. I must try. She cleared her throat, just about to open conversation when the maid, Frau Miller, came into the room. Melly remained silent, observing how the maid selectively arranged a breakfast tray of tea and rolls, discussed with Ilse the menu for this evening's supper, then carried the tray from the room and up the circular stairway,

"I'm sorry you won't be meeting Simon this morning." Ilse sipped her coffee and tapped the corners of her mouth with her napkin. "He sends his apologies but it's his habit, you know. He takes his breakfast in bed and spends a good part of his morning in his room, reading his books and grading students' papers...but perhaps later...."

"Oh, but I won't be staying...but it's all right...another time maybe," said Melly, hoping to conceal her disappointment. She cleared her throat once more. "You know, Kurt has told me about your husband. About how they were children together."

"Oh, yes, Kurt." Ilse leaned back in her chair and nibbled on a buttered roll. "Truthfully, Simon did tell me a few things when you and Kurt first married. Since then there's been nothing until we received Kurt's letter last week. They've been out of touch for years...you see."

"Oh, well that's all right...I understand," while truly not understanding at all.

"And now I must apologize again, this time for my daughter, Ursula, who sleeps until the very last minute before getting ready for school. I don't know if she will even have time to come to breakfast this morning. She'll probably have a tray in her room." Ilse rose from the table, refilled her coffee cup and resumed her seat.

"That's all right," said Melly lamely, feeling her insides sink. Nothing this morning was as she had envisioned. She came all this way and nothing was working out. First Hoffmann...now this...this...snub. She studied this rich imperious woman, who never wanted for a thing. The way she sat, so removed, so distant, hardly looking directly at her, never noticing Inge. What kind of person ignores a baby, she wondered? What goes on inside such a person? How do I begin to...Melly set aside her plate. She folded her napkin into a square, then into a boat, like a preoccupied child. Well, I'm not going home without going after the help I need, and without saying why and what I came for. However it comes out, that's how it will be. She handed her napkin to Inge, who grabbed it and promptly stuffed it into her mouth.

"You must be wondering why I'm here."

"Yes, we all are."

"I've come to get help for my business," Melly blurted. "It's going under because I can't get merchandise, because my suppliers won't ship. I came here because you know people, influential people. I hoped that you could connect me with business people who can help me. That's why I came here."

Ilse leaned back in her chair and looked upwards as if collecting her thoughts. Then meeting Melly's eyes she said, "There have been shortages all over since that boycott on Jewish business. It was only for one day but it did a lot of harm, and still does. Some have recovered, some have not. Yours is not a unique situation." Ilse leaned forward in her chair and suddenly exploded, "My God, it's not up to me to cure the problems in our country." Her face reddened, "Right now there is a rumor that Simon will be dismissed from his position at the university! All these years, a prominent professor of literature and philosophy, now facing a likelihood that he will be thrown out of his work. Can you imagine what he is going through now, what we are all going through?" With clenched teeth she hissed, "And you came here, to me, to this family for help. What possible help can I give you? I haven't even a way to help my husband. If it's money you came for...?"

"Not money! Never! Melly jumped to her feet then slowly lowered herself into her chair. Incessant worry, the restless night before, now this woman's totally unsympathetic manner brought Melly's nerves to the breaking point. She must keep calm, she told herself, not let desperation take over. She forced herself to keep her voice even, to keep control.

"No, it's not money. What I'm asking for is a connection to a supplier to sell me goods. Not give!" She took a deep breath, ran her hands along her thighs and said quietly, " I'm prepared to buy." But immediately upon saying these words her thoughts flew to her depleted savings and to how in the world she could even pay for a shipment. But I don't care about that now. I'll get the money somehow if I need...my sisters maybe....

Melly peered closely at Ilse, examining the effect of her words. But, if they had any effect at all, Ilse wasn't showing it. Instead she busied herself with studying her fingernails, first one hand, then the other, then switched her attention to a monster beetle forged in silver and pinned to the shoulder of her dress.

Suddenly she sat up straight, looked in the direction of the door. For the first time since entering this house Melly saw her hostess do the unexpected: Ilse smiled.

"Ursula," sang out Ilse, "Good morning, *Liebling,* my dear sweet girl. Come here to your mother and give me my morning kiss."

Melly followed Ilse's glance; a dark-haired, dark-eyed girl about twelve or thirteen, Melly guessed, padded into the room directly into Ilse's outstretched arms. Some of Melly's earlier conceived notions about Ilse dissolved in light of this altogether loving demonstration. Well, she's capable of some warmth, thought Melly. There is a heart there, after all.

"Ursula," said Ilse, "I want you to meet Melly. Melly is a relative...a cousin."

Solemnly, Ursula walked around the back of Ilse's chair to Melly, put out her hand and said almost in a whisper, "How do you do."

"I'm very pleased to meet you, Ursula." As Melly took Ursula's hand, she shifted Inge onto her lap. "And this is my baby. This is Inge. She is one year old."

Ursula leaned her face into Inge's, then turned toward to her mother and asked, "*Mutti*, can I show Inge my doll-house?"

"No, no. I'm afraid not today. Inge is leaving in a little while. Then pretending irritation, "And you know the rules about coming to the table in nightclothes. And you should be getting ready for school...no?"

"*Ja*" sighed Ursula in a long breath. She shuffled to the doorway, stopped short, then called a merry goodbye over her shoulder, *"AufWiedersehen,"* and scooted from the room.

"She is a lovely child," laughed Melly, thankful for the small bit of gaiety in these otherwise dismal two days.

" Ilse stood and pushed her chair back. "And she's an excellent student," she said proudly, "Attends lyceum...preparing for university," as she straightened her dress, carefully positioned her fox over her shoulder and pinned her quilled hat into her blond chignon. She placed her handbag under her arm and stood ramrod straight opposite Melly. "I must be going. But please don't rush. I have an Opera Guild meeting and I can't be late. After that there is a meeting with the Jewish Women's League.

"Now, about your problem. There is really nothing I can do for you. My circle of friends, connections, as you call them, grow smaller each day. Yesterday I had the shock of my life. I called upon Helga Baumer, my friend for years. She had invited me just last week to her home for lunch. We've sat on committees together, been involved with the same charitable works. Our daughters grew up together, sisters practically, they are so close. Well, when I came to her door, she did not welcome me inside. She pretended there was no invitation. At first I thought she just forgot; either that, or she was playing some queer joke for some reason. I tried laughing it off outside there on her doorstep, jokingly tried to refresh her memory, but she cut me off. I tried stepping inside, but she blocked me. Then she said, 'I do not invite Jews into my home.'

"That is what she said to me. I could see she was upset, embarrassed. She said that she was sorry. She closed the door.

"I don't know how long I stood outside staring at that closed door before leaving. When I turned to walk away I saw a woman, I don't know who she was, a neighbor most likely, standing near the gate, listening to what had just taken place. She just stood there and stared at me, and I could feel her eyes on my back until I turned the corner and was out of her sight."

The room fell silent. Ilse's eyes were now cast down as she searched in her handbag, withdrew a miniature bottle of cologne, and dabbed a drop behind each ear. She replaced the bottled and inched into a pair of pinch-tight black leather gloves. "So you see why it is that I cannot help you." She smoothed down each individual finger, stretched out her gloved hands, examined backs and palms, then secured them with two tiny buttons at each wrist. Her preening completed, she looked up.

"But please finish your breakfast. Stay as long as you like, and please help yourself to whatever you would like for the trip back. Frau Miller already knows to take care of your taxi whenever you're ready." Then in a voice unexpectedly softened, she offered gently, "I do regret that I cannot help you with what you came for...the times being what they are. And I understand that you did not come for money, Melly, but just the same we will send some from time to time, whatever we can." She walked to the back of Melly's chair, put her hand lightly on Melly's shoulder, then turned on her heel and walked away, leaving a scent of lavender water behind.

Melly, anchored to her chair, watched Ilse depart into the hallway then out of sight. Above the throbbing in her temples she heard Ilse's clicking heels grow faint, then silent as the front door closed. Ilse's dreaded words, "I cannot help you," beat time like a drum. It, took all her strength not to scream, come back, come back. You must come back and help me.

She stood to leave, conscious of the heaviness in her chest and the fluttering in her stomach, like butterflies trying to escape. As she tucked Inge into her basket, she turned and saw Frau Miller approaching with a box. "For you and the baby," she said gently, "Take, take, you will get hungry later."

Mechanically Melly accepted the box, "Danke." She had pushed all thoughts out of her mind, but one: home. I can now go home. She climbed into the waiting taxi, then whispered in a tear-choked voice to her precious, sleeping Inge, "We're going home Liebling,....home."

Dusseldorf
1935

CHAPTER FIVE

A Snub and A Celebration

Six passengers disembarked at Dusseldorf. Melly was one. The others, the Schneider family, hurried past Melly in a nervous flurry, quickly casting their eyes aside as each one caught Melly's stare. How many dozens of times, Melly thought, have these children run into my store for a cookie or my special holiday stollen? Or Frau Schneider, how often has she dropped by to exchange gossip and pass an hour or two on a slow afternoon? Now they walk by me, pretend they don't see me. The shunning, this is the hardest part of everything.

Two Brownshirts, Hitler's Auxiliary Police, strolled along, glanced casually at the six travelers and their baggage, paused to light their cigarettes, then continued on. Melly, unnerved at the sight of them, shivered slightly and drew together the corners of her upturned collar. "It's getting older," she muttered into her coat. She peeked inside the basket on her arm and lowered Inge's bulky, knitted hat to her eyebrows, leaving visible only Inge's wide, watchful eyes. Then after raising the blanket to make a tent over the basket, Melly proceeded on her way.

A slate colored sky cast a reminder of the coming winter, and the smell of burning wood traveled in the air. Already the stoves are going, she thought. Melly always welcomed the coming of the new season: the approaching holidays, the foods, the smells, the family joking and teasing around great-grandfather Alonzo's ponderous table. " So many Gold-schmidts before me gathered at that table," she often said to herself. "So many holidays celebrated."

She quickened her pace as she crossed the deserted park bordering the cobblestone square, the other side of which stood, "Goldschmidt's". A shower of leaves, freed from their branches by a sudden blow, swirled crazily around her ankles and onto the pathway, crunching under her shoes. Soon, soon, she thought, as she finally emerged and faced the imposing red brick building where she lived and had worked all her life.

For a few moments she stood and thought back to when she was a child and to her grandfather, so many times, telling the story of Goldschmidt's: of how his father came to Dusseldorf from Bavaria with new bride; of how with his last *pfennig* he built this flat-iron brick edifice; of how against strong opposition from his soon-to-be-neighbors in their timber frame houses, he built it anyway facing the town square; of how he laughed when the townspeople called it a monstrosity. "Oh, *ja*" her grandfather had said proudly, "he was one smart man, because now you see Goldschmidt's is a landmark. When people give directions to the park or to the market, they always say first go straight to 'Gold-schmidt's, you can't miss it. Then go left to the park, or right to the market. Wherever anyone wanted to go, first they must find "Goldschmidt's.' Oh, he was one smart man all right."

Just then a clattering milk wagon jolted Melly from her thoughts. She rested Inge's basket on the pathway and looked across to the lighted windows in the apartment over the store. There was something comforting in the drawn shades and her sisters' shadowy figures moving busily about the dining table. They're all there, she thought, Kurt, my sisters and their husbands. They're all there to make a homecoming for me. Away one night and they do this for me. She swelled with the warmth of it, and all at once felt rested and serene as though she had just returned from a leisurely stroll; as though the disappointment in Berlin and those hours on the train never happened.

Melly sighed and proceeded across the square. "They'll want to know everything, what Hoffmann said, what the cousins said," she said aloud. She shook her head quickly from side to side, embarrassed to have spoken aloud, thankful to be alone in the square. *Ach du lieber,* she thought, somebody walks by me they'll think I'm *verruckt,* looney in the head or something.

Home at last. Melly stepped inside the side door into the wallpapered foyer, placed Inge's basket on the downstairs landing, and waved her arms overhead until she located the cord to the ceiling lamp.

She could hear Rosi's robust laugh mingle with her sisters' disagreements about the best time to start the noodles. A sudden burst of good cheer from the men and the clunk of mugs made her smile. Overhead, footsteps scampered about the rooms and the smells of food welcomed her as she climbed the stairs.

We have to make a change, Kurt and me, she thought. We can't continue the way we have, like everything is normal, like everything is fine. At the top of the landing she stopped to catch her breath. Hearing the excited voices of her family on the other side of the door, oh *Ja,* she thought, there'll be plenty to talk about tonight. But, when the talking is over, we'll have a good meal and a good time and even a good laugh when I tell them about Otto Hoffmann's napkin and Ilse Steinhardt's hat with the quill.

CHAPTER SIX

Seeds of Change

The first morning home from Berlin, Melly lingered under the eiderdown, watching the window curtain caught by the early autumn breeze. Just like a dance, she thought. She sank deeper into the bedclothes to escape the chill in the room and thought about the approaching winter and her failing business.

"Kurt must help out," she whispered to herself. "There is no other way." She remembered promises she made: to Kurt, to his sisters, made before God, when they married in 1927. She would always take care of him. A solemn promise eagerly made when life was safe and secure; when there was no reason to think that anything could change. Back then, it was inconceivable that her livelihood, so carefully nurtured by the generations, and then by her, would be taken away. Knowing that Kurt had no assets to speak of, financially or professionally work-wise, but certain that he was a good, decent man who would be a faithful husband and a loving father to their children, if they were so blessed, the promise to always provide for him was easily made. *Ja,* but that was then and this is now...a very different world now....

Her eyes roamed the bedroom and rested on the large family portrait opposite her bed. There they were: her parents standing proudly behind their four daughters, all dressed in their best, all smiling gently. A reminder of once better times touched her spirit. Someday it will be good again. She would make it good again. She was home and the sights and sounds were all around her. Entrusted with this legacy she would do whatever needed doing to keep it for herself and for those to come after.

Now this morning standing at the side of her bed, pushing her feet into worn, plaid flannel slippers, tying a blue chenille robe around herself, Melly glanced at Kurt's side of the bed. The covers were thrown back, and in a peculiar habit that Kurt could never explain, he had turned the face of the clock to the wall upon arising. So odd, she thought, that in all these years he never skipped a morning. All around him changes are happening, but inside himself he keeps change away.

She shuffled across the hall where she filled the chipped enamel basin from a pitcher of water left standing overnight to take off the chill. With much sputtering and foot stamping she washed her face. On her way she stopped to look in on Inge, still sleeping soundly, then walked into the kitchen. She sat down to her usual breakfast of blackbread and tea.

She thought about the night before: the excited talking and the festivities. But then an unexpected announcement from her sisters cast a cloud over the evening. They said that they were thinking about moving to Frankfurt. They said that I shouldn't worry because it's not going to happen soon. They had heard that it's better there. Here, in Dusseldorf, they can't find work. They said that no one will buy from them. And no one will hire them, even to clean houses. They're using up their savings. It's better in Frankfurt. But don't worry, they had said. Everything will work out all right. But in her heart Melly knew that their leaving day would come, and soon, How could she not be heartsick.?

"Well, Melly, *guten Morgen,* I'm so glad you're home. I missed you. Even for one night I missed you. Now you must tell me all about it." Eager to hear the news, Kurt seated himself opposite Melly at the table, poured a cup of tea and relaxed back in his chair. With the manner of someone about to be entertained he moved the ashtray stand closer, lit a cigarette, then looked expectantly into Melly's eyes. "So, how are my cousins in Berlin? Tell me about Simon. Is he well? How does he look? I heard he became stout. I hope you remembered me to him. Did he ask about me? Tell me."

In a composed, almost monotone voice Melly related, in detail, about how she was treated by Kurt's family. But then, in all fairness, she said, "Your cousins, Kurt, are having troubles of their own. I don't expect anything from them. But with Hoffmann it's a different story. I have hope that something will come from him. You'll see...Hoffmann is a good man with a conscience. He feels his obligation to this family. You'll see, one way or another Hoffmann, or his son, Hans, will send a shipment and then we will be able to get back some of our business.

Melly stood and began clearing the breakfast things. "Of course I understand the business can't be the same, not the way it was." She placed her washed cup and saucer on an overhead shelf, rinsed the teapot and carefully wrapped the remainder of the blackbread for tomorrow's breakfast. "But not everyone is going along with the ban on Jewish business. I see people every day bringing their shoes to Walter Stein's shop for fixing. And the bakery, Frau Alterman never closed that store even for one day. People still go there for their breads and pastries.. I see it every morning. With Hoffmann's shipment there might be enough business to keep us going until this Nazi nonsense is over."

Inge's stirring two rooms away, then her call, "*mutti, mutti*" grabbed Melly's attention. "*Ach,* Inge needs me." She rose from her chair to leave, but paused to summon her courage and say what needed saying. Her voice shook. "Kurt, until the shipment comes, you'll need to bring in some money." She pretended not to notice Kurt suck in his breath or that he blanched then slumped in his chair. "The little bit of money from Julius every once in a while buys your cigarettes and sometimes a book. But these days we need for food and coal because it's already turning chilly, especially the nights. Winter will be here before you know it. Maybe Julius could spare more."

Kurt stood. Melly saw his color return as the astonished look on his face slowly receded. At first he said nothing. He mashed out his cigarette, carried his cup to the sink and into the basin of soapy water. "Of course, I'll take care of it right away...right away." And in a troubled voice, "I'll do whatever I can...right away"

Days, then weeks, passed with no response from Julius and no word from Hoffmann. Melly found some work with the the local tailor, fixing trousers for his customers. But the work was not steady, and her earnings were small. Since she was not currently using the store for her business she decided to take her sister Rosi's advice to get a tenant and rent it out.

"Kurt," she began over supper one evening. "I spoke to Herr Feinermann a few days ago. You know who I mean... the man who fixes pots and broken things from that shed behind his house."

"*Ja*, I know who you're talking about. So what's the gossip from Herr Feinermann?" teased Kurt lightly, always ready for neighborhood news.

"No gossip. But we made a business deal. What happened is that he inherited a printing press, and now he wants to try and make it a business. But he needs a place to put it. His shed is too smal l. So for some rent money every month I told him that he can put his machine in my store. He wants to move in right away. So I will need you to help me box up some goods from the store to clear some room for him."

As she spoke Kurt slowly raised his eyes toward the ceiling, just enough to avoid facing Melly, but not enough to hide his confusion as his eyes shifted from side to side. After a few moments he found his voice, barely above a whisper.

"What are you saying?"

"You may need to bring some boxes upstairs into the dining room," she continued, "any corner so they're out of the way."

"What is all this about?" Kurt gasped.

"And I guess some boxes can stay in the upstairs landing by the kitchen door, if you leave room enough to pass."

Kurt, his dinner half eaten, rose from the table. He stood alongside his chair. "Yes, of course, I'll pack up the boxes, but why? Why go through all this trouble? For what? So times are a little hard right now, but it's only temporary. So there's a little less food on the table these days. So what! We're not starving. We've been through this before. First it's bad, then it's good. All this will pass. You'll see." His voice was serene, calming, as though soothing away a bad dream. Then seeming to dismiss the whole idea, reseated himself at the table and quietly resumed his supper.

Melly closed her eyes, leaned back in her chair and crossed her arms over her chest. It's unbelievable, she thought, how little he understands. Nothing I say gets through to him. She reminded him about their desperate need for money. "Maybe Julius will send money. Maybe not.

Maybe he has no money to send. One way or another we must get money, any way we can!"

All at once the strain of the past few weeks released in a torrent of tears. Melly covered her face with both hands and sobbed until she could no longer endure the pain behind her swollen eyes. She heard Kurt scampering about the room, running water, then squeezing a cloth before gently blotting her face and neck. "It's not good for you to get so upset. Everything will be all right. You'll see... times will change.... you'll see."

"I don't know what else to do," she wailed. "I need you to help me."

All at once Kurt slammed the washcloth onto the table. "Don't I always help?" he exploded as he stood over her, hands on his hips. "Don't I always do what you ask?" He dredged up the past , things he did, the events leading to those things. "What more can I do? What do you want from me!" he cried out. He seated himself opposite her at the table. Pushing aside his dinner plate he leaned toward her and asked, "How, or from where ,do you expect me to get money?"

Melly sat quietly, calming herself, thinking about how to make him accept reality; how to deal with a way of life that he had never experienced and can't understand.

"You must find a way to earn it," she said gently. " Get some work, any work. It doesn't matter what....It's different now, Kurt. You must bring in some money."

Melly rose from her chair abruptly and looked into his eyes, now dull and expressionless. I did that, she thought, I drove the light from his spirit. I did that to him... may God forgive...."I'll be in the store packing boxes. So whenever you feel like it they will be ready for you to move." She said these words to the man she loved with all her heart;

a man, who she sensed in one instant finally understood, at last. Yet who, in that same moment became a different Kurt. No more the man-child giving in to her decisions, but instead a dominant presence, a husband in charge. In one brief instant Kurt became, in every sense, the kind of man she never would have accepted to be her husband. Yet she would always deeply love him. She knew that. And he would always love her. She knew that also.

CHAPTER SEVEN

A Visitor and an Offer

The next two months passed quickly. On New Year's Eve, Melly and Kurt ate a quiet, simple supper of red cabbage and, unexpectedly, a cold blue carp brought by Herr Feinermann that morning. "Gerda had extra," he smiled patting the package as he handed it to Melly. "And don't forget," he called over his shoulder on the way out, "I heard there'll be fireworks and church bells at midnight."

Just before midnight Kurt woke Inge. Melly objected saying it was too late for a two year old baby to be awake, but Kurt woke her anyway. He said that it was only for a short time and that just this once couldn't hurt. Who knows what will be next year.

By half-past midnight, Inge was tucked back into her bed and sleeping, the plates and platters put away into the special cupboard reserved for holiday dishes, and the stove banked for the night.

Melly undressed quickly in the dark and slid into bed against Kurt's warm back. She wondered if he was still awake, he was so still. Timidly she slipped her hand under his nightshirt around to his chest, his soft hairs against her palms, hoping he'd turn to her gently, sweetly, be again the tender lovers they once were. But like all of Kurt's responses to her attempts at lovemaking over the past months, his breathing held at her touch, his body straightened and tensed. Slowly

Melly withdrew her hand and turned away. Instantly she heard his breathing begin and felt his body loosening as if suddenly unlocked from bonds.

She thought about his heartsickness, his despair, never mourning the loss of property, but only social position he felt he was born to have: a gentleman who would fill his life with beauty and ease.

Instead despondency claimed his days, ever present, tugging at him like the hidden pull of gravity. She saw it in his eyes, in the humiliation that haunted his once clear, serene expression. She heard it in his voice, in the many stories he told two year old Inge, who sat wide-eyed and filled with wonder at Kurt's remembrances of times past, even though it was all beyond her understanding.

"See, Inge, this is my Iron Cross for Bravery," he would say as he opened the satin lined case to show her. "This is from when your papa was fighting for our country, and I did such a good job that I was given this special medal of honor. It's beautiful, no?" And Inge, filled with awe, would gingerly touch the precious item and whisper, "*Ja*, papa, beautiful,"

Kurt's distress cast a far reaching gloom, infecting their holiday celebrations, once joyful, but now only a sadly acknowledged duty quickly cleared away. How very different from previous New Years with her sisters and their families. How they had chattered and clattered around a bountiful table. Then always with the table cleared and the cups and plates put away, a flushed and excited Rosi, swaying on the rickety piano bench and thumping a military style fanfare on the old mahogany upright, signaled the start of the evening's songfest. Behind her, seven raucous, off key voices boomed their favored folksong of love:

Du du liegst mir in Herzen
You are in my heart.
Du, du liegst mir in Sinn
You are on my mind.
Du, du machst mir viel Schmertzen.
You cause me much pain.
Weist nicht wie gut ich dir bin.
You do not know how good I am for you.
Ja, ja, ja, ja, weist nicht wie gut ich dir bin.
Yes, you do not know how good I am for you.
So, so wie ich dich liebe........

Sometimes they'd alternate with a drinking song or two, but always returned to their most loved Du, du...And always the little ones clowned at their caterwauling, pretending to gag, clutching their throats, hooting into each other's faces. And as always the elders with dogged persistence never missed a note and raised their voices even louder, while the children with equal persistence rolled their eyes, and twirled on their heels until dizzy and breathless, and finally flopped on their backs, their tongues dangling like thirsty pups.

Just before midnight an exhausted and hoarse Rosi would announce that she was "Getting deaf already," and bang down the lid on the yellowing keys. The festivities, except for hugs and kisses and happy new year's wishes, were over.

Then, afterward with everyone gone and the house still, Kurt, would seat himself at the dining room table, rest his crossed wrists on crossed knees, and with his last cigarette for the day loosely held between his fingers watch Melly move about the room. And Melly, anxious to finish clearing away the last remnants of the evening, would smile shyly as she caught his eye, and murmur how much she loved the quiet of the place after a party. Then undressing before a still warm stove, they'd slip into bed. Always he reached for her. "Happy New Year *Liebling*" he'd whisper, "happy New Year." And Melly, her being filled to bursting, silently with pounding heart, would fold into his arms.

But not tonight. Not this New Year. Melly sighed, drew the covers to her chin and turned her thoughts to the next morning. I'll make a special breakfast to start the new year. Kurt loves stewed fruit and a boiled egg with a hard crusted roll, and chicory instead of tea. *Ja*, that's what I'll make. Maybe his spirits will pick up. *Ja*....

But as in all mornings these days, Kurt's cup and plate were already in the sink. "So," Melly muttered into the air, "He wants to be by himself...even on this special morning...already 1936...."

She sat Inge on books stacked on a chair and pushed her to the table. Quietly they breakfasted on blackbread with a bit of honey, which Inge solemnly drizzled over the tops. Tea was sweetened with homemade jam from Hildy Frankel, who three days before exchanged it with Melly for two spools of thread, and a small box of pins from the packed boxes in the hallway.

Thoughts about her sisters were constant. They filled her mind from the first day they left for Frankfurt. Amid tearful "goodbyes" they swore to visit often.

"You'll see,'" Rosi had said, "It won't be so bad."

"We'll keep the holidays together like always," said Sabine. And as soon as we're settled you'll take the train to Frankfurt and stay for a nice visit."

"And we'll come to Dusseldorf," assured Bella, the trains run all the time. You'll see, you'll hardly know we left."

But no amount of assurances could quiet Melly's heart-break or smooth away the loneliness of total separation when neither Melly nor her sisters could put money together for train fare.

In the beginning letters between Dusseldorf and Frankfurt softened the blow of being apart, which up to then, except for the passing of their parents had been the biggest upset of their lives. Newsy and filled with hope for the future, from Frankfurt they wrote of the work they had found in spite of the boycott. Rosi went door-to-door and sold aprons that she made on her sewing machine, and all three husbands found kitchen work in the Jewish Hospital. Things were going well, they wrote, in face of the almost worthless mark. But best of all, the three families found apartments within a few blocks of each other.

From Dusseldorf, Melly wrote of Inge's progress and of Kurt's work, running errands and occasionally helping Herr Feinermann in his printing shop downstairs. Two days a week she found work cleaning houses. The pay is small, she wrote, but a meal is included, and I can bring Inge with me. Sometimes I get food to take home, and sometimes, there's a treat for Inge. Herr Feinermann, she was glad to report, became a permanent tenant, who paid his rent on time, in Deutchmarks when he could. But mostly he paid in food and fuel, which was the best arrangement since the mark hardly bought anything anyway. She never wrote of Kurt's unhappiness or even of her nights without sleep or the days of constant tiredness and fitful crying when she was alone. Why bring them worries?

As the months went by, letters from Frankfurt came less often. And when they did, once bursting with talk and good cheer, now were sparse and strained. A duty, it seemed to Melly. Not at all the lighthearted interchanges they had started out to be.

Melly's days, as well, were long and leaden. Outwardly she was doing, going, taking care, but except for Inge, Melly found no joy, as she once did, in the daily routine. Inwardly she wished for change. Only change could restore hope. But she was uncertain how, or even if change could be possible, especially with no resources and with no other roof than the one over the store.

The banging of Inge's spoon on the table and Inge's sing-song "la,la,la la," brought Melly's attention to the present. She began clearing the breakfast things when heavy footsteps on the stairway, then persistent knocking at the door called her from her work. "*Ja*, who is it?" she called, as she half-ran, half-walked through the rooms. "I'm coming, I'm coming," she called as she threw open the door.

"Herr Hoffmann! Oh, *Gott!* Kurt, Kurt. Oh my God! Kurt come here," shouting in the direction she believed Kurt to be. "Look who is here. Look who came to see us, such a wonderful surprise...my head is spinning. Come, come in," as she took hold of his arm and led him into the living room. "Sit, sit, I make tea. Kurt, Kurt ...."

"Melly, you make too much fuss," laughed Hoffmann, who, upon Melly's introduction to Kurt stood to shake his hand, then fell back into the chair .

Over tea Hoffmann began, "I came here Melly, Kurt, to explain what I am doing."

"But you are here," she said, "that's what's important. I knew you would not abandon me. I told that to Kurt many times, didn't I?" She turned to Kurt for his affirmation then turned back to Hoffmann. "You will be sending merchandise, *ja*? That is why you came. To tell us the good news."

"Melly, my dear Melly, I am so sorry to say what I am about to say. But the truth of the matter is that there will be no shipment." He slumped further into his chair, hands on his thighs, smoothing away tiny specks of crumbs.

THE TRIAD TREE

"What are you saying?" Melly's voice was raspy, shaking with disbelief. "Why else would you come? Why are you here?"

"To say goodbye. We are going to America, Hilde and me. We're leaving Germany."

"America?" Melly said dully. "You are going to America?"

"Hans gave up the business. Abandoned everything. He and Gisele, that's his wife, went to Norway to live with her family. With Germany rearming, and conscription a certainty, Hans is frightened for himself and for his little boy, who is almost old enough to be pulled into the Hitler Youth to be made into a soldier."

"But when was all this decided? You should have let me know…something… some word. All these months we've been waiting to hear from you."

Hoffmann rose from his seat, walked over to where she stood and took firm hold of her shoulders. "I could not say anything, Melly. Could not tell you anything when you came to see me in Berlin because of the servants. They could have made trouble for us, especially for Hans. It's hard to know who to trust these says. We couldn't take a risk. Our plans had to be kept secret." His voice trembled. "Tell me you understand," he pleaded, "You do understand, *ja?*"

"*Ja,*" she whispered into his troubled face, "*Ja.*"

Hoffmann smiled, sighed deeply and resumed his seat. Between gulps of tea he spoke about the distressing political climate on the one hand, on the other he spoke excitedly of the Olympic Games coming to Berlin " In just a few months. *Ach,* if I have any regrets at all about leaving Germany, it's only because I will not be here for the games. But it is settled, We are leaving next week for New York to live with Hilde's sister and husband until we find our own place."

Melly walked to the window and watched children play-ing in the town square. So there it is, she thought. His unsettled manner that I sensed in Berlin.... his reluctance to give me firm assurances...yet he let me leave with hope. He was wrong to do that...to treat me that way. "Dear God," she whispered, "What are we to do? She spun on her heel, faced Hoffmann, and cried out, "What are we to do? What will become of us. Every day is worse than the day before." She sank into a chair, covered her face with both hands and rocking back and forth wailed, "What will become of us?" over and over.

"Melly," Hoffmann's manner was stern, commanding and filled with concern. "I speak to you like a father, and if your dear papa were here he would say the same. He would tell you to go America. Life in Germany is not good. For the Jews it can only get worse. He would tell you to leave."

Melly's head reeled. She felt suddenly dizzy and groped for Kurt. who took her arm..

"Your papa would tell you and now I tell you. Leave! I will sponsor you and your family once I'm settled, or I will get you a sponsor. If you need financial help I will supply it, or I will get someone who will. I promise you this. I will do this for you."

Melly sat with her eyes cast down, her shoulders rounded as she rocked in her chair. Several weeks back Hoffmann's offer would have been shocking, absurd, not to be given serious thought.. But perhaps this opportunity for bettering their lives, now offered like a precious gift, would end her despair. If she were free to choose, she would seek an environment more familiar than America. Perhaps Holland....maybe Austria, or even Switzerland where some German is spoken.

She had heard stories, horror stories of New York City filled with Italian gangsters, their hair smelling of garlic; drunken Irish hooligans always fighting and making trouble; and Polish Jews with their vulgar Yiddish and coarse ways.

Yet now, facing an uncertain future, and Hoffmann's offer within her reach, some of the old fears of living among foreigners began to crumble. She could build a new life for her family. Maybe even open a new Goldschmidt's with Hoffmann's help, right there in New York City. She thought about her sisters and how lonesome she was for them. But maybe they would also move to America , and we could all live nearby each other again and be together, and we could have our holidays and parties just like always, just like old times. In America we can get jobs and Inge would be able go to school, and it would be good for Kurt also. He could throw off his old idea of special privilege. In America everyone is the same. He could start over, fresh, hold his head up.

As if he could read Melly's mind, Kurt, no longer the timid man who had once deferred all life's decisions to Melly, now with a small, smile shook Hoffmann's outstretched hand. "We appreciate your coming here, and we sincerely thank you for your offer to sponsor us, but we will not be leaving Germany. To leave is to surrender. The Germany we know and love will return, but only if we stay and hold onto what is rightfully ours."

Kurt helped Melly to her feet. He put his hand on her shoulder."My family and I are not, and never will be, in serious trouble. Hindenberg had promised faithfully that Germany will always take care of its war heros. And he made Hitler make that same promise. So you see why we will never leave Germany. We don't have to. But I wish you safe journey and good luck in what you do."

Hoffmann reached for his muffler. He grunted as he struggled into his bulky coat. "I disagree with you, Kurt. Hindenberg is dead and I do not trust Hitler. I believe your decision to stay is a mistake. But my offer will always be open. So, goodbye to you both, and give your Inge this sweet I brought," as he reached into his coat pocket and extracted a wrapped candy.

Melly watched him walk through the rooms, heard his footsteps recede as he clumped down the stairs and closed the downstairs door behind him. She turned to Kurt.

"I think we should think about Hoffmann's offer. Maybe we should go. Maybe going is the right thing for us to do after all."

For for the first time in all their years together, he shouted at Melly in anger. "*Nein, nein,* absolutely not. We do not leave Germany. Never! Never!" Then in a calmer voice continued, "If we go anyplace at all we'll go to Frankfurt. My family is there. Your sisters are there already." In a loving gesture he embraced his wife and said, "You will see, we will be much better off in Frankfurt," He daubed her eyes then offered his handkerchief.

And Melly, who never before this moment allowed her opinions to be dismissed, fell under the spell of Kurt's long withheld tender attentions, accepted his handkerchief and softly uttered, " *Danke.*"

Berlin
1936

CHAPTER EIGHT

"But I'm Protestant."

"*Bitte*, everyone, your attention!"

Ursula Steinhardt Wallerstein looked up from her studies to see her teacher, Herr Schultz, in his customary brown rumpled suit and brown rumpled tie spanning the classroom over the top of rimless eyeglasses. He stood alongside his desk smacking a ruler onto its top. His face, she noticed, was redder than usual, while his white knuckled hand holding the offending ruler struck in perfect cadence as though marking time for a military march.

Almost at once a stirring traveled among the students. Feet shuffled, pens dropped, some into proper slots, some to the floor and books snapped shut while papers shifted into disarray.

The bustling in the room finally subsided. The striking ruler stopped. The room fell into silence.

"I want all the Jews in the class to stand. Stand up!" his voice, clear and commanding, rang through the room.

Ursula, pale, petite with long black hair worn back behind her ears and secured with a simple mother-of-pearl clasp, looked more like twelve than her I sixteen years. And, indeed, neither parent could place her resemblance to anyone, neither Steinhardt, nor Wallerstein. "If I hadn't pushed her out from my own body, in my own bed, in my own house,

I'd think that she belonged to another family," Ilse had joked when the subject came up, which it frequently did.

Now, midway into her schooling at Lyceum, Ursula excelled well over the heads of her classmates. She looked forward to each new year at school, to take up the challenge, to nourish her competitive spirit, to learn and prepare her for the next higher level: entrance into university.

But never before in all her years in school did those words just spoken by her teacher come into the classroom. She was aware of the anti-Jewish laws and the problems they created for her Jewish friends. Most especially that new law barring Jews from admission to university. Margot Meysel, her friend and classmate, was devastated at first. But then later confided to Ursula that her parents were making plans to send her to university in America where they had family. And while she was glad that her friend would be able to continue her studies, still it troubled Ursula that many of her classmates were not so fortunate.

"Did I not make myself understood?" This time Herr Schultz shouted, "I want all the Jews in the class to stand up!"

Ursula turned in her seat, as did mostly all the students, searching each other's faces, questioning by their expressions if perhaps they had misunderstood their teacher.

"Stand! Stand! Stand."

Ursula watched several students rise slowly and take places behind their seats.

"I mean for all the Jews to stand!" Herr Schultz exploded while pointing a finger at Ursula, "That also means you, *Fraulein,* does it not?"

"Me? You can't mean me Herr Schultz. I'm not Jewish."

"You are a baptized Jew, are you not? Stand up!"

"But I'm Protestant."

"Stand up! He strode to where she sat and screamed into her face. "Stand!"

It was close to dismissal. Ursula began a trance-like gathering of her things. Ordinarily at day's end the room filled with activity; bustling students eager for home chatted and joked and rough-housed their way from the classroom. But this day a death-like quiet claimed the room. And Ursula, the model student, the always obedient student, nevertheless, this day defied her teacher and stood only to leave for home with Herr Schultz's parting words reeling in her mind, and lodging in her chest like a fist sized rock. "You will see "*Fraulein,*" he hissed directly into her ear, "More will come from your insolence."

There was never any doubt that Ursula was a very different child. "Unique" was the word family used to describe her. Not only in face and form, but bearing a precociousness that from babyhood on confounded, yet at the same time, amused and delighted her parents, as well as Sunday company.

Worried that her young charge might one day "Blabber away family secrets to the company," Frau Miller, the housekeeper-nanny usually stayed within hearing whenever Ursula was brought out to recite or sing for the guests. There in a bright, light-filled sun room, from Frau Miller's carefully selected repertoire, Ursula, at three years of age, recited from memory the first two stanzas of Heinrich Heine's "Die Lorelei." After that she concluded with a drinking song or two, much to everyone's merriment.

"I must confess," said Ilse as she walked with her guests into the dining room for a light buffet and afterwards a game of Skat, " Frau Miller taught me the same songs when I was little. But, Die Lorelei? Well that was beyond my capabilities.

One Sunday in 1924, Ursula at four years of age, did the unexpected: she regaled her audience, not with songs or poems, but instead with a detailed story of Alma, the kitchen maid, who had to go back to her parents' house in the country. In a most serious tone Ursula whispered, "To have her baby." Then in a loud voice continued, "She was disgraced. Frau Miller said so."

Ursula then sighed deeply and curtsied and began exiting the room. Suddenly she turned back and announced, "And I know where babies come from."

"You do?" teased her chuckling father, struggling to catch his breath. "And from where would that be?"

"From some good-for-nothing *grober Schwanz* in Strausberg. Frau Miller said...." when an arm suddenly appeared in the doorway, and amid howls of laughter yanked Ursula out of the room. From the sunroom in the front of the house the Sunday company could hear Frau Miller, now in the back of the house, loudly and sternly reproach Ursula for "Telling such a naughty story." Above Ursula's small bird-like protests, "But you said....and it's not a naughty...." Frau Miller extracted Ursula'a reluctant promise never, never to tell it again.

For her sixth birthday she was given a set of colored pencils. Immediately, she knew how to use them. At first she began by copying pictures from her own storybooks. Then she turned to drafting portraits of the rooms in the house. Over time the entire interior was depicted, room by room, each effort showing more and more skill and sophistication.

Before reaching her ninth birthday she astonished her parents when she presented them with her rendering of the exterior of the home. It was just before evening on a Sunday. Ilse and Simon were in the sunroom, side by side in the wicker settee, watching the last bit of lowering sun, when Ursula tiptoed over the where they sat and wedged herself between them.

"*Mutti,*"she said just above a whisper, not wanting to startle them yet eager to present her gift, "I made this for you and *Vati,*" as she handed the drawing to her mother; a drawing containing such exact proportions and artistic precision that even the curlicues and gargoyles adorning the outside metal works were included.

Ilse, so moved by this stunning rendition of her beloved home that after passing it to Simon, blubbered '*Danke schon*" repeatedly as she thanked and hugged her precious, talented child. And Simon, for the first time seriously considered the notion that his daughter was truly a brilliant child. He sat speechless, staring at the drawing in his lap, then absently handed it back to his wife.

On the evening of her tenth birthday, Ursula sat oppo-site her parents at a late supper. It had been a day of open house festivities, a double celebration. One to honor her birthday and another to mark her enrollment and the start of her studies in Lyceum. Now with the well-wishers gone and the day's excitement behind her, Ursula slowly picked at the meal before her, a worried frown between her eyes.

Suddenly she pushed aside her plate, sat forward in her chair and said, "*Mutti,* I want to say something."

Ilse and Simon both put down their forks and turned their full attention to Ursula.

Then with all the bravado she could muster, Ursula blurted, "I'm going to be an architect. I've decided....

Ilse tapped her napkin to the corners of her mouth, reached across the table and took hold of Ursula's hand. "Well of course you will...one day...when you are ready."

"But I don't want to wait. I want to study right now to build opera houses and museums, even churches. I want to go to school to learn that now. I don't want to go to Lyceum."

"Oh my darling Uli," said Ilse lapsing into her pet name for her daughter "Going to Lyceum is very, very important. Afterwards you can enter university and study whatever you wish. But it is imperative to first finish studies at Lyceum. Then you will be qualified for university."

At this point Simon had gulped down the last of his beer. He reached across the table and replaced Ilse's hand on Ursula's with his own. His face glowed like a lamp turned on. He squeezed her hand. "I have a wonderful surprise for you...a wonderful gift I've been saving."

Ursula sat straight in her chair and fixed all her attention on her father. I hope he's not giving me a silly puzzle with hundreds of pieces, she thought. Of course, I'll tell him thank you and pretend to be pleased if it is. But I hope it isn't.

"Now listen to this. I know a young man, a fine young man. His name is Peter Brettschneider. He is a student of architecture at the Bauhaus in Dessau. But almost every week he comes to Berlin, to the University to use the library." Simon gripped her hand tighter and in his excitement at what he was about to say, gently, rapidly thumped the top of the table. "I will ask him if he would agree to come here from time to time and privately teach you architecture. Would you like that?"

"Oh *ja, ja* papa, *ja,*" as she loosened his hold on her hands, ran around the table, and embraced him with the tightest squeeze she could manage. " Oh *danke, danke shoen, danke.*"

Simon's voice, barely choked out his words, "A*ch,* so many thank yous. You're so very welcome *Liebling,*" a special word reserved for his darling and most special child. He reached for his handkerchief and dabbed at his eyes beginning to fill. Then, with the sound of a trumpet, he blew his nose.

Berlin
1936

CHAPTER NINE

Curious House. A Work in Progress

Now, a deeply troubled Ursula, five years after Peter
had brought uninterrupted architectural studies, and after
five flourishing years in the Lyceum, upon reaching home
went directly to her room, without making the customary
stop in the kitchen to chat with Frau Miller. The booming
commands of Herr Schultz, "Stand! Stand! Stand!" filled her
mind. No matter how hard she tried to obliterate his voice,
she could not make it stop. She watched the clock, anxious
for her parents to come home. They would know what to
do, to make things right, to ease her misery. When finally,
she heard their voices downstairs, Ilse's pride and Simon's
darling joined her parents at the supper table.

There, in a shaking voice, Ursula related in detail the incident in the classroom with her teacher, Herr Schultz. First,
she confessed her wrongdoing: she disobeyed the teacher.
And then she sobbed when telling of his veiled threat about
her "insolence."

"He's going to do something terrible to me," she wailed.
"I just know it...something awful...."

In an instant Ilse jumped to her feet. "How dare he!" she
exploded. "How dare he say those things to children? How
dare he treat my Uli that way. Tomorrow I will go to the
school and take care of this. Herr Schultz and the Administrator will hear from me. And they will also hear that

my funding, my very generous funding for their special programs, is in serious question now because of this. How dare they!" as Ilse dropped down into her seat. She glanced at Simon as if to gain his approval. But he bit his lip, returned her glance, and said nothing before turning away.

Except for the clock on the mantle, its pendulum clicking the minutes forward, the room fell into silence. Ilse had just reached for the bell cord to signal the start of the meal, when a clattering, rolling food cart, steered by Frau Miller down the length of the dining room interrupted the quiet and prompted Ilse to ask, "Where is Greta this evening? Why are you doing her work?"

Seeming not to hear, Frau Miller continued moving around the table, setting places, filling plates and glasses. At Simon's place, she unfolded and laid an extra napkin across his lap, "Just in case," she muttered. Then straightening and striding from the room, this time pulling the cart from behind, she called over her shoulder, "Greta left this morning...new law...under forty-five years of age... can't work in Jewish homes. I'll be serving the meals from now on."

Once again the room became silent, yet Frau Miller's words hung heavy in the air. Sounds from the kitchen, clanging pans and clattering utensils, familiar as they were, brought no comfort. Not even the aroma of pears baking in the oven, their favorite dessert, could lift their spirits. For Ilse and Simon, believing all along that their wealth, their influential friends and relatives, and their elevated social position protected them from the chaos growing around them, a different reality arose. In spite of their determination to continue their well ordered, predictable and harmonious life, trouble had reached them, after all; each new day brought changes. Life was falling into disarray.

Suddenly Simon placed his knife and fork alongside his plate, rubbed the back of his neck and seemed to be studying the ceiling fixture above the table. He cleared his throat, pulled an envelope from the inside pocket of his jacket, sighed deeply and in a shaking voice said, "This letter came today. I found it on my desk when classes ended."

Ursula removed the napkin from her lap. Dinner was over as far as she was concerned. She leaned toward her father. "What is the letter about, papa?

Simon, holding the letter at arm's length began to read:

This is to answer your letter in which you asked for a reversal from our decision to dismiss you from your position at the University. You say that you are a veteran and hold the Iron Cross for Bravery and, therefore, entitled to special privilege to continue in your work, That privilege was given, which allowed you to remain in your post for the past two years. However, the Law of Reconstitution of the Civil Service Act of 1933 commands dismissal of all non-Aryan Civil Service Workers. Your special exemption has expired. You are immediately dismissed.

"And it is signed by Administrator, M Rodenkirch."

For the next few moments Ursula could only stare into her father's face, absorbing and trying to make the most sense she could from that letter. Trying to fit what she just heard into the life of her family she began, "But what does this mean...?"

All at once Simon slumped into his chair. Shaking hands covered his face. Cries, howls, like those of a caged hound came from his throat. He rose abruptly, stumbled from the room like a blind man and climbed the stairs to his study where, from her place at the dining room table, Ursula could still hear his cries.

" *Ach, nein, nein,*" Ilse whispered as she rose from her chair. "It's a mistake….a mistake". She walked around the table to Ursula. "I must go to your father, Uli." In a pleading voice she continued, "You understand, *ja?*"

"*Mutti…*" Ursula began, but stopped at her mother's troubled face. She felt her mother's hasty kiss on her cheek and the quick nervous strokes of her mother's fingers through her hair.

"We'll talk later, Uli…tomorrow…" as Ilse quickly turned and hurried from the room, calling ahead as she mounted the stairway, "Simon, Simon, I'm here ..my dearest…I'm coming, Simon…."

Feeling weighted and wedged into her chair, both hands held tightly between her knees, Ursula trembled. No *Mutti* sat across the table reaching for her hands, gently explaining, offering solutions, giving guidance. No V*ati* sat on her left at the head of the table excitedly presenting a wonderful, extravagant, feel-better gift. Nothing in her sheltered, doted-upon life had prepared her for anguished parents or personal strife. And never before this evening had she ever felt excluded from her parent's concerns, not welcomed into their discussions. This evening they had retreated into a special, private sphere, remote and inaccessible. Feeling strangely alone, deserted, with rising alarm Ursula realized that she, at that moment, had become an outsider in her own family.

She tried making sense of it, but it escaped her ability to understand and analyze. It was not like drawing on a grid where interlocking ideas produced a blueprint to follow, a forecast, a knowing of what was to come. No, this was very different. This had to do with a world beyond school, beyond home. A world in which she had no experience and almost no knowledge.

Her mind raced in circles. It was all about Jews. But what about them? What about her parents?. It was difficult to think of them as Jews when neither gave any attention to it. When both having no loyalty to any faith and finding all faiths "pure nonsense," yet, nevertheless, on a Sunday morning in 1920, had her baptized in the Lutheran Church, naming Frau Miller, the housekeeper, Godparent. Years later Ilse had explained that life as a Jew could be problematical. As long as one had to be something, one might as well be Protestant. Recalling that conversation with her mother, those words, for the first time in Ursula's life, had meaning.

She thought of her father's dismissal from the university. She thought about Greta, the kitchen maid, thrown out of work and she wasn't even a Jew. And she thought about the students made to stand for being Jews. For what purpose?

All at once Peter Brettschneider came into her thoughts. She pictured his slight, slender frame, dark wavy hair and thickly lashed dark eyes behind horn rimmed glasses. She recalled her father saying that they looked more like siblings than teacher and student. But there was no doubt that Peter was the teacher. A brilliant, strong-minded mentor with the same passion for learning as she. He taught her about stresses and girders and materials; about construction differences between private houses and opera houses; between museums and concert halls; between bus depots and railway terminals.

Together they designed and constructed a doll house that evolved and expanded into sixteen rooms, showing the most forward thinking in architectural design. Peter's Bauhaus studies influenced and dominated the project's scheme.

Seltsamhaus, curious house, is the name they agreed upon. They also agreed that it would be a never ending work in progress; that together they would incorporate the newest, latest ideas. He would always be in her life to continue the work, he had assured her, as long as she allowed.

Remembering his words of assurances brought her back to the present, to the dining room, to her parents' vacant chairs. She wondered if now, like Greta, the maid, Peter would have to discontinue his sessions with her.

She recalled a recent, playful remark made by her mother.

"You know, Uli, what I think?" teased Ilse. " I think you have a secret admirer. I think Peter is sweet on you."

"Mutti, that's ridiculous! "

"Smitten, Uli, totally, completely smitten".

Not interested in the direction this conversation was headed, Ursula had planted a quick peck on her mother's cheek and escaped into Simon's library, where she located, Plato's Republic," her next school project.

But now, this evening, her thoughts quickly moved away from that light conversation and her mother's romantic fantasies. Concerned only with continuing her studies with Peter, her mind spun with "what ifs." She tried to imagine her life without Peter but she had no idea how to proceed... no idea....

In a sudden rush of fatigue she wished now to be in her room, a warm, soft place, a welcoming space. With elbows on the table, her head held between her hands, her parents' vacant chairs, told her as much as she needed to know for now; that it was unrealistic to take for granted that her parents would always and unconditionally champion her causes; that all their strengths were needed for each other; that they recognized and responded to a foe, and that foe, indeed, was formidable. Somewhere lurked an enemy she did not yet know. . She rose from the table, a very different Ursula from the one who sat down earlier. Yet not so different that she did not tremble as she shuffled through the swinging kitchen door into Frau Muller's waiting arms.

CHAPTER TEN

Frau Dietz-Meyer's Hat Fell Over Her face

It had been many weeks since Ursula and her mother, hand in hand walked Unter den Linden. Strolling this grand Berlin boulevard had been a Saturday routine, one that mother and daughter eagerly anticipated as the week drew to an end. Even more than Sunday church with Frau Miller, Saturdays on Unter den Linden had always been the highlight of Ursula's life.

Having her mother all to herself, the news of her studies, her classmates, and her sessions with Peter tumbled from her lips. Sometimes the words came so fast that some syllables were swallowed and only half words escaped. She paused only to catch her breath, taking in great gulps of air, then with the same exuberance continued on.

If now and then her voice trailed off it was to examine details on many of the elegant buildings along the way. Sometimes she and her mother entertained themselves by playfully speculating in which of the buildings Hermann Goering might be residing with his movie actress wife. "This one." "No, that one." "No, no it must be this one, it has his nose."

Other times they lapsed into gossip, nodding in commiseration with the misfortunes of those they knew, and of those they only knew by name. With heads together and arms linked they walked and giggled like conspirators in a secret society.

But always the topic came back to Ursula, her concerns, her achievements. Nothing was said of the hardships of unemployment throughout the land; nothing about Hitler's pronouncement of rearmament; nothing about the anti-Jewish legislation, so clearly aimed at the destruction of their comfortable lives. Not even the coming of the Olympic Games to Berlin held any interest for them. All interest was centered on the details of Ursula's world.

If the weather was especially beautiful, the crowning feature of Saturday's walk was an adventure through Tiergarten Park, where they tramped the wooded brush, meandered the garden paths, and exited where a nearby café served, according to Ursula, "The very best gingerbread." A taxi ride home concluded the Saturday walk.

But recently Ilse had suspended the walks. Running into old friends, or committee associates, or even some shopkeepers she knew since childhood, who rebuffed her friendly overtures and turned their eyes away, brought unbearable humiliation. Posted along the way were Nazi Flags and hateful signs about Jews, although presently, they had been removed for the sake of the thousands of foreigners expected to pour into Berlin for the Olympics. Nevertheless, she was forced to face a painful reality: with a stroke of a pen she was now among the underclass. For her it was a reality easily avoided; she stayed indoors.

So it was unusual that this Monday morning, Ilse and Ursula were again walking on Unter den Linden. But this time it was a very different walk. With short quick steps, elbows hugging their sides, they charged ahead with purpose and obvious determination toward a goal: a conference with Herr Director Paul Josef Loeber, the head of Lyceum and a friend of Ilse's since childhood.

"Ilse, my dear Ilse, I am so glad to see you." A lanky, white haired man, wearing thick, heavy horned rimmed glasses and ill fitting dentures that clacked as he spoke, the Director rushed from behind his desk and extended his hand. "Here, sit, sit please. Sit." Herr Director Loeber brought a chair close to his desk. "And this is Ursula, of course. We are very well acquainted, Ursula and I." He pointed to a chair across the room. "So, my dear bring a chair and sit next to your mother. Did you know that your mother and I were children in school together? That's how far back we go...*ja,ja* so many years."

Of course I know, thought Ursula. Mother spoke about it often. It's the major reason for giving money to the school for special programs. But we are here because of my serious problem, and it's best if *Mutti* did the talking. With this resolve Ursula cast her sweetest smile in his direction, sat quickly, said nothing and began examining her fingernails.

With the fussing and seating amenities done, Herr Loeber took a seat behind his desk, folded his hands and placed them atop a file on his desk clearly marked, "Ursula Steinhardt Wallerstein."

"So," he began, I believe I have an idea of why you are here. But tell me in your own words."

Ilse moved to the edge of her seat. "Ursula has been telling me about Herr Schultz and his treatment of her. He is a horrid, despicable man and should not be allowed in the classroom, any classroom." Her voice was clear, her manner firm. She went into the details of the incident, while Herr Loeber with each detail, expressed shock and dismay.

Ilse leaned toward him, her wrists resting on the top of his desk. "Are you not aware of what this man is saying and doing to these children? In your school you allow this?"

Red faced and clearly shaken, Herr Director Loeber opened the file before him, glanced quickly at the contents and just as quickly closed it. "*Nein, nein*, I was not aware of anything you have just told me." In a worried voice he continued, "I thought you came to discuss Ursula's failing grade, which truthfully, surprised me. I did wonder about it because she never failed before. But I had no idea about....."

Sitting quietly, twisting a loose button on her sleeve, Ursula tried to erase the classroom incident from her mind, from her life, if she could. Her mother's angry voice seemed far away, dimmed by Herr Schultz's command to "Stand! Stand! Stand!" still relentlessly churning in her mind like a monstrous, unstoppable wheel.

She saw herself back in the classroom as she must have looked: red-faced, tight-lipped, near tears, defying her teacher's pointing finger as she remained in her seat.

Months later she wondered if that act of disobedience was the moment her courage took root; when she learned to say "No" out loud, even though her voice trembled; when she learned to hide fear even though her insides quaked and her knees twitched.

But now, this moment seated opposite Herr Director Loeber, Ursula strained to recall what her wrongdoings at school were that would cause her teacher to become so filled with contempt.

Well, she admitted to herself, there was the time when I caused a disturbance when my bag broke and all my books fell out right in the doorway and students had to wait outside until I cleared the way. But no, that was an accident and Herr Schultz saw that it was an accident and he never said anything about it. But there was the time when Frau Dietz-Meyer was giving a talk to the class and her hat fell down over her face and I giggled. But so did everyone else. Even Herr Schultz laughed because it was so funny.

Becoming increasingly upset as she thought about incident after incident she finally concluded that she did nothing wrong; she did her lessons, she earned many scholarship awards, and she wasn't, and isn't, even Jewish. But even if she were why would that be wrong? Why be made to stand?

Unable to hold back the tears any longer, Ursula crouched over and hugged her knees. In muffled sobs cried, "Why, did he do this to me? I don't know what I've done. I don't know what to do."

Herr Director walked swiftly to Ursula and helped her to her feet. "*Ach*, here *Fraulein*," as he handed her Ilse's held out handkerchief. "Here, dry your eyes. No more crying."

Once Ursula seemed composed he helped her back into her seat and turned to Ilse, his voice a mixture of worry and confusion. "I can assure you, my dear friend, that until this moment, I knew nothing of this. But I know what the times are like these days, and I am familiar with Herr Schultz and his sympathies. And I know he is not alone in them. It is a terrible time for everyone. Mostly terrible for the Jewish people, but terrible for the rest of us who are helpless to challenge the government. And I can tell you it would go very bad for us if we did. I just don't know" he wailed softly. "I just don't know...."

After some quiet moments, Herr Director walked to where Ilse had been stroking Ursula's hair and whispering soothing words. "Well," he said, "Here's what I can do. If I thought it would make a difference I would talk to Herr Schultz. But it would do no good and it might even bring suspicion to the school. On the other hand, what I can and will do is remove Ursula from his class, but that will have to be for the next term. But it is the best solution. And I, personally, will hand pick the teacher myself. Would you like that Ursula?"

"*Ja, danke,* Herr Loeber, *danke.*" A small smile touched the corners of her lips.

"In the meantime, do the best you can with Herr Schultz. I regret that you will have to repeat the class next term from the beginning. But it is the only way to remedy the failing grade."

"*Ja, danke.* " Ursula rose from her chair and held out her hand, which he eagerly clasped and tapped against his chest.

"You are most welcome, *Fraulein*"

On the way out, walking between mother and daughter, with his arms on each one's shoulder, Herr Loeber bent towards one, then towards the other. "I'm certain times will get better. The Olympic games are coming here, right here in Berlin soon. The whole of Germany is preparing. The entire world will be watching us. You'll see, Germany will be on best behavior. Normal times will return."

Ilse held out her *hand.* "*Ja,* my friend, my dear friend, let's hope that you are right. *Danke, aufWiedersehen,* You should stop by some day."

With those words Ilse took hold of Ursula's hand. "Uli," her voice was light, almost carefree, "I think today, instead of a taxi, we enjoy a nice leisurely walk home."

Hand in hand, arms swinging, their strides long and lei- surely, Ursula, glanced sideways at her mother. "Do you think, *Mutti,* that Herr Loeber was correct?" She spoke slowly, measuring each word. Maybe things will return to normal, like they were before. And school will be good again and papa will be called back to work at the university and Peter, who is is still coming regularly, will always come regularly, for our lessons."

Suddenly, Ursula brightened. "I just remembered. Peter is coming this afternoon." Her voice filled with excitement. "And he'll probably be earlier than usual because Frau Miller promised him strudel and he always comes early for strudel. Maybe he's already at the house."

As if by signal, mother and daughter quickened their pace toward home, toward a hope of normal times captured by the expected visit of Peter Brettschneider and his love of strudel.

CHAPTER ELEVEN

An Inappropriate Love

Peter Brettschneider completed Gymnasium in Hamburg in 1930, where he lived with his parents. His father, Fritz, a carpenter, and his mother Helga, a housewife and sometime pastry maker for the local baker, called a modest, but adequate apartment, home. There they raised an only child, an exceptional son. While proudly acknowledging his brilliance, both were at a quandary to know who he took after. "Certainly not Fritzy or me," his mother once remarked to a school official.

But Peter was destined to move on from Hamburg He announced his intention to study architecture and move to Dessau to begin classes at the Bauhaus, a school controversial for a curriculum that stressed modern design over classical. Considered vulgar by many in the profession, nevertheless, it fired the imagination of young architecture hopefuls. Peter, among them, enrolled in the Bauhaus. He was eighteen..

Once there, although living the barest existence, he managed almost every week to scrape together train fare to Berlin, to the university, where archives with rare documents were available to further his studies, and where admiring faculty took him under their wing. On occasion, while hanging their coats in the cloakroom, a faculty member would initiate a chat with Peter, often offering Peter supper with his family and a bed for the night. Peter became a familiar figure around the halls, the library, and even the washroom. It was at a washroom encounter that, Simon Wallerstein offered Peter a tutoring position for his ten year old Ursula; an offer that Peter readily and gratefully accepted and put into practice the next day.

Two years later the Bauhaus moved to Berlin. Excited over the move Peter scheduled more sessions with Ursula, now twelve and flourishing under his teaching. The additional money was welcome, even necessary; his room in Berlin cost three times more than in Dessau. He rationalized the frequency of his sessions over the next few years: she was an exceptional student and working partner, he told himself; she fired his imagination with her creative ideas; and she became a best friend who listened and offered solutiions to his concerns with a maturity beyond her years. Especially so when one year later the Nazis had closed down the Bauhaus entirely, and he worried about continuing his studies. After long talks together, both concluded that since he needed someplace to be, he should enroll at the University in Berlin. Even if it meant curtailing his architectural courses for the time being, they would still be able to continue their studies together, designing magnificent homes, museums and government buildings, the same as always.

But one day after a session had ended and he had called a cheery "Auf "Wiedersehen," on his walk home. Peter finally, honestly confronted long held feelings; he, a man of twenty-four, had inappropriately fallen in love with his student, who at fifteen was barely beyond childhood. There was nothing he could do about it except to keep it secret and hope for nothing more than to continue as her teacher, her mentor, her best friend. He thought about her parents and the kindnesses they had extended to him. They included him in family matters, confiding about their fear of Hitler, about their fear for the Jews, and about their fears for Germany. They became his family, albeit a second family, yet his family all the same. Offending them was inconceivable.

As for Frau Miller, watchful and fiercely protective of the Steinhardt-Wallerstein family, she would certainly run Peter off if he brought distress to the household. And while Peter took great care to avoid causing unhappiness to anyone, family, friend or stranger, he was doubly careful when it came to Frau Miller.

CHAPTER TWELVE

Underneath Frau Miller's Umbrella

A trusted family housekeeper since before Ilse was born, Frau Miller, always on the move, doggedly ran about the rooms, tidying, dusting, plumping, always slightly out of breath, yet always thinking of the next thing that needed doing, then the next. She never considered her work too hard or too demanding of her time. On the contrary, she prevailed upon Ilse to fire the ironsmith because " His work was sloppy and unreliable and he always had too much beer in his belly and often fell asleep before finishing his work." She could take care of the outside wrought iron railings better than he.

Unfailingly beautiful, the railings surrounded not only the house and garden but encircled the Summer Tea House, as well. There, Ilse's guests chattered, consumed fancy cakes and sipped Chinese tea, shielded by a lattice enclosure from the eyes and ears of the curious. It was an afternoon to boast about for weeks afterward. For an invitation to the Tea House was highly prized and aggressively sought, but available only among the Steinhardt's private, privileged circle.

Frau Miller knew the importance of the Tea House to the family. She understood that these occasions demanded perfection, and eventually removed Gertrude, the kitchen maid, from preparing the Tea House for guests. "She does not know how to set an elegant table," she explained when

Ilse questioned the substitution. "She knows only her country ways." And *"Nein,* nein, no, it is not too much work for me," she assured in response to Ilse's concern.

Steinstrasse-6, the Steinhardt home in Berlin, was Frau Miller's home too. After a hasty marriage, a stillborn baby and a husband who abandoned her, she came to work for the family as a young woman and stayed on over the years, never giving thought to living and working elsewhere. She felt privileged to belong to this prestigious household, and in her gratitude created a caring umbrella, under which the needs of the family dominated her days from early morning to late evening. She reserved only Sundays for herself.

On those days she carefully combed her greying hair, clipped short to below the ears, and donned her special blue Sunday dress for church, On each wrist she spritzed a smidgeon of "Evening in Paris," a Christmas perfume from Ilse, and headed off to worship at St. Paul's Evangelical Church and afterwards to teach Sunday School. Later in the day she visited her married sister and family and took bit of supper with them. Always at the end of each visit she called their attention to their poor church attendance and suggested that they reform. And as always, with a wink behind her back, they promised that they certainly would.

Having a major part in raising Ilse had always delighted Frau Miller. Frequently over the last years she thought back fondly to when her "little girl," was put in her charge.

But there came the time when Ilse at 27 years of age was unmarried. She appeared contented and seemed to enjoy her single, busy life. But, nevertheless, Frau Miller began to worry that Ilse would remain an old maid and grow old alone, without family, most especially, without children.

Ilse's family, the Steinhardts, were among Germany's oldest, wealthiest and most socially prominent. Their fortune, which originated from small scale money lending, burgeoned over the generations into world-wide banking, then expanded into Germany's growing chemical and dye industries and broadened into various business ventures throughout Europe. By the year 1920, the family's wealth had grown so vast that, where only a few in the family could actually put a number to it, Ilse could not.

Known for their money, they were, however, most noted for their devotion to the arts. Over time they had established foundations to promote and fund cultural events for the greater good over which Ilse presided, filling her days, fulfilling her life.

"You're being too particular," Frau Miller had announced to Ilse, who softly declined Kurt Rosen's marriage proposal, bid him a polite "goodbye," and closed the front door after him. "Sometimes," Frau Miller added as she trotted after Ilse into the living room. "I think you really don't want to marry at all."

It wasn't that Ilse hadn't considered marrying. On the contrary, she looked forward to meeting the "right man:" one who would not expect, or require, her retirement to become soley his Frau. She knew that she was eligible, desirable, and sought after. Yet, when suitors came, suitor's departed, one by one. For no matter how handsome, moneyed or brilliant, she would neither resign from the Steinhardt Foundation or from her various social clubs, where as leader of the smart-set, she reigned unchallenged.

Saddened that she might never find that man and becoming fearful when she imagined her life without a partner, at times she considered Frau Miller's urgings to "compromise."

But each time Ilse turned away saying into Frau Miller's set expression, "Just the thought of being with him, makes me miserable."

Then one evening at the grand opening of the Steinhardt Art Gallery, Ilse's newest venture, Simon Wallerstein entered her life.

Wallerstein's Emporium, a chain of high-end men's clothing stores, established in every major city throughout Germany, was the source of his family's wealth. Simon though, stubbornly independent and wanting no future in the family business, privately invested in German and American film industries. He accumulated a fortune aside from that into which he had been born. His life's ambition had been to live an intellectual life among peers in the academic world.

The Wallersteins were considered pure German and old family, owing to their family tree that could be traced back into the 1800s. Their wealth, rather the manner in which their wealth had accumulated, placed them among the "nouveau riche," new money, an elevated social station but somewhat below the Steinhardts.

If they were noted for anything special, it was for their clientele. For only the wealthiest could afford the Wallerstein label. Representing the finest tailoring, finest fabrics and fanciest prices, there were no bargains to be found at Wallerstein's Emporium. By even suggesting such an idea, one would find himself being shown the door.

This was the life Simon left when he chose the life of the mind and achieved his dream of Professorship at the University of Berlin.

Yet he desired more: a weekend retreat where he would invite his colleagues for intellectual talks and invigorating hunts; a place to indulge his occasional yearnings for solitude to read the philosophers and smoke his cigars before a fire in his someday wall-to-wall book lined library. But most of all, he longed for a family of his own: a wife, a child, perhaps several children, and a comfortable home to provide creature comforts. Yet, here he was at 33, still a bachelor, trying, but failing to content himself while living with his sister's family in Berlin, where cigars were forbidden, where constant quarreling among the servants forced him to retreat to his room to seek quiet. But the room was cramped, leaving no space for a library. His growing personal publications, on the lives and opinions of the worlds' philosophers, had to be housed at the University. Equally bothersome, the only window in his room faced the street, and was nailed shut to keep burglars out. Simon, who preferred the night air for sleeping, could do nothing but grumble and yearn for a home of his own, someday.

Family dinners and social gatherings among the academic community, solely to introduce Simon, hopefully. to his future bride had come to nothing. And Simon often voiced his dismay and raised the question, "What could be the matter?" as *Fraulein* after *Fraulein* discouraged his attempts at serious courting. He believed he had all the necessary credentials for attracting marriage minded young women. If one looked past his pudginess and beginning baldness, but noticed the monocle, which he flaunted to call attention to his personage, he believed his handsome chubby face and Wallerstein name should engender some interest among the opposite sex.

Also, aside from family wealth, which would always be available if he so chose, and his motion picture interests, he was also financially secure as a University Professor and employee of the government, especially so as holder of the Iron Cross for Bravery. Young maidens should be standing in line for an introduction, he believed. But instead, after so many polite "I'm truly sorry," or "I'm already committed," or "I'll be traveling for the entire next year," in response to his " May I have your permission to call on you?" he surrendered to his destiny: hopeless, lifelong bachelorhood.

There were, of course, young women and those not so young, who sought him out for his wealth and prestige. But Simon, desired more that just wedlock. Simon also wanted love. "Am I unreasonable?" he frequently asked himself in the mirror. And as always, looking into his own eyes, the face is the mirror always answered "Why no. Not at all."

Then one evening, desperate to escape his sister's house, a sudden impulse moved Simon to persuade his best friend and colleague, Wolfie Holzer to accompany him to the opening of the Steinhardt Gallery.

"Come, come," he said to the reluctant Wolfie. "It's a beautiful evening for a nice walk. We have no other plans. And it's not even far, just around the corner. Listen, even if the paintings are disappointing, the buffet spread would make up for it, *ja?*"

They agreed, food first, art second. While making selections from the bountiful buffet, pondering the varieties of smoked meats, cheese delicacies, goose liver spreads and pickled herrings, Simon heard an animated stirring from the entrance behind him. He turned to see a blonde, stout, Wagnerian-like woman, wearing a black hour-glass fitted gown, stride into the room. Smiling broadly, she regally acknowledged her subjects to the right then to the left.

In open-mouthed awe, Simon poked Wolfie's arm, upsetting his friend's newly filled plate. "Who is that magnificent, blonde goddess over there?"

Wolfie brushed the front of his coat from the aftermath of Simon's exuberance and whispered, "Why that's Ilse

Steinhardt. Everyone knows Ilse," and quickly walked out of harm's way to refill his plate.

"Well," muttered Simon to himself, "Not everyone."

Of course, he knew the name. Often he heard stories about the Steinhardts and how the next best thing to being a Steinhardt is to marry one. But never before that moment had Simon given it any thought. Now standing in the crowded gallery, observing majestic Ilse, a full head and shoulders taller than he, a smitten Simon vowed, "This woman I will have."

He placed his still empty plate on the table behind him, pasted a Cheshire smile on his excited reddened face, and strode to where "his Ilse," quietly conversed amid a small group of wine sipping guests. He excused, then introduced himself, elbowed his way to her side, and smoothly squired her to a quiet corner.

"Yes," said Ilse, "you may call on me." And "yes," said Ilse to his marriage proposal some months later, "but only if you discard that silly monocle."

" Of course, of course, yes, I promise anything, anything."

They had fallen deeply in love. She for his mind. He for her amplitude. If marriage to Ilse also meant that he give up his hope for a country retreat, his wish for a private library, his treasured monocle, he would gladly do so. For more than anything he wanted Ilse for his wife.

At the celebration of their first year of marriage, a curious Wolfie Holzer asked, "Simon, if Ilse were dark haired and slender would you still love her so much?"

Whereupon, Simon rubbed his chin and considered carefully. "You know something, Wolfie, that is a very difficult question."

The following year, 1920, Ursula was born. Ilse and Simon considered their family complete. Surprisingly Ursula's baptism which had been just for convenience, took on a life of its own. They were amazed at how totally Ursula embraced her faith while growing up, eager for Sunday morning church and Sunday School with Frau Miller. While Ilse and Simon could not understand their daughter's religious zeal, they saw no harm in it. They called a merry "Auf Wiedersehen" as Ursula, wearing Sunday's finest red velvet dress and black patent leather shoes, hand in hand with Frau Miller, waved goodbye and left for Sunday worship.

As for Frau Miller, to her delight she again had a little girl to raise. That Ursula was a child of her own faith to raise in her own Evangelical Church, made Frau Miller's joy complete.

Over the years, continuing their busy lives, secure in their devotion to each other, their work, and their prominence, and with Frau Miller at the helm maintaining their well-ordered household, life was good. Ilse and Simon dismissed the calamity of Nazi rule declaring, "It does not pertain to us."

Then came the horrifying realization at the dinner table in 1936. Only then, did the family of three face a sobering reality; regardless of their wealth and personage, Nuremberg Laws, enacted the year before, depriving Jews of their citizenship, and whatever might follow, did, indeed, pertain to them.

CHAPTER THIRTEEN

A Second Failing Grade

Even though it was the final day of classes until the new term, Ursula was made to sit at a back table where the non-Aryan students had been reseated. But with renewed spirit, Ursula was determined that the change would not affect her studies. After all, she told herself, it's nothing more than different seat and Director Loeber promised her a new teacher next term. Then everything will be the back to normal.

This particular morning more than just a seat concerned her. The students had been given intricate mathematical problems: a segment of tests to be graded, their results entered into permanent records for university entrance.

As she began the assignment, Herr Schultz's footsteps broke the silence as he walked about the room. The sound of his shoes, halted behind her seat. Ursula felt his eyes at the back of her head, and heard the creaking of the floor boards as he shifted from leg to leg. Waiting for his meanderings to resume, she put down her pen, paused momentarily, then turned slowly in her seat. Her eyes, wide and questioning, traveled upwards until they met his, unblinking, narrow slits that stared downwards into her face.

"Is something the matter, *Fraulein?*" he boomed.

At first, startled by his volume and the way his voice seemed to bounce around the room, she took a few seconds to compose herself. Then in a timid, most respectful tone, for above all she did not want to anger this man, Ursula whispered, "Oh, no, not at all, Herr Schultz, nothing is the matter. I was just wondering why you stand there behind me.

A small, cold smile touched the corners of his mouth. He looked away and spanned the classroom. Again his voice boomed, " To answer your question, I stand here because from here I am able to view all the students, but most especially to keep an eye on you."

Gripped with fear Ursula realized that she was still his target. But she kept composed, pretended not to notice, and assumed her sweetest expression, the one that without fail moved her father to smooth her problems away. "Please, I mean no disrespect, but I am not able to concentrate on the assignment while you...."

"Just do the best you can," he shouted in a whiny sing-song voice. "I'll be right here until the test is over. It's timed for two hours. And I suggest that you get started, that everyone get started," as he waved his arm in a circular motion to include all the students. "You've all wasted valuable time."

With these words there came a general shuffling of papers and shifting in seats as the entire class, up to then transfixed by the verbal interchange in the back of the room, now turned their concentration to the test before them.

With racing heart, Ursula, picked up her pen to begin, yet she was unable to ignore the figure standing over her, or quiet the throbbing in her head. She stared at her paper without comprehension.

Time passed in the hushed classroom. Students began putting down their pens, indicating the completion of the assignment. With trembling hand, in broken penmanship, Ursula scrawled her name at the top of her blank paper.

Dazed, she sat back in her chair as Herr Schultz called, "Pens down. Time is up."

Over her shoulder she heard his words, "I'll take this now, *Fraulein*." He picked up her paper and smiled his cold, stiff smile into her tortured face. Then, "Everyone," he boomed, "Bring your work to my desk and return to your seats."

Now, for a second time, a failing grade would be entered into Ursula's school record. She fought back the urge to cry. Crying in the classroom was undignified; it generated punishment from some teachers and often brought ridicule from classmates. She saw it happen to Berta Schroeder when she forgot to bring a handkerchief and sneezed into the air. For punishment, poor Berta was excluded from sports. And then, because she cried, she was made to sit with folded hands for three hours.

Ursula watched Herr Schultz stuff his briefcase, struggle into his overcoat and tip his hat good day calling " *Guten tag*'" to Frau Brunning, who passed him in the doorway.

In her dark blue skirt, white shirt and knotted tie, representing the approved Nazi dress, Frau Brunning dropped her satchel on the desk, and faced the class, all of whom had jumped up and stood at their seats as she entered the room. "You may be seated," she instructed. She then extracted a hard bound folder which she held above her head. Silently she slowly turned so that everyone had an opportunity to view the cover. From where she sat at the back of the room, Ursula clearly saw the title: "Race and Nationalism: The Struggle for Racial Purity."

Lowering it, now holding it face out against her chest, Frau Brunning began, "Dear students, my talk today is...."

Whereupon, Ursula, now lowered her head, face down on her folded arms, and quietly let the tears come.

CHAPTER FOURTEEN

Two Jewish Grandparents Are Sufficient

It was the first day of the new school term. As she walked to Lyceum, she thought about the signs that had lined the streets and storefront windows saying "Jews not welcome" and "No Jews allowed." They had all been removed at the start of the Olympic Games. Even though it was beyond Ursula's imagination to connect political agendas with sports, even Olympic ones, she did connect with Herr Director's parting words at their meeting several months ago. And those words proved true; school, home, church, every aspect of her life had returned to normal.

Even her father found work teaching Jewish children in one of the special schools quickly set up by the Jewish community. It wasn't university teaching but he seemed thankful for the work. He became his enthusiastic self again, retired his schnapps to the back of the cabinet and joined his wife and daughter at supper. And as always at every opportunity, he lit up a good cigar.

Ilse rallied as well. She became her proud buxom self as her appetite returned and the gradually acquired gaunt facial lines and furrows filled out to rosy plumpness. In her grande style, she resumed committee meetings and, the same as always, returned home with stories of this one and that one, who didn't do what, and who did it wrong. "Hopeless inefficiency," she complained at supper. "Just hopeless." Daily life became the same as before, although the social invitations which she craved, and which she believed would be extended once "This Nazi thing is ended." did not resume to include her.

Even Frau Miller was in a much better temper after she took on a new kitchen helper. "An old maid," she had stated with satisfaction. "A Jewish old maid. Now what are they going to say about that?" she harrumphed.

It seemed to Ursula that the worst had passed. Now, that the requirement to repeat last term had been forgiven and expunged from her record, she looked forward once again to new studies, new challenges and new commendations to add to her collection.

Except this day as she walked to school, some worry returned. For the Olympic games having ended, and the city having said "goodbye" to the last of the foreign visitors, Berlin returned to its pre-game oppressive measures. The dreaded signs not only reappeared, but one after the other larger, bolder and more numerous then before, lined the route to school.

But she was determined not to let anything spoil her first day, Ursula pushed unwelcome thoughts aside as she strode into her new classroom. There, a smiling Frau Hofer, her teacher, calling attendance and assigning seats, motioned for Ursula to "Come forward please, and your name please?" She held a red-inked pen in the air ready to check off the name from her student list.

Impressed with her teacher's soft manner, simple dress and welcoming smile, Ursula waited to be seated after her name was marked. But instead Frau Hofer said, "You must go directly to Herr Director's office."

"But why? I don't understand. Why?" All at once Ursula, overrun with old fears, suddenly paled. "For what reason?" Her voice trembled. Her knees began to shake.

"*Ach* do not look so troubled, *Fraulein*. It's probably nothing serious." She lifted a paper from her desk and waved it in the air. "This note left for me just said to notify you as soon as you arrive. It doesn't say a reason. So, go, find out what he wants. I'll seat you when you return from the meeting. It can't be anything serious. School hasn't even begun."

But Frau Hofer's kindly assurances did not dispel Ursula's feeling of dread. Maybe its over that Jewish thing again, she thought. But no, it can't be. That's all been corrected. She stood in the hallway outside the Director's office door and thought more about it. It's probably something good, she consoled herself. Maybe since the two failing grades have been removed from my record, Herr Director wants to congratulate me for earning another scholastic medal. Now fully calmed and prepared for a new commendation, Ursula, after timidly knocking and hearing a rather hoarse "Come in," seated herself in the visitors' chair alongside his desk.

After a moment's silence, Director Loeber cleared his throat and pushed his lopsidedly perched heavy glasses back from the end of his sweaty nose, only to have them slide back. He clicked his tongue over the annoyance, impatiently removed, then dropped, them into his desk drawer.

Ursula quieted her inclination to giggle as she watched his face grow serious and tight-lipped. He rolled his shoulders backwards, seeming to relieve a tightening in the neck. So many times she saw her father resort to the same shoulder rolling when he became upset. No, she thought, this meeting is not about anything good. Once again a premonition of trouble claimed her.

"Ursula," he began, " I've been made to examine the records of all the students here and then send a report to the District Leader. I have just received his findings and I am required to inform you of his conclusions and recommendations."

Her face got hot and, she was certain, red. Her insides shook. She wanted to run, run fast and far, get away, not hear the next words, dreadful words she knew were coming. But all she could do was to sit there, take it in, let it happen.

"Ursula," he cleared his throat, "You have been classified as *Geltungsjude,* a full Jew. Your classification is based on having two Jewish grandparents. In your situation there were four, actually. But two are sufficient for this classification." Her head was reeling. She tried to digest his words, put them into a place in her life. "But Herr Director," she cried out, "I'm Protestant! I'm baptized, registered in the Protestant Community. I've been confirmed in the Evangelical Church. And you already know this. So why....?"

In an instant her thoughts traveled back to the previous Palm Sunday. Dreamily she pictured herself in her new black velveteen dress, as she held a small bouquet of tiny white roses tied with her confirmation veil. She recalled the excitement of wearing, for the first time, grown-up silk stockings and new shoes with heels, low heels, but heels all the same.

She remembered the altar and Pastor Munk reciting the bible verse from Jeremiah especially selected for her... *Say not I am a child....* her thoughts trailed.... *for thou shalt go to all that I send thee, and whatsoever I command thee thou shalt speak. Be not afraid of their faces:* for *I am with thee to deliver thee....*

In her mind she could hear the church bells upon leaving the church. And in her soul, still so deeply touched by their music, love for the Lord and for her church welled up inside her to the point of tears.

"I receive communion," she cried out." I attend Church every Sunday. How can that be taken from me? How can I be Jewish when I'm Protestant. My parents...."

"Ja," Director Loeber crossed his legs and shifted in his seat.."Your parents, I was coming to them." His voice was gentle. "You see, in your school records, when they first registered you, they indicated their own religious affiliation as 'dissident'."

"Dissident? meaning....?"

"Meaning simply that they disagree with all religions."

Ursula 's stomach began to hurt. Her head began to throb. The Director turned in his chair, away from her eyes.

"In your situation, Ursula, it means nothing. It does not factor into your classification."

"But I'm baptized. I'm...."

"Ursula," he interrupted, his voice subdued, "your classification comes under the Racial Laws. It is a racial identity. Yes, you are baptized and with that baptism you are Protestant. But racially you are considered Jewish. Race cannot be baptized away. That is the position of government on matters of race."

With labored movement he rose from his seat, and with stooped shoulders paced about the room. His voice trembled with the next words. "I have hoped with all my heart that this day would never come; that somehow the country would change; that all these racial laws would be abolished. But they keep coming up, one after the other, after the other. And, truly, I never thought for a single moment that any of them would involve you....and...."

Suddenly, Ursula sprang from her chair and blocked his way, stopping, what seemed to be, his incessant babbling.

"No!" with rising panic, she shouted into his face. "No! No! all this does not involve me. It has nothing to do with me. I will not listen to you anymore!"

He straightened then. His was the saddest expression that Ursula ever saw in all of her seventeen years. "You will not be allowed to go to university. Your category restricts you. I am so very, very sorry my dear child....So very...."

Ursula stared into his face and collapsed.

When she opened her eyes, faces were hovering over her. Somehow she had been maneuvered into a chair and a cold rag placed on her forehead. Chorusing voices asked, "How are you feeling?" "Are you all right, *Fraulein?*" "You gave us a scare." Then she heard her mother's voice, "Oh my God, Uli! What happened.? Uli, *Liebling* I'm here. It's... M*uttii*," as Ilse pushed aside the huddlers and knelt before her child.

On wobbly legs, with her mother's arms around her, Ursula shuffled to the doorway. Behind her she heard the Director's voice, "Things being the way they are, Ilse, there is no point returning her to school here. There is no seat for her. Better to find another way." Then in a choked voice, "I'm so very, very sorry Ilse, so sorry."

Ursula turned then to see him gather his staff together and heard him say, "I have several students yet to see today about this matter. Contact the parents to be here. *Gott im Himmel*" he moaned, What next, what next?" he blotted the sweat from his face, went back to his desk and dropped into his chair.

CHAPTER FIFTEEN

BDM:The League of German Girls

"Hitler means trouble! Hitler means war!" Manfred Zinmann shouted when any of his five children displayed an inclination toward the Hitler Youth Program. His children considered him unreasonable, but steered clear of the organization all the same.

A four room clapboard and shingle dwelling, needing whitewash, was home to the Zinmann family: Beate and Erika, his daughters, Max, Fritz and Willie, his sons, Hansi, his wife, and her mother, called *Omi,* who had been living with the family since before Beate was born, comprised this household of eight.

Beate, his youngest, had no real interest anyway in the League of German Girls, the BDM, but her curiosity rose unexpectedly when her friend, Elsa Stern, was denied admission because she was Jewish. It was great fun, Beate believed, for the much younger girls as they marched through town in their white blouses and blue skirts, jiggling little flags while smiling and singing the Horst Wessel Song. But she was already fifteen. The BDM seemed to be a silly waste of time.

Mainly occupied with school, church, and her duties at home, Beate's need for companionship was satisfied, in part, with the company of her friend, Elsa Stern. Her father owned the butcher store, saving the meatiest soup bones for Elsa to bring along on those afternoons she spent with

Beate. Each time when offered payment, Elsa declined, saying each time that "Papa would not hear of it".

But Beate's closest friend was her older sister Erika. Together they enjoyed long walks, shared secrets and, best of all, at the insistence of their father, Manfred, Beate chaperoned Erika when she met with Karl Kaufman, "Her beloved, her one and only," teased Manfred as he raised his eyes to the heavens. He considered Karl to be a nice young man, with whom he had many pleasant talks. When Hansi raised her concerns that he was Jewish, Manfred waved her remarks away. "There's plenty room in this world for everyone," he had said. Nevertheless, when Karl came to court Erika, to take "My daughter," for a romantic walk, with pointed finger and sternest voice to Beate, commanded, "You! You go with them!

Manfred Zinmann, stooped and sickly from a lifetime of poor nourishment, made the law in his family, ruling with strong beliefs and few words. Often with nothing more than that *look,* his three sons and two daughters abandoned their arguments and wordlessly obeyed. On the other hand, Hansi, his wife, returned that *look* with her own, then went about doing as she pleased...most of the time.

Predictably, when two years before, the Hitler Youth organization came to their village of Schoenbach to recruit members, Manfred objected and forbade his children to join; most especially his young sons, who he believed would be trained for war, But also the girls, who would be lured from the family.

For now, Beate at fifteen, unable to fathom how the BDM, with its seemingly benign agenda of sports and hikes, could raise such anger in her home when the subject came up, nevertheless, decided to attend a meeting to express her objections over Elsa's treatment. She did not seek her father's permission. He would forbid her from going; that was a certainty. And rather then violate his express command, she considered it safer instead to violate his general opinion. She would go and keep it secret.

First she thought about her appearance, to make herself presentable so that she would fit in with the other girls and not look strange. But all her clothes, hand-downs from a shorter, rounder Erika, looked "shabby" to her. After adding to the length and subtracting from the waist, Hansi declared them "Serviceable" and that Beate looked "Just fine." But Beate didn't feel fine at all. She felt frumpy, inadequate and self-conscious. She vowed to have all new clothes, someday.

She brushed her shoulder length hair, fly-a-way, the color of wheat, and secured the sides behind her ears with clips secretly borrowed from Erika's personal box of treasures.

"There," she said to herself in the mirror over the wash basin "I guess I'll do." She was pleased that she grew up to be pretty. That her teeth were straight and not protruding like Therese Brandl, who sat next to her in school. And that her face was not blotchy and pimply like Clara Menschenfreund who had no friends. Even Hansi, who withheld compliments from her children for fear they would become conceited and ungrateful, nevertheless, broke that rule several times to remind Beate how closely she resembled her great Aunt Hildegard, "The family beauty, may she rest in blessed peace. All the young men hoped to marry her, you know."

But the only thing Beate knew for sure that afternoon as she made herself ready, was that she was going to the BDM meeting. And the only thing for which she prayed, was that her father would never find out.

The first BDM meeting in Schoenbach was held in a clearing in the woods. Months before, Frau Gertrude Helmut, BDM Leader, was astonished when Herr Priester refused her request to hold BDM meetings in his Church. "The Church does not feel friendly towards Adolph Hitler," he said. "The Church does not support his policies or his programs, The BDM is not welcome here." Not to be undone, Frau Helmut declared the woods to be the official, scheduled meeting place, weather permitting.

On this cool, clear, late afternoon Beate walked the road to where the trees grew dense. Sidestepping fallen limbs, pushing away thorny brambles, she reached a clearing near a pond. There, huddled around a campfire, poking sticks into a low flame and singing lively and loudly a song about noodles and strudels, sat six girls wearing BDM outfits: blue skirts, white blouses and knotted bandanas at the neck. Surrounded by her girls, Gertrude Helmut sang heartily along with them, slapping the tops of her thighs with both hands to keep time.

Enchanted by the lightheartedness and good cheer of everyone, Beate stood quietly out of sight. The song came to an end with a rousing "Noodles, strudels and cock-a-doodles," then all broke into gales of laughter. Even Beate couldn't help giggling herself, it was so silly.

Still out of sight, she searched the faces of the girls for someone who might recognize her. To her relief she knew no one who could tell her father where she was. Her secret was safe, at least for the time being.

Beate stepped into the clearing. "Excuse me," she said in a shy voice. "I'm sorry to interrupt everyone's good time. But I was wondering if I may ask a question?"

As she spoke all chattering ceased and all eyes turned to their leader, who glanced up, smiled and patted the vacant space beside her.

"Please do sit down. I am Gertrude Helmut, Group Leader, and these are my girls," pointing in a sweeping, circular motion as though she were conducting an orchestra. "Now tell me your name and where you live and, most importantly, have you come to join us?"

Carefully, Beate straightened her skirt, and as gracefully as she could manage, settled herself beside Frau Helmut. One of the girls handed her a twig for fire-poking. Mesmerized by the crisp cracklings of leaves and pine cones and the feel of the fire's warmth upon her face, in a low trance-like voice she said her name and town.

"Well Beate," Gertrude Helmut began, "We are all glad that you are here. We hope you will join us. We have many enjoyable activities you can see. One of the things we do is talk about our concerns. Sometimes because of family, or because of other girls, matters begin to trouble us, and we discuss these troubles and find solutions so that afterwards when we go home after a meeting we are unburdened and joyful."

As she poked and stared into the fire Beate heard the words. But more, she absorbed the sincerity in the words themselves. She looked up and saw, in the eyes of the other girls, adoration for their Leader. Sitting among them, she felt their acceptance and respect.

Assured that her concern over Elsa would be treated with kind consideration, Beate plunged right in. She questioned Elsa's rejection when she had applied to join. She aired Elsa's disappointment. "She was so upset she came to me crying and asking if it was really because she was Jewish. I said that I didn't know, but that I would try to find out and maybe change their mind." Beate's eyes were fixed on Frau Helmut's face. She could hear the shuffling and whispering of the girls during the brief silence before their Leader's response.

Frau Helmut cleared her throat and began, "I understand you are upset for your friend and I know it seems harsh, but it really isn't harsh if you think about it. The Hitler youth is reserved just for German children. Just like the German Women's League is just for Catholic women, or the Hitler Youth for Boys is just for boys. In the same way, the BDM is just for German girls of certain ages. You see how it is then? Now your friend has Jewish organizations available to her, but not to you. And I am sure if you were to apply to any one of them you would be refused. You see?"

Ja, Beate did see. It was all very reasonable when put in correct perspective. She felt relieved that she had an explanation for Elsa, who certainly would understand. She was glad that she came to the meeting even if it might mean trouble at home.

Surrendering her twig to the fire, brushing and shaking off small bits of leaves from her skirt and hair, Beate hoped that the odor of smoke was not on her. She stood and turned to Frau Helmut. With a simple *"Danke"* to her, she then waved goodbye to the girls and turned toward home.

She thought about the girls around the campfire, whose voices in a goodnight song followed her as she walked the path to the road; Even when the melody faded beyond her hearing, nevertheless, their song played again and again in her mind. She thought about their closeness to each other and their acceptance of her as though she had already belonged to the BDM. It was like having six more sisters. Mostly though, she thought about speaking to her father. Maybe if she explained what they actually did, and what they were truly about, maybe she could overcome his objections, and he'd allow her to join. Maybe.....

CHAPTER SIXTEEN

Rescue From A Dismal Destiny

"So!" Hansi shouted to Beate, who had just walked in from that meeting in the woods. "Guess what has happened!"

Beate stood in the kitchen and stared into her mother's face; a wild-eyed mixture of grief and horror told a now terrified Beate that the worst had happened: She was found out Seized with dread and panic Beate half expected her shaking knees to give way..A fleeting thought suggested that if she did collapse, her father would be so relieved that she was only clumsy, not dead, he would forgive anything.

Without waiting for Beate to reply, Hansi continued shouting. "Erika and Karl are married! Do you hear this? Married!"

At first, faint with relief that this was not about her, Beate took a moment or two for her head to clear. She lowered herself into the nearest chair, stupefied, speechless. Her heart slowed its racing and her voice returned.

"Married?" she croaked. "What do you mean married? How can they be married when everyone knows about the marriage ban between Jews and Aryans?"

"A Rabbi!" Hansi screamed. They were married by a Rabbi. City Hall refused to marry them so yesterday they eloped to Munich, and a Rabbi there married them.! My Erika," sobbed Hansi, "My little girl.....no official record....no

Church......no Priest.....how can she say that she is married? My little girl, living in sin!" She blew her nose, slumped into a chair and stared up into Beate's face "She was just here, a little while before you came home. Just walked in and give us this news, and packed a few things and left."

Her composure now completely restored, Beate questioned, "But what happened, why all of a sudden....?"

"Well, I'll tell you what happened," said Hansi sarcastically. She pointed to the empty chair at the kitchen table beside her for Beate to sit. Holding her deeply lined face between two hands she leaned towards her daughter and began.

"You know, don't you, that Karl is a student at the University in Munich?"

"Well, yes, yes I do...so?"

"So," said Hansi, "what you don't know, what none of us knew, except Erika, of course, is that he belongs to an underground anti-Nazi organization; that he is involved with people distributing leaflets for the Resistance and writing on storefront windows and all over the streets in Munich in large letters, 'Freedom, *Freiheit,* Freedom all over everything."

"Gott in Himmel" a red faced Beate whispered reverently to God in Heaven. She leaned toward her mother who seemed as though her body had shrunk into itself.

"So," continued Hansi, "if you think that's bad enough, there's more, much more. Erika said that there is an underground leaflet called, 'The White Rose' and that is was put out by two people, a brother and sister, and they got caught and put to death. Erika told me that she and Karl are terrified that maybe they are looking for Karl, so they married to run away and hide."

Hansi slumped lower into her chair, shaking, hugging her chest, rocking back and forth, all wordless gestures telling Beate that Erika, in her mother's thinking, was doomed.

Hoping to bring some comfort Beate said, "but Erika isn't...I don't understand.... if Erika isn't involved with this organization, why is she running away?"

"To be with him!" screamed Hansi. "She's in love...that stupid, stupid girl! What kind of life will she have? Always running, hiding all the time, always afraid."

Beate walked to the back of Hansi's chair and hugged her mother's shoulders. "Does Papa know?" she whispered.

"Yes, of course he knows. He was right here when she made this announcement."

"What did he say?" Beate drew in her breath. Her heart began to race at the thought of his reaction.

"Well, it was not as any of us expected." A now calmer Hansi stood and filled the kettle with water for tea. "At first, he didn't say anything. Then he threw up his hands and walked out of the room mumbling about one less mouth to feed. A minute later he came back, walked to Erika, advised her to take care of herself. Then he wished her good luck, and said, 'We will miss you." Then he lit his pipe and walked outside to go to the woods.

To the woods? Beate's thoughts suddenly left her family and returned to the campfire in the woods, to the girls and their songs, and to the Leader, Frau Gertrude Helmut, who was so kind.

With Erika gone, Beate's life became one of endless chores, church, and useless study, each one a misery. Study especially, always her biggest burden never held an interest. Upon reaching her thirteenth birthday she had decided that her removal from school was long overdue.

After all, she had explained to her startled parents, her future lay in marriage and children, the same as her mother, the same as every girl. She considered her destiny dismal enough without the added torment of schooling which, she argued, "Held no usefulness anyway." Then because her mind was made up, she emphatically announced, "I intend to leave school."

Just as emphatically her father corrected her intentions. His mind was also made up. He pointed his finger and shouted, "You, go to school!" So, go to school she did, but Beate never earned a passing grade again.

As the weeks went by Beate's loneliness without Erika intensified. She became moody, withdrawn. She thought often about Gertrude Helmut, the girls, the singing and companionship. She asked questions of the girls she knew who already belonged. She read pamphlets and learned about overnight and weekend trips, wandering and hiking in the countryside, engaging in sports and sporting competitions. Such activities which had only been available to boys in Schoenbach, were now also for girls in the BDM.

If she joined she would be in the company of other girls, marching and singing and doing good deeds. Most of all, she'd belong. It was so important to belong. She learned that sometimes speakers came to their meetings to talk about women's role in Germany's future. "But," said classmate, Sophie Schroeder, "No one really pays attention. We're young girls. We have no head for politics. Who cares about all those things? We just want to have fun."

But the more Beate learned, the more her desires extended beyond the usual goal of fun. Pride touched her spirit and shaped her thinking. She was proud to be German. She would be prouder still if she had a part in creating her country's future. In the BDM she would have such a part. In the BDM she could become somebody. She would have it, whatever the cost.

CHAPTER SEVENTEEN
A Brazen Stand

The Zinmann house stood back from an unpaved road. "Too far back," Manfred often complained when the winter snows held him captive inside.

Along the same road, were two additional houses, the Zinmann's only neighbors, a quarter mile apart. Identical on the outside, inside the similarities ended. Except for a pump in the kitchen supplied from a well, Beate's family had no inside water. The privy behind the house, treated periodically with lime, and a makeshift shower hooked onto the back of this dilapidated structure, was the extent of the plumbing. And while Beate noted that her neighbors also had very little in the way of modern comforts, she noted as well, that her family had even less.

The road itself, never officially named, known simply as *Der Waldweg,* the forest path, meandered for another half mile beyond the third house, then disappeared into the woodlands, where hunters pursued large game and trapped rabbits for food.

But Manfred Zinmann had no stomach for hunting. He hated guns, never held one, and forbade his sons to shoot, or even set animal traps.

"Only barbarians torture animals," he shouted amid loud protests from his sons when they asked to join a local rabbit hunt. Manfred slammed his hand down on the table. "No, not my sons!"

On the other hand, he did teach his sons to fish, and took them along whenever he heard that the fish were running. Sometimes the catch was so plentiful, they brought back enough to share with neighbors. Other times they were not so lucky and Hansi made her emergency bread soup for the evening meal. It had no taste, but was better than nothing.

Once, Hansi mumbled barely above a whisper, but within Manfred's hearing, "It would be nice to have some fresh meat sometimes, for a nice sauerbraten with dumplings, or even sometime maybe a nice chicken with noodles.....sometime....".

"Oh *ja*" he sarcastically whined three inches from her face, "Sometime" will come when prosperity comes. In the meantime we do our best not to starve to death so that when 'sometime' comes, we will be alive to enjoy it."

A locksmith without work, Manfred, who was among the country's unemployed millions, grumbled each morning while preparing to begin the day. "Every year it gets worse," he hissed, as he pushed his feet his feet into boots before leaving for the countryside to seek work. "Any work for any pay?" he'd asked anyone who seemed less destitute than he. At times he returned home with some money. Frequently he was paid with food or given food to bring home even if there was no work. And sometimes there was nothing to bring, only to try again the next morning, and the next, and the next....

A small garden tended by the children provided vegetables in the summer. But the growing season was short and the yield too meager for so many mouths. Hunger was constant. .

Manfred, harbored no hope or expectation that Germany would ever recover from its bankrupt condition. Daily life would never improve, he was certain. Life's pleasures were beyond his reach, except tobacco, his only indulgence He grew his own; some of which he sold. But most went into his own pipe.

A post office, general store, bakery and meat shop held together the tiny Village of Schoenbach and its environs of scattered, modest houses. Situated nine miles outside of Munich, Bavaria's capitol, the townspeople of Schoenbach relying mostly on bicycles for transportation, stayed close to home and remained largely insulated from the turbulent political climate that prevailed in Munich during the 1930s.

The Catholic Church, central to daily life, tended to the religious obligations of its parishioners, and the parishioners looked forward with mounting excitement to the next christening, or confirmation or wedding celebration. Wearing their traditional folk *dirndl* dresses and *lederhosen* trousers the townspeople plunged into every festivity, dancing polkas and waltzes, downing beer and sausages, singing sad songs and drinking songs, until dawn.

But for Beate, these same celebrations once shared with Erika, were no longer joyous without her sister. Instead, she missed her even more, and many times thought about the campfire in the woods, and relived every detail of that BDM meeting.

"I'm old enough now to make my own decisions," she confided to Elsa Stern, who came to say that her family was moving to Berlin to live with relatives. "The Nazis closed papa's store," Elsa explained.

Beate hugged her dear friend. "I will miss you so much, Elsa. Now more than ever I have reason to join the BDM and I will. My mind is made up. I'm not certain when to tell my father, but it will be soon."

"Oh my God," whispered Elsa, her eyes wide with horror. "He will surely do something terrible to you. Maybe you should change your mind. Maybe you....."

"No," Beate interrupted her friend. "This is what I want. This is what I will have."

"But he will punish you. Remember when he made you stay in the privy all day just because you walked in the woods with a boy. And the other time when....."

" I don't care. When the punishment is over, I'll join the BDM"

For the next several days Beate thought about the best time and the best way to speak to her father, although she fully realized that it probably wouldn't matter. So choosing this Sunday, after returning from Church, Beate stood quietly before him, her hands folded behind her back. She waited as he lit his pipe, settled himself into his favorite chair, and finally acknowledged her presence.

"You wish to say something to me, Beate?" His voice tinged with impatience also held the tone of dismissal. Sunday afternoons were sacred to Manfred. He asked nothing from his family except, on Sundays, to be left in peace.

Drawing on all her courage, speaking slowly in hushed tones, Beate delivered her carefully rehearsed circumstances of her life. She spoke of her loneliness without Erika, of the monotony of her days. She ventured one step closer to his chair where he sat sucking on his pipe and brushing bits of tobacco from his lap.

"Please, please," she begged, "please understand what I am going to say."

" *Ja*, so say it. Then go help your mother with the food."

"I'm going into the BDM." She had sucked in her breath. Half speaking, half crying. "My BDM Leader, Frau Helmut, said that I need to have a uniform for my family to provide and...." With this said, her voice trailed off. Her legs trembled and she sank into a nearby chair.

"Are you crazy!" he screamed. He rose from his chair and held a fist to her terrified face. "Do you not understand what you are saying! Never! I forbid it!"

It was not in Manfred to understand loneliness or the need to escape it. Born into a large family and having produced a large family of his own, he lived a lifetime of bumping into children, relatives and oftentimes, furniture. One person more, or one person less in his household was not even noticeable. Even though he wished that Erika had not run off like she did, nevertheless, he looked forward to his children being settled and in their own houses; that the clamoring and squabbling and racing around, especially the boys, would be replaced with quiet, just he, Hansi, and his pipe.

"You are unhappy!" he thundered. "So who is happy? Tell me, who do you know who is happy! Lonely!" he roared, "You do what everyone else does" as he raised his arms to embrace the world. "You do the best you can!" he shrieked. His face reddened, his voice cracked then gave way entirely as he continued his tirade, but with no sound from his throat.

Her steady gaze into his eyes challenged his rage, his dignity, his unquestioned authority over his household. Beate, never more miserable than at that moment, also knew that at some point his tirade would end. Her stare followed him as he moved to leave the room. She noticed her mother in the doorway, wide-eyed, one hand covering her mouth as if to stifle her own outcries.

Breathing rapidly, his hands on his hips, Manfred stood and unrelentingly glared at her, while she just as stubbornly returned the glare. For the first time in her life Beate brazenly and openly defied her father. She watched him leave, passing his wife in the doorway as if she were invisible, while Hansi, wordlessly followed behind.

Now alone in the room, relieved that the confrontation with her father and the anguish leading up to it that had preyed on her mind for so long, was now behind her, Beate's despair dissolved. Even though she lived at home, and would face her father each day, she knew that, for punishment, he would not look at her, or speak to her for weeks, maybe longer..... still, her thoughts raced with a new optimism. Now her life held the promise of a future to do meaningful and important work; a future in which she would escape the poverty and the loneliness of her days; a future to be somebody, someday.

In an ironic twist her father's words just moments before screamed in rage, "Do the best you can!," now held a different, never intended meaning. "*Ja,* she said to herself. "This is the best I can do." Briefly she worried about the required uniform. But then remembered that Frau Helmut offered to help if her family could not.

"Imagine," she whispered in awe at her reflection in the mirror the next morning. "It will be a brand new uniform, never worn before, first hand."

CHAPTER EIGHTEEN

Romance

"Welcome to our camp, Beate Zinmann, to *Landjahr*, to the start of Reich Land Service." Leader Guida Dietz, her dark hair tightly braided and wound into a crown, stood proudly and sternly in her BDM uniform and personally greeted each newcomer. "Your stay here will be different than your past experience in the BDM. Here you will not be camping or engaging in sports as before. You will not march in parades. You will not attend rallies in Munich. You will not sit around campfires and sing silly songs.

"Here, for the next six months is where you will live and work." With pointed finger she encircled the compound consisting of fields, ramshackle barracks, barns and outhouses. Then lowering her arm she continued, "You will share your sleeping quarters with the other girls. At 6am every morning, you are required to attend the flag raising ceremony. After breakfast you will be trucked to the fields to help with the harvesting until dark."

Beate had not been given a midday meal. She was weary and needed food. "Excuse me," she began, "but could I...."

"Do not interrupt me when I speak. Now, to continue. You'll then be brought back for the evening meal and leisure. Sometimes we will have a guest speaker to talk about the importance of your work here as young girls and then as women in your own families. Several times we have been honored when our great Leader Gertrude Scholtz-Klink herself visited us. Perhaps she may again. After six months you will be transferred elsewhere to fulfill your *Landjahr* obligation.

At this point Beate's attention traveled to her own thoughts. The voice of Leader Dietz faded from her hearing. *Omi,* her grandmother had caught pneumonia and died. Willi and Fritz, her younger brothers, were recruited into the Hitler Youth when it became mandatory soon after she herself entered the BDM. Max, the oldest and the scholar, who at the urging of their Priest, tutored children, began attending Nazi rallies in Munich. Eventually, he declared his eagerness to be part of the Nazi Organization, "But, of course, on a high level," he had said.

Her parents, however, concerned her. Manfred spent less time with his family, and less time searching for work. He had little to say if anything at all, and frequently went off alone to fish, whether or not the fish were running. Hansi, in despair, sought comfort with the parish priest, who offered counsel and wine, mostly wine. "My mother cries. All the time she cries," Beate had once confided at a meeting around the campfire.

She was relieved to be no longer at home. I'm beginning a new life, she told herself. I'll work hard, harder than anyone else. I'll become a Leader, be independent, respected, free. Her mental wanderings drifted to anticipation of the evening meal.

"Romance!" shouted Leader Dietz, as if to call back Beate's attention. "If you are looking for romance, you will not find it here. Your purpose here is to work for the good of the people, to fulfill a duty."

"There are no boys or men here," she shouted even louder. "BDM emphasizes comradeship among girls. If you show any interest at all in romance you will be assigned someplace else to work. And it might be that you would have to start *Landjahr* all over again."

With Leader Dietz's emphatic proclamation against romance and men, Beate was astonished several weeks later to see a tall, slender, most handsome man crossing the field towards her. She brushed the back of her hand across her forehead, then shaded her eyes as she watched his approach, then poked her field companion with the handle of her hoe.

"Erna, look. Who is he? He's walking straight towards us."

"Towards you," corrected Erna, "not us," as she quickly resumed her work.

"Guten Morgen, Fraulein, I truly hope it is a good morning for you."

Dumbstruck, Beate could only stare at this man, terrified to return the greeting, or say anything..

"I have been observing you as you work and I am most impressed with your diligence." His tone was light, playful, teasing. His smile was broad. Beate, transfixed, wondered if the corners of his dark eyes always crinkled like that when he smiled, or only when he teased.

Still smiling he said, "my name is Franz Westermeyer. I am Reich Youth Leader. Do you not know who I am?"

Fearing to utter a sound, Beate shook her head "no" and clasped her hoe more tightly.

"I visit the work camps every now and then just to see for myself how everything is going." After several silent moments of meeting each other's eyes, he prompted, "And you are...who?"

Beate said her name, but it sounded to her as though it came from somewhere else. She said it a second time and realized that she probably sounded foolish to him. She wished he would leave because her heart was beating so fast. She couldn't tell if it was because of him or from the heat of the day.

"When your work is over, would you walk with me later?" He was still smiling, but this time his voice was serious, sincere.

"Oh, I couldn't. I just couldn't." Beate's words tumbled out as she remembered the warnings of Leader Dietz. Only yesterday wasn't her friend Charlotte made to sit in a hard chair in the sun all day until she collapsed, just for complaining about the work. Terrified at what might befall her if she violated the rule against romance, Beate sputtered, "Nein, nein, no. Don't ask me such a thing. It's against the rules. I'd get into very serious trouble." She would have liked to soften her refusal by first saying that she would very much like to accept his invitation, but....

"Please go," she said softly. Please."

"Well, I will if you really mean it. But you see I can bend the rules. I made them, you know."

"Please, please go," she begged.

"Very well." His voice barely above a whisper, "Another time then." He turned and strode into the fields toward a small black car. Beate watched as he settled himself in the back seat behind a driver. As his car disappeared around a bend, she knew in her heart, that she had not seen the last of Franz Westermeyer.

Almost breathless with excitement she called to Erna, who, immediately moved to the end of the row as Franz Westermeyer approached. "Did you see, did you hear this?"

" No, I saw nothing, nothing. I don't know anything." as Erna crouched even further away from Beate.

Beate quickly hunched down and resumed cultivating the asparagus beds, her assigned task for the day. But all her thinking was focused on Franz Westermeyer, this man, who held keys that could open doors to her future, This stranger who in a single, brief encounter had stirred her feelings in a way she had never before experienced.

In her final one-half year of service Beate was assigned to a farm family to fulfill the domestic duty requirement. More than disliking field work, she hated domestic work. If it was up to her she would have stayed in the asparagus fields. But she was sent to work in this new place to test her endurance, she felt certain. She would not allow herself to fail.

The work was harder than she could ever have imagined: she scrubbed the farmhouse floor on her hands and knees; every day, rain or shine, she washed mountains of filthy work-clothes worn by the fieldhands, beating them on a scrub-board in a giant vat, then pinning everything onto seemingly endless miles of clothesline to dry. Tending to the outhouse, taxed, disgusted and frequently nauseated her. Many times she felt so sick that she left her work to go behind a nearby shed, where she couldn't be seen, and retch until her insides were emptied. It was unthinkable to display weakness openly.

But every evening when the workday ended, Franz came to the farmhouse where she worked. Together they walked the countryside. They spoke about their childhoods, their work, their ambitions. And every evening they lingered a little longer than the night before to say goodnight.

"You are worrying me ,Beate," he said one evening. They had just returned from their customary walk and were ready to say their goodnights, when Franz, with concern in his voice asked, "Are you not getting enough food? You are getting so thin. If it's a matter of food I will make certain...."

"Oh, please no. I'm fine, really. There is more than enough to eat. It's just the work...but it doesn't matter. I'll be eighteen soon and my six months here will end in a few weeks, and then I will go to a new assignment, to a real job in the Organization."

Just the thought of the new work waiting for her, important work that would pave the way for future promotions, excited her. Her dreams of success were within reach. She would endure anything she had to endure.

Not quite ready to end the evening, Beate sat down on the farmhouse step and motioned Franz to sit beside her. "Wouldn't it be wonderful," she began, "if we could both work in the same city?"

"*Ja,* it would be wonderful," he said lightly, "so I have already begun the process. Your next assignment will be in Frankfurt. You are going to Frankfurt."

"Oh stop," she laughed. "You are teasing me. All the time you tease me. Be serious. This is important."

"I'm quite serious, Beate," he replied. "I don't know exactly where you will be assigned, but I am certain we will be in the same city. He stood then and drew her to her feet. "So what do you think of that, my almost eighteen year old, almost a woman, my beautiful love."

Beate, incredulous at this man's ability to capture all that he desired, whether people, or tightly held information, could only smile into his eyes. "What I think, Franz, is that you are wonderful," she responded. To herself she thought she was truly blessed to have such an exceptional man in her life.

CHAPTER NINETEEN
A Formula For Success

Franz Westermeyer never knew his parents. Abandoned in the back pew of Saint Lukes Lutheran Church in Hamburg shortly after birth, he was discovered by the Pastor and turned over to the Church Orphanage. The year was 1911. He was given a birth date, and simply because he needed a name at baptism, he was named for the Pastor, who, not having children of his own, delighted, and took special interest, in his namesake in the years to follow.

Saint Lukes Orphanage sheltered between thirty and and thirty-five foundling boys. It was headed by visiting Deputy Administrator Walter Schacht, who arrived every Monday morning to manage the funds, oversee the seven matrons supervising the boys' daily life, and then take a hasty evening meal with Pastor Westermeyer before leaving. Except for an occasional surprise visit from Pastor Westermeyer, who always inquired about "My little Franz," or *"mein kleiner Franz,"* the orphahage ran on its own and provided the necessities of life, albeit frugally. Treats for the boys at Christmas and an occasional outing sponsored by the generosity of congregational offerings, were the only frills. But decent treatment and an ordered daily life made their world secure.

After early morning chapel, breakfast, chores and a seven hour day at the church school, little time remained for leisure. Preparation for when the boys, at eighteen, would leave the orphanage to build their own lives, was the main focus of classroom learning, which included a mix of religious and secular subjects.

But Pastor Westermeyer went one step further for "my little Franz." For his fourteenth birthday an apprenticeship with a printing shop a short distance from the church was arranged by the Pastor. "You will attend after school," he explained, "So you will have a trade and be better prepared to leave here when that time comes," as he handed over the apprenticeship papers and a new pair of socks for Franz's birthday.

For the next few seconds, Franz stared at the papers. As far as he knew no other boy had ever been singled out for a special advatage. He stuttered an astonished, *"Danke,"* and folded the papers into the back pocket of his trousers.

Ironically though, it was not so much his work in the print shop that prepared Franz for life outside the orphanage, but his realization that special favors come from those in special and higher places. At the age of fourteen Franz began to plan his future, not in the print shop, but there in the orphanage where he lived.

His life's plan began as a campaign. Starting with the head matron, he captured her interest by assisting in supervising the younger boys at recreation. Affable by nature, bright and overall good natured, he had, from his youngest years, been well liked by peers as well as by those higher-up.

Gradually, over time he assumed more responsibility during recreation, to the delight of the matrons who enjoyed more free time to linger over afternoon tea and gossip, confident that their charges were in capable hands. Even the Monday Deputy Administrator was so impressed that when Franz, at sixteen, asked for a meeting, he readily agreed to take some precious time from his duties to "Honor the young man's request," as he put it.

By the end of that meeting, Franz had outlined his idea for a structured recreational plan, one that would separate the boys by ages and into age compatible activities. "The way it is now," he explained, "The older boys rough-house and race around like wild monkeys. I constantly break up fights and stop the racing. Now, even though they get less bruises and black eyes than before, the brawling has not entirely stopped, and injuries still happen. Just last week, Hermann Hauser broke his arm from a fight with another boy. And the younger boys....well, they are afraid to be around them. So they watch and keep a safe distance and never play games anymore because the older ones are rowdy and interfere and often ruin their fun.."

Having caught the Monday Administrator's attention, Franz continued. "What I thought is that the older boys can be in sports, like soccer, and have teams and competitions. Apart from them, the younger boys will be given constructive games to enjoy without interference."

Franz outlined the details of his plan, estimated when and how his program could be installed at Saint Lukes, and then took the next step–a giant step—and boldly convinced the Monday Administrator that he, Franz, was the most suitable one to undertake its implementation.

Several weeks later Franz's program went into effect at his orphanage. The news traveled. The plan was so successful that it was installed in a number of district orphanages, as well as in some secular schools, as an experiment.

Franz's objective, promotion of his own self, gained momentum, and even exceeded his own anticipated outcome. As his recreational program became widely adopted, his reputation widened as well. In a short time he became

a frequent topic of conversation among orphanage adminis-
trators. But Franz's reputation peaked a year after he first
introduced his ideas to the visiting Deputy Administrator.
He won the attention and admiration of Herr Administrator
Werner Sell, head of the District's Church Orphanages. The
name, Franz Westermeyer, became associated more with
"little Franz" than with Pastor Westermeyer. And, as would
any parent, the Pastor spoke proudly of, and took a bit of
credit for, Franz's celebrity.

In 1929, at eighteen, Franz entered the world with glowing letters of recommendation, a maturity far exceeding his
biological years, and the trade of a printer, which he had no
intention of pursuing. Instead he headed directly to District's Head Administrator Sell, who immediately put Franz
to work overseeing and reporting on the newly named,
Westermeyer Recreation Activity Program, currently in
place and operating throughout his region.

The work included travel and Franz welcomed it. Excited
over entry into his future, anxious to see it all, determined
to do it all, he was impatient to become the large presence upon which he had set his sights at fourteen. Yet it
was an innocent Franz who emerged from his childhood at
St Lukes. Orphanage life had sheltered him from most matters beyond its walls.

Widespread poverty, unemployment, trade unions, com-
munism and socialism were ideas with which he collided as
he paused in his travels to listen to soap-box speech mak-
ers. He was enraptured with their passion, caught up in
the fervor of the moment. Their voices, their words, the
content of new ideas, never before encountered, played
over and over in his mind, frequently ruining a good night's
sleep.

Political rallies became Franz's entrance into the world of political ideas and personal betterment. Rallies drew large and spirited crowds, more thrilling than soap-box speeches. Rally speakers wore uniforms and, in Franz's thinking, carried credibility and legitimacy. More and more he absorbed the excitement of political causes. It became obvious to him that Germany was headed for a monumental change. He wondered about goals for the greater good of the German people, for the *Volk*. He thought about how his personal goals could connect with those ideas and what it would mean for his future. But he was in no hurry. Franz knew the formula for success, and when he considered himself ready, he'd use it. In the meantime, he still had much to learn, much to consider, and much more life to experience.

In 1932, at twenty-one, lured by an intense interest in politics, he left his work with the recreation program and relocated to Munich, the birthplace and capital city of The National Socialist German Worker's Party, the Nazi Party.

Short of funds, unable to find work for several weeks, in desperation Franz accepted a janitorial job in the Munich Hospital. He was paid a small salary, which included a basement room and one daily meal from the hospital kitchen. But of major importance to Franz was his now close proximity to Munich's political events. As for only one meal a day, well, he would certainly require more than one. His immediate goal became two meals a day, at the very least, and three if he worked it right.

He started working his charms in the kitchen. The staff soon considered Franz "Such a nice young fellow, always smiling, always going out of his way to make things easier for us." They were grateful that he often put his own work aside to assist in distributing food and even feeding the sick, who were too sick to feed themselves. As a consequence, Franz very often worked late into the evening hours to complete his janitorial duties. Such sacrifice did not go unnoticed by the kitchen staff or the Hospital Administrator; they looked the other way when Franz helped himself to cocoa and a bun or two in the morning, then returned later in the day for a main meal, and once in a while for something extra before bedtime.

Rallies and speeches were frequent in Munich, and Franz single-mindedly dedicated every hour of his free time to attend. He also paid visit upon visit to Nazi Headquarters at Konigplatz. There he studied their literature, their faces, their bearing, their posture and manners. Soon he received their permission to distribute leaflets to the general public. On two occasions, the staff invited Franz to an afternoon snack..

In July, 1932, he heard Joseph Goebbels' stirring call to the German Youth: a call to eliminate the existing Social Democratic Party in favor of the Nazi Party at the upcoming vote.

Some months later, a small man with a small moustache railed against Germany's collapsed economy, against seven million unemployed, against the unspeakable injustices of the hated Versailles Treaty, the cause of Germany's present crises. Franz, hearing these words, hearing the passion behind them, with racing heart and swelling chest did as the hundreds upon hundreds in the arena: he zealously raised his arm in the Nazi salute.

But it was Adolf Hitler's words and ideas that the youth belonged to Germany, his vision to develop a strong youth, athletic and fully trained in physical exercises, that excited Franz's spirit. The Nazi Party became his life. Adolf Hitler, his God.

It wasn't long before Nazi officials recognized Franz Westermeyer as "Quite exceptional." At official meetings as well as in social conversations, "invaluable," "special," "gifted," and "enormously talented," were some of the words used to describe Franz. If he had one flaw it was that he was not blond, they joked. They dismissed as unimportant Franz's close resemblance to Tyrone Power, the American movie star, " In view of his extraordinary attributes," they joked further.

At twenty-two, Franz was made Leader of the National Socialist German Student's League. At twenty-three, he was Leader of the Hitler Youth Organizations, and at twenty-four, he reached the position of Reich Youth Leader, the highest administrative post in the Hitler Youth.

Everything for which he strove he had achieved. Except now in 1937, at twenty-six, during a periodic farm inspection, he looked across an asparagus field and saw a beautiful young woman, with hair the color of wheat. At that moment he realized that missing in his life was such a woman. In that instant Franz took upon himself the pursuit of Beate Zinmann.

CHAPTER TWENTY

A Place To Live

Upon her arrival in Frankfurt that first morning, Beate walked from the train station directly to 35 Bachstrasse where she had been assigned.

Along the way she admired homes, austere yet dignified, streets lined with Linden trees, some with small plantings surrounded by pristine white pickets, gates of black wrought iron, spired and almost as high as the homes they fronted. She wondered about the people who lived in such fineness, about their lives, their clothes, their foods...

She pictured herself fitting into this beautiful city, absorbing and becoming part of its culture. Saying proudly to anyone who asked, "Why, I live in Frankfurt," knowing that she would be looked on and considered in a much different way than if she were to say, "I live in Schoenbach."

Now standing at her destination, with rising excitement, Beate's thoughts were racing. Here, she thought, is where my life truly begins. Here is where my hard work will be rewarded. My capabilities for leadership, for self reliance, for my steadfast loyalty to the Party will be acknowledged with promotions and advancement within the Nazi Organization.

During the train ride to Frankfurt she had entertained herself by imagining 35 Bachstrasse as an imposing, official structure having a grand entrance flanked with pillars. A gleaming brass-knobbed double doorway would be opened by a special guard, who would have her name on a list, allowing her entry. Once inside several smartly uniformed government officials wearing serious expressions would inquire about her business. Then one would leave his post and escort her to the correct department, while along the way pointing out the different offices and their functions.

Instead, she faced a dingy, stucco, factory-like structure with a run-down side door and no one in sight to direct her. Once inside, she seemed to be walking in circles amid a confusion of soundless, dimly lit hallways until finally, there it was: the Office of Administrator Guida Erhard, head official and Beate's immediate work supervisor.

Blonde, chubby-faced and stout, wearing a mannish shirt and tie, Guida Erhard barely glanced up when Beate, after several moments standing in the open doorway waiting for some acknowledgement and permission to enter, finally strode into the room to Administrator Erhard's desk.

With lowered eyes Frau Erhard shuffled papers, and made red check marks here and there. Finally raising her eyes she said, "Ah yes. You must be Beate Zinmann. Please sit. You make me nervous standing there. Your file is here someplace," as she moved the papers around the desk top. "Well, no matter," she began. "This is a Childrens" Shelter. Your duties here are to care for children who are brought just for the day. Children, whose mothers are called away.... Others just live here because they have nowhere else to live. But those children are not your concern. Not Yet."

A Children's Shelter! Beate thought. I'll be working with children! I expected an appointment higher than this, considering all my achievements. She could feel her insides sink, but she knew better than to complain or show disappointment. So she smiled and nodded and pretended enthusiasm, consoling herself that this was only a beginning. From here she would rise to higher positions of leadership. She reminded herself of all her achievements, of how she excelled in athletics, first aid and map reading. She complied with all the rules against smoking and wearing make-up, and earned badges for never missing a meeting, and for her superior work during Land Year. She won praises for her loyalty and acceptance of her role to become the perfect German woman. Even though in her heart Beate never endorsed or accepted, for herself, the ideological destiny of children, church, and kitchen, or that motherhood was the highest calling for women, nevertheless, she behaved as though she did.

Now at eighteen, standing before this woman whose high evaluations were crucial for her advancement, and seeing the large envelope with her record which was sent ahead, but still unopened on Frau Erhard's desk, Beate took heart. She was certain that once Frau Erhard read the reports she would be highly impressed. Especially, Beate thought, when she reads that her BDM Leaders held her in such high regard, that she was selected for special Leadership Training at Coberg Castle when she was barely seventeen; and that she completed the training in just two weeks.

On the wall behind Erhard's desk hung a photograph of a bucolic woodland scene, reminding Beate of the beautiful woods on the outskirts of Schoenbach. But it also reminded her of the brutal poverty, the misery from which she had escaped. Yet none of that mattered anymore. She had put herself on a path towards a future of achievement and advancement. She would do important work, essential work for the good of the *Volk,* for the good of her Germany. Praise would follow then recognition, commendation, and then promotions. She considered that she might feel overwhelmed sometimes by her chosen path. But she brushed those thoughts aside. Intertwined with duty to Germany and to herself, she would succeed. She would be unstoppable. She would make it so.

Now, impatient to begin her duties, and waiting for some instructions from Erhard, Beate nervously smoothed her hair, pretended to search through her pockets, played with the buttons on her shirt—anything to get her supervisor's attention.

All at once, Erhard, as if suddenly remembering Beate's presence, brought her attention up and suddenly blurted, "Have you located a place to live?"

Up to that moment Beate hadn't given any thought to living arrangements. If she had, she would have supposed that a place to live would be included in her appointment. She was astonished to learn that it wasn't.

"Well no...I was not informed about that and I only just arrived and...."

"So, I understand." Erhard, now on her feet but still sorting papers, instructed, "You will take the rest of today to look. Nothing extravagant you understand. A place nearby, convenient to your work here, is best. If you are not suc-cessful, come back here and someone will put you up either at their home or here in the shelter. I'll leave word...."

Confused, with tiredness setting in, Beate asked, "What time do you close up?"

"We never close," Erhard was emphatic. "Staff is here all day and all night with the children. At some point in your duties you will be staying overnight. We rotate overnights here."

Beate's heart sank. *"Ja,"* she said, dragging out the word, all the while thinking that being put up with a co-worker or being put up in the shelter was equally intolerable. Never!

She had enough of sharing beds and tight quarters at home and afterwards in the BDM camps living in barracks with not an inch to call her own. No! I'm sick of it!

She felt awkard, self conscious as she stood at the desk of the now reseated Guida Erhard, who, Beate observed, stood up and then sat down, every so often for no reason that Beate could fathom. Wondering if there would be further instructions, Beate hoped for words of encouragement, even some hint of how to proceed in her search. But after a few moments of silence she realized that the meeting, short and to the point, had ended without even a cursory, "Heil Hitler," to send her off. Wordlessly she had been dismissed.

Beate drew on her back-pack and stood in the doorway she had just entered some moments before. Glancing at her supervisor, still absorbed with her papers, shuffling here to there, then back to here, making clicking, disapproving noises, with her tongue, Guida Erhard seemed not to notice or even care that Beate was about to leave. And Beate, having no clear idea of how to go about finding a place to live, nevertheless, swore to herself that she would stay the night in the train station or sit up all night in a church pew, rather than accept either of the other two choices. Never!

Wandering the streets, inquiring of strangers along the way, it seemed as though the city was closed to her. The idea that she might, after all, end up living in the shelter even if only for a short time became an agonizing possibility.

She paused in her walk to whisper a short prayer for help, said "Amen," then hoisted her back-pack higher on her shoulder and continued on. Her walk led to an open courtyard and once inside to a Church; not a Catholic Church but a good place all the same for information. She whispered a fast, "Thank you God, Amen," adjusted her skirt, smoothed her hair and entered the outer vestibule.

No sooner had she stepped inside when a well dressed, proper and, in her view, important man entered from an opposite doorway and barred her further entry.

"And what can I do for you, *Fraulein?*" His voice was formal, his smile, forced. He did not introduce himself and was not in cleric's clothing, but from his manner, Beate was certain that he was the Pastor.

Part way through her explanation he held up his hand. "Please," he said in a gentle voice, "I think I can help you." He removed a matchbook cover and pen from his vest pocket and began writing on the inside cover. "I know of a room that's available. It's been vacant for a long time. For what reason I do not know. I speak to the woman every so often. Sometimes I hire her to do some cleaning for me. So I know she is very anxious to have a tenant."

Returning the pen to his vest he smiled while handing the matchbook cover to Beate. "Here is the address and the name of the woman. It's only a few short blocks from here. When you leave the courtyard go four blocks and you'll come to the street."

Beate glanced at the address: Goethestrasse 19. *"Danke schoen, danke,"* She couldn't say "Thank you" enough times to show her gratitude. She pushed the matchbook cover into her bag and strode from the Church. In her excitement, she forgot her manners to say goodbye.

The nearer she came to Goethestrasse the more she noticed that the streets were not as lovely or as welcoming as they had been during her earlier walk. Nowhere to be seen were trees along the streets, or small picketed gardens gracing the walkways, or the elegant charm of high spired wrought iron gates. Instead of gracious homes, houses with shabby exteriors barren of even the most meager greenery presented a sorry introduction to a street named after one of Germany's most famous poets.

Finally she came to a narrow brick building, its only adornments: a grey stone planter with no plants and the number 19 painted in green on a weathered front door.

She had expected to find a place, even to some degree, as pretty as those homes she had admired earlier. But then she consoled herself with the thought that inside most likely would be better than outside. She brushed aside her disappointment and knocked several times, each time harder and louder until she heard the door unlatch from the inside.

Now facing her in the open doorway stood a plump, dark-haired woman holding tightly to the hand of a little girl with blonde Shirley Temple-like curls, who, Beate guessed, to be about five years old.

"Ja?" asked the woman as she wiped a floured hand across the front of her apron.

Beate dove into her bag and dug out the pastor's matchbook cover. She flipped it over, glanced at the name then at the woman and asked, "Frau Wallerstein?"

"Ja, ja."

"Oh. Good day. My name is Beate Zinmann. I came about the room for rent." Peering into the hallway she spotted an inside doorway with a Mezuzah nailed to its frame; and now she knew why there was a vacant room.. Why, this woman is a Jew, she thought. I came to the house of a Jew. Now what am I supposed to do? Her thoughts were in turmoil. I have to live someplace. But in a Jewish house? My superiors all said to avoid Jews. They were firm, almost hysterical, it seemed, when they warned us about Jews. But it's almost night. No time to look further. And actually, it's not really a rule that must be obeyed. It's more like a suggestion, or advice. Not a rule. Anyway they should have provided me with living quarters, suitable ones. Just sending me on my own to a strange city, expecting me to know things.... Anyway I never cared about all those things they told us about Jews. My sister, Erika, is married to a Jewish man and he is nothing like they say. And my dear Elsa......

For a few seconds her thoughts returned to Erika, now underground, who, changed locations frequently, but could be reached by word-of-mouth messenger through the Church in Hannover or Mannheim. A sudden gust of wind caught her breath. Beate shuddered. She was exhausted. She needed a place to live, and here she was, standing on a doorstep with lodging just a few steps beyond. If I ask for consent, she thought, Guida Erhard would say absolutely not, unthinkable, and order me to live in the shelter. But as long as I don't mention it, and as long as she doesn't ask, and it probably would never come up anyway, and even if it should come up I'll smooth it over, somehow....such a small thing. Suddenly a picture of the shelter, then the train station flashed through her mind. She shoved the matchbook cover into her coat pocket, lifted her bag and looked into the face of her new landlady. "I'd like to see the room, please."

Walking closely behind she followed Melly, holding tightly to Inge's hand, through an unlighted hallway leading to a back door, through a closet sized courtyard, then through another door that opened to a house behind the main house.

"We live in the *hinterhouse*," Melly explained over her shoulder. "The room for rent is our attic above where we live." She grunted as she pushed the door open then proceeded up a steep, narrow stairway.

Faced with yet another door, a troublesome door that creaked and groaned upon opening, Melly tried to quell the noise by opening the door very slowly, pausing between creaks and groans. In desperation, it seemed to Beate, Melly finally resorted to shushing the door, as if it were human.

Beate fought off the impulse to laugh. It might hurt her new landlady's feelings. But the comedy of it brightened what, up to then, had been a dismal day. Impatient now to view her new home, Beate peeked over Melly's shoulder to catch a glimpse, if she could, while Melly, seemingly oblivious to Beate's craning, continued opening and shushing until the doorway cleared.

Once inside Beate slowly spanned the room: a small three drawer chest faced a bare bed across the room; a corner table held a shadeless, lopsided pewter lamp; and a bedside table, missing the top drawer, comprised the contents of the room. Another disappointment.

On the other hand, she thought, the size is ample, enough for herself and maybe sometimes for Franz if he visited. She delighted in the window that faced the front where she would be able to see across to a neighbor's garden, whenever it bloomed.

She wondered about her new job and if there would be time to seek another place. Here at least was something. She took in again the shabbiness of the room. On the verge of tears her resolve against living at the shelter began to crumble. If nothing else, she thought, the shelter is at least decent.

She turned to Melly. Her voice quivered. "I'd like to take the room if I could move in right away. But I don't know... you see...all I have are some books and clothes and a little money for rent."

Overtaken by weariness Beate sat down on the edge of the bed. "I have no furnishings of my own," she sighed, "and I can't live this way, with nothing...so I...."

"Of course, you can't," Melly interrupted from the door-way where she stood. "No one can live this way. Come, come with me downstairs and we go through what you want and we fix you up."

With Inge's hand in her's Melly descended one step at a time, calling over her shoulder with each step, "You'll have the privilege of the bathroom, a nice large bathroom, but no tub." Next step, "We go to the public baths once a week, sometimes twice if we need to. Step. "And the kitchen is also included whenever you like." Step. "First, we settle on a rental fee then we'll go through what you need and help you get settled and comfortable so you get a good night's rest, *Ja?*"

With her eyes fixed on Melly's back, a relieved Beate, filled with gratitude, smiled broadly and suppressed the urge to giggle as her Jewish landlady, one step at a time, endeared herself in a way that Beate had never experienced before.

That night alone in her room, Beate changed into night clothes and sank into a bed of starched sheets smelling of lavender and oversized pillows stuffed into cases with fancy embroidery along the edges. She surveyed her new home while under a plump eiderdown, remembering how Melly withdrew it from her cabinet and folded it into Beate's out-stretched arms. "For a special occasion," she had said.

A dotted-swiss curtain printed with pink roses, faded with the years, but elegant all the same in Beate's eyes, graced the lone window. A lace table cloth now dressed up the bedside table with the missing drawer, "So no one will ever know," said Melly. And the pewter lamp now propped with a book and topped with a shade "borrowed" from a lamp in the downstairs hall cast a warm, welcoming glow.

Made from wool and knotted by hand from China, "So many years back I can't even count," said Melly, as she laid the floor runner alongside the bed. "So when you step down your feet won't touch the cold floor," Melly whispered in Beate's ear, like a secret.

But to Beate, most wonderful was Herr Wallerstein's treasured writing table. Made of dark mahogany and fitted with a center drawer below a black and white marble top, she saw him rub his land lovingly over its top after positioning it under the window, "For the best light ," he had said. Then added, "I never use it anymore, and you need somewhere to put your books and send word to your family."

So overwhelmed at the kindness of this family in whose home she was now living, Beate could only manage wide eyed wonder and a simple soft, *"Danke schon."*

"You're most welcome, *Fraulein,"* Kurt answered tenderly. Then, "Come Melly, we let this young lady get some rest." On the way down he called, "I hope your stay here will be in good health and comfort. And, oh, I will look for a stove, something to bring some heat in. But in the meantime when you need it we can leave our door open and the heat from downstairs will come up."

Before going to sleep, Beate sat down at the writing table, drew a sheet of paper from the center drawer and began her letter:

Dear Erika....

Berlin
1937

Chapter TWENTY-ONE
A Proposal

Cut off from school and with no hope of entering university, Ursula seldom left her room. She busied herself with
carefully chosen books from Simon's library, settling herself
in the overstuffed window seat overlooking the garden and
Ilse's tea house. In a year's time she had read all of Tolstoy,
some Flaubert, all Shakespeare's plays and various versions
of his biography. When she tired of reading, she tinkered
with her doll house. When she tired of the doll house she
went downstairs to the kitchen to Frau Miller.

"Go outside for a while. Get some sun on you," Frau
Miller often urged.

But Ursula's reply was always the same. "I have no place
that I want to go." She never mentioned the other reasons:
that the Nazi signs on the street frightened her; or that she
would be embarrassed if she came upon a former classmate;
or that she would be conspicuous to people, who would
note that if she wasn't in school at that time of day, then she
must be a Jew.

Once again Simon fell into inconsolable distress as the
Nazis closed the Jewish Schools. His private students, fearful
of the streets, showed up less and less, and then not at all.
He returned to his schnapps, his solitude, and to an occasional search for work. But the issuance of Employment

Books, required for work eligibility, but unavailable to Jews, prevented success.

As for Ilse, when her committees and board meetings began scheduling without her, and needing something to fill her life, she filled it with Simon and seldom left his side.

It seemed to Ursula that once again her mother had become thinner. Her clothes hung loosely from her shoulders. Her face, pallid and pinched, showed her unhappiness.

"And besides," said Ursula as she reached into a pan of freshly made biscuits from Frau Miller's oven, " Sometimes mother comes downstairs to have *mittagessen,* a main meal, with me. And anyway, Peter is coming today and I want to be here...."

"*Ja, ja,* I know all about it. But you should go outside anyway, I can keep Peter here with these biscuits until you come back."

Ursula just smiled. She left the kitchen, returned to her reading, and then to the doll house. Crouching before it, elbows on her knees, hands on either side of her face, she studied the many rooms, remembering Peter's admonition, "Always always put function first," whenever her designs fell into detailed ornamentation with no useful purpose.

"All these rooms facing North," she muttered, "Need more light...larger windows....maybe glass bricks...talk to Peter."

She pulled her chair to the drawing table, rolled out a large sheet of paper and tacked it securely at the corners and across the top. As she began drawing her thoughts strayed to the time, two years before, when she came downstairs and met for the first time Cousin Melly and her baby, Inge, and wanting to show Inge the doll house if there was time. She lingered with these thoughts. A smile touched the corners of her mouth as she imagined Inge's delighted response. She saw herself showing the rooms and explaining the furnishings amid Inge's excited squeals, and letting her touch and hold some articles, and even letting her keep a special item if she wanted.

Abruptly her thoughts returned to the present as she heard the front door open and close and then heard voices in the downstairs hallway. Thinking that the house needed some fixing and that workmen had arrived, she cleared her mind and turned back to her project, when she heard her mother's voice.

"Uli, Uliiii... can you hear me? Come downstairs please. We have company. Come down."

Company, thought Ursula, how exciting. Who can they be? No one has come for months. Our Gentile friends don't come because they are afraid of the warnings. And our Jewish friends don't come because they are afraid of the streets.

She hesitated long enough to comb her hair and straighten her skirt. A quick glance in the mirror, one last pat to her hair and she galloped down the stairs to the voices in the sitting room.

There on the sofa sat Peter, filling his plate high with Frau Miller's special Christmas biscuits and strudel, his favorites. On his left, a blonde woman stirred a spoon in a teacup, while a paunchy man concentrating on lighting a cigar sat at Peter's right. Opposite these three sat Simon already puffing on his cigar, and Ilse, busily arranging the tea things, who glanced up to see Ursula enter the room.

"Oh," she called. "Uli's here. Come, come *Liebling,* my darling girl. Bring over a chair and sit by us."

Ursula, puzzled over who these two strange people were, stared and continued to stare over her shoulder as she dragged a chair from the game table under the window, causing tracks in Ilse's heirloom Chinese rug. Seating herself alongside her mother, she looked questioningly into Ilse's face. And Ilse, reading her daughter's mind said, "Uli, this is Herr and Frau Brettschneider, Peter's parents." Before Ursula could utter an astonished "oh," Ilse turned towards her guests and with unabashed pride said, "And this, this is Ursula, my Uli,"

In the customary way, Ursula rose and politely extended her hand to her mother's company and smiled. Frau Brettschneider. plump, with short curly hair that framed her face like an ornate picture frame, exuded a country-like essence. Hearty, robust, direct, she accepted Ursula's hand, and with a friendly squeeze covered it with her own. She wore a simple green sweater and black skirt, and except for a cameo on a chain, no jewelry.

Herr Brettschneider, occupied with lighting his cigar, acknowledged Ursula's outstretched hand with a tap on her fingers and a small, shy smile. In many ways, Ursula observed, Peter's father closely resembled Simon, except in dress. Papa, she thought, would never wear a cut-away coat and striped trousers, unless of course, Ilse insisted. On the other hand, both being stout, short-legged and almost bald, made for a striking similarity. And even more so since they both enjoyed, with open and profound appreciation, a good cigar.

Ursula resumed her seat. She glanced at Peter, brushing crumbs from his lap while refilling his plate, this time with gingersnaps and sections of dried fruit. Ilse poured a cup for herself. Ursula examined her fingernails. Simon puffed a succession of smoke rings. And Ursula wondered about this odd visit, but could think of nothing to say. The room was silent.

All at once Simon;s voice boomed, "Can I get for you something special, Herr Brettschneider?"

"*Ach, nein, nein,* Herr Wallerstein, this cigar is sufficient," as he held it out at arms length. "Tell me, where did you find....?"

Suddenly, Peter's mother, declining a second cup of tea, sat straight in her seat, folded her hands in her lap and said, "Well, shall we get down to the business at hand?" She looked nervously from Ilse, then to Simon, and then to Frau Miller who unexpectedly rolled in with a pastry cart containing a platter of assorted fruit breads and a second pot of tea.

"I apologize for interrupting, said Frau Miller, but I must leave for the market. Can I bring anything before I leave?" She glanced over at Ursula, who saw in her face, unabashed disapproval of the company and also, it seemed, their reason for the visit.

"*Ach, nein,* Frau Miller, thank you. We have everything we need for now," said Ilse. Waiting for the door to close behind her housekeeper, she then turned to her daughter, but before she could say anything, Ursula remarked, "Business?" almost giggling at the thought that her mother's company came for business.

"Uli, listen and do not interrupt," said Ilse. "Peter's parents are here because Peter has asked to marry you and we, your father and I, have given our consent."

All at once the activity in the room ended. Cigars were relinquished to nearby ashtrays. Cake plates were surrendered to the cart. Even the sound of rain that had been pelting against the house, ended abruptly as if by signal. And in that silence all eyes fastened onto Ursula.

She stared at her mother, open mouthed, not knowing what to make of her mother's words, not wanting to believe her mother's words, thinking that she had misunderstood. Before she could utter an astonished utterance, Peter's voice broke the silence.

"No," he shouted, "let me. I want to speak. It's up to me to explain...to tell her...." He scrambled to his feet and to where Ursula sat. He took hold of both her hands and drew her to her feet..

Standing before her, his eyes never leaving hers, Peter revealed an amazing story to his 17 year old best friend, soon to be his bride, he hoped.

"You already know," he began, "That I was past the age for the Hitler Youth when it first came in. I escaped that madness. But two years ago the Nazis made military service mandatory throughout the land. I was so terrified...I can't begin to tell you....that I would be called up. I thought I would go crazy from fear." Even now as he spoke about it his voice trembled and cracked. He paused to calm himself.

"I had to find a way to get out of it," he continued. "I knew eventually I would be tracked down and pulled in, or arrested ,or God knows what they would do to me. I tried to make myself invisible so I left my classes at the university."

"But Peter," said Ursula, "I thought you....."

"*Ja, ja,*" I know what you thought. And I did start classes there and it was fine for a while. But when the Olympic games ended and the Nazi's activities returned. I was an easy mark. So I tried to blend into the crowded streets of the city."

Ursula removed her hands from his, and placed them on either side of his face. Her voice was incredulous, dazed. "But why, Peter, why did you keep this from me? Why didn't....."

"I could not tell you...involve you...don't you see....?" He reached for his tea, finished the contents, and resumed speaking, seemingly unaware that he was still holding his empty cup. "I carried no identification. Many times the SS stopped me, or the Gestapo. 'It's in my other pants,' I'd tell them. Or when they'd ask me where I was going I'd say 'To

Synagogue,' because Jews are not permitted in Germany's army, you know. Sometimes they called me a foul name and walked away. Other times they beat me up. I preferred the beatings to the army."

"Peter, Peter, my God, Peter...." Ursula's voice rose, astonished, alarmed, "how awful for you....to go through such...."

"So you see," he interrupted, "I'm in trouble two ways. For avoiding the army I broke the law. For assuming a Jewish identity, I'm subject now to those cruelties. And now it's worse than ever ...the pressure to serve...the treatment of Jews, I'm in terrible jeopardy. I must leave, get away from Germany." His voice rose with hysteria.

Helga Brettschneider leaned forward in her seat towards her son. Removing the teacup from his hand, she said, "Peter please, come sit here by me. Everything will work out, You'll see. Come sit down."

As Peter slowly lowered himself in the seat alongside his mother, he sighed, a groan-like sound. "I have no funds, Ursula. I'm practically penniless. My parents have no money. Your parents....well....they have been like parents to me over the years. I turned to them for help and they said 'Yes.' They said they would help me....and...."

Helga filled a plate with biscuits and handed it to her distraught son, who stared at it dumbly. "Here, Peter, don't say anything more right now. Just sit and compose yourself." She leaned toward Ilse.

"Frau Wallerstein, I want you to know that Fritzi and me, we appreciate what you are doing to help our son. We are not fancy people, Fritzi and me. We finished our schooling at sixteen and have worked hard and lived simply all our lives. We do not like what is happening in our country. But we pretend to go along with everything because we don't know what else to do....because it can go very bad for us otherwise," Her voice trembled as she spoke. Extracting a handkerchief from her purse, she dabbed at her eyes, sat back and helped herself to a biscuit from Peter's plate.

Ursula, dazed and dumbfounded, now sitting alongside her mother, wondered how anything of what she had just heard, had to do with her marrying Peter. I know nothing about being grown up or about how to be a wife, she thought. She looked across at Peter. Yes, she had seen the love in his eyes so many times. She wondered if those same feelings would ever grow in her; if he would ever see that same love returned in her eyes.

Suddenly, she felt her mother's hand on her arm. Ilse, leaning forward, about to speak, first glanced at Simon, who nodded affirmatively, retrieved his cigar, then with an extended index finger, signaled for his guest to do the same.

"Uli," Ilse breathed deeply then calmly and simply told her daughter that they must all leave Germany. She explained that who they are and who they know can no longer shield them. "The Nazis will confiscate our funds, everything, all our assets, except maybe not the house. All my jewelry, family heirlooms, I have already given over to Frau Miller for safekeeping. Wallerstein's Emporium, all the stores, have already been taken over."

"Oh... *Mutti*," a trembling whisper barely escaped Ursula's lips. "Oh...."

With a small squeeze of reassurance to Ursula's arm, Ilse continued. "But our holdings in other countries are safe, and....well we didn't want to say anything to you until the right time.... but we have been making plans to leave, leave the country....we must....."

She then explained that they have applied for passports and have completed all the paperwork, and that they are now waiting until they are cleared for travel.

"But you, Uli, as Peter's wife, you have an opportunity to leave soon, right away. All the arrangements are completed. Peter is going to Holland, where we have funds....where we have connections....to Amsterdam...to the University. And you'll see, times will change and we'll all be reunited. But right now this is the best that can be done...the best for all. Do you see....?"

Ursula stood and stared across into Peter's face. He rose and walked to her and said, "You know that I love you. With all my heart, I love you. We can't do anything about our ages, or about the times being what they are, but I know that we will have a good life together. We will make our way." Peter reached into his pocket and held out a small tissue paper package. "Will you marry me.?"

Ursula thought about her mother's words. All her life, she respected and trusted her mother's advice, but her thoughts were in turmoil. I have no idea of the best thing to do. But *Mutti* always knows and......

Just then the front door opened and slammed shut and Frau Miller's voice sailed from the hallway into the sitting room.

"*Ach du lieber Gott,* you'll never guess what's going on outside. I couldn't even get to the market. The streets are filled with crowds and parades and soldiers marching on Unter den Linden carrying flags and banners with Hitler's face, the size of an elephant's behind, swaying higher than the trees, and people cheering and raising the arm...." as her voice faded behind the kitchen door.

With Frau Miller's outrage still ringing in her ears, Ursula looked into Peter's eyes and saw again the love. She extended her hand for Peter to place the ring, contained in the tiny tissue package, on her finger.

"*Ja,* Peter, *Ja,* I will marry you."

" Right away? Tomorrow?"

" *Ja*, tomorrow."

Holding hands, they began walking from the room. Ilse called after them, "Uli, remember to take your Baptismal Certificate when you go the Registrar's Office tomorrow."

CHAPTER TWENTY-TWO

A Sign Nailed To The Gate

The window shades were not yet raised that morning, leaving the room in half darkness. Melly, in a red upholstered rocking chair, a sewing basket in her lap, kept one eye on her mending and the other on five year old Inge, sitting cross legged on the floor near the stove, removing labels from a stack of phonograph records.

"The government buys these to melt down for who knows what," Melly was told while being handed the dusty box of old Jewish records from the hospital basement where she worked. "But better to remove the labels," she was advised. Melly wondered but never learned why the government needed the records. But she really didn't care. She cared only for the few pennies they brought. So she gave that job to Inge, who eagerly undertook the task on Melly's promise to take her on an outing for a reward.

Watching her child Melly felt saddened that Inge had to be indoors so much. "It is not good for the child," she complained to Kurt many times. Tomorrow, she thought, I will take Inge to the zoo. It will be her first time to see the animals in real life instead of just pictures.

That evening amid much excitement Melly and Inge prepared for the next day, selecting the perfect skirt to go with Inge's favorite blue sweater and rolling Inge's hair in rags to make curls, "Just like Shirley Temple," demanded Inge.

Someday, thought Melly I'll have to tell her that Shirley Temple is really an American little girl in an American movie. But not yet. Why spoil her fun.

The next morning between much shouting and protesting and drawer slamming. Melly threw up her hands and let Inge select her best black shoes to wear with her pink and white fanciest party dress.

"You are too dressed up for the zoo," warned Melly. "None of the other children there will be in party clothes. You'll see...."

"I don't care," interrupted Inge, "I want to look pretty."

Before leaving, Melly packed a lunch with a little extra bread "for the birds... to feed.... when no one is looking." At the last minute Inge decided to change to a red hair ribbon instead of the black already in place, and Melly argued that the black looked best. Kurt called, "Go, go already, you are giving me a headache," as Melly and Inge scrambled out the door and ran to catch the street car, already taking on passengers.

As they neared the entrance to the park Melly noticed, and thought it odd, that people were turning back and walking away. Then she saw the sign, NO JEWS ALLOWED, nailed to the gate. She stood before the sign and read it several times. Shock still and numb she held tightly to Inge's hand until the words sank in. Then turning to Inge, now hopping with anticipation on one foot and then on the other, her curls bouncing and jiggling, her hands pulling on Melly's arm, she heard Inge's urgings, "Come *Mutti* come."

Hard as she tried, Melly was unable to keep the sob from her voice. "The zoo is closed today, little one. We can't go in today." She had turned her face away from Inge's to hide her heartbreak, to hide her fear.

"*Nein, nein,*" insisted Inge, still pulling on Melly's arm. "We have to go in to feed the birds. Remember.....we're supposed to...." as her voice trailed off.

For a few moments Melly watched as people came to the entrance, stared at the sign then turn back. Others stood outside the gate, turned to those nearby, and whispered among themselves.

Melly took hold of Inge's hand. "We can't go in today little one. The zoo is closed. See some people have left already. We have to go home now."

Melly was prepared for further protests and urgings, but there were none. She did not expect that Inge would withdraw her hand from Melly's and then step sideways to create a distance between them. Nor was she prepared for Inge's mute stare into the distance, or for her flushed, strained face and clenched jaw. It seemed to Melly that Inge had moved into some quiet, private place inside herself, into a refuge where even Melly was not welcome.

This is not good , thought Melly. She is only a little girl, barely five and already knows so much hurt. Someday she might stay too long in that place of hers...or not come out at all. We have to do something, Kurt and me. We'll talk later... see what we can do.

Melly reached out, pulled Inge close and began the walk home. Inge, holding tightly with both hands to a thermos pressed against her chest, remained silent and continued to stare straight ahead.

Even before the incident at the zoo, Melly's concern over Inge was constant.

"Your worry is no more than hysteria," was Kurt's sharp retort whenever Melly brought up discussion about Inge's future. "She'll be all right," he assured. "These times will pass and she'll be all right."

"So, how long do we wait, Kurt, until these times pass. In the meantime she has no childhood. No school, all closed to Jewish children. How can a child not go to school?"

"We teach her ourselves, at home. At her age whatever she needs to learn we can teach her."

"And after that?" Melly challenged.

"After that! After that!" an irritated Kurt would explode. "By that time things will have improved! Good God in Heaven! I have no more patience. Why do you not understand!" And as always these talks became arguments and ended with Kurt throwing his arms up and rushing from the room to his record player, to the voices singing his favorite arias, to his haven, safe beyond the reach of anything outside.

At an unhurried breakfast with yesterday's upset at the zoo a large presence, Melly sat alongside Inge, still distant and mute, whose downcast eyes seemed to be fixed onto her hands clasped between her knees.

Melly peeked under Inge's lowered head. "Later today we bake cookies... *ja?*"

Inge slumped in her chair and lowered her head even further.

"Your favorite cookies, Inge. You know....the big, big kind with the sugar sprinkles on top to make the funny faces.... and then we'll surprise papa and have a party.... and....and....."

Inge looked into Melly's eyes, then away and stared at her uneaten breakfast.

Melly's heart sank. It's no use, she thought. She won't talk now. I'll try again with her a litle later. Maybe after she eats something, she'll feel better.... feel more like talking. She helped Inge from her chair with one hand ,and carrying Inge's breakfast in the other, Melly maneuvered into the front parlor, where side by side on the floor they resumed the task of removing the last few remaining phonograph labels.

"There, finally." Melly sighed and handed the last one to Inge, who tip-toed toward a completed stack across the room. Pausing at a nearby window Inge studied a wispy, fern-like plant on the sill, a special plant that she had raised from two carrot tops. The carrots from a neighbor's garden were bartered by Melly for a packet of six sewing needles and two yards of black velvet ribbon, treasures from Gold-schmidt's. The carrots went into the soup and the tops to Inge. Nothing was wasted.

"Mutti?"

A feeling of relief swept over Melly. Her litle girl is bet-ter. *"Ja, ja,"* she called.

"Do dead plants go to heaven?"

Startled, not so much at Inge's question, but more that her thoughts were morbid..... about death.... about ....

"Where did you hear about Heaven, Inge? Such a ques-tion from such a little girl."

"From papa's opera records," Inge sat down next to Melly. "People die there and go to Heaven...all the time. ...Does Heaven have a zoo?"

Melly had no idea when Kurt came into the room or how much he had heard. His face was pale, and wore a mix-ture of worry and profound sadness. But his outstretched arms into which Inge ran, and his words, "Come *Leibling,* we listen to a new opera today," told Melly that he had heard enough. Upon Inge's excited nodding, Kurt hoisted her onto his shoulder, and stamped from the room warbling the over-ture from the Barber of Seville. With a choking voice he explained "You see, Inge, there was a beautiful maiden named Rosina, who lived in a faraway land called Spain, where the sun shone all the time, and she met a young, handsome...." His voice trailed away beyond Melly's hearing, beyond her lingering feeling of doom.

CHAPTER TWENTY-THREE

A Change in Duties

From the start of Beate's tenancy in Melly's attic, a closeness grew between the two women. Often they visited for tea and talks in Melly's kitchen. Frequently, Kurt, who always had a ready ear for gossip joined his "Favorite ladies," for "the latest news."

So it was not unusual this morning, several months after Beate's eighteenth birthday, for all three to have tea together. They spoke of the times, of the Olympics held in Berlin the year before; of how the Games brought not only international prestige, but also better conditions throughout the land.

My father writes that he has been working every day for the past year," said Beate, "and that daily life is stable and orderly again. But he is upset that my brothers were forced into the Hitler Youth to be soldiers. He always said that Hitler means war. He's very frightened for my brothers."

"Do you see now, Melly?" said Kurt, who, it seemed, ignored the prospect of war, and continued excitedly, "Do you see how the country is coming back; just like I said it would. You can see it for yourself, *ja?*"

But Melly, feared war more than anything. She thought about everything that was stolen from her: her business, her home, the life she had treasured in Dusseldorf, But wanting to be carefull not to cast a cloud over the morning's optimism, muttered a cautious "We'll see." She refilled Beate's tea and placed a pastry by the cup. "Eat something," Melly ordered, "You're too thin."

The next morning, before her mirror, Beate dressed with more care than usual. She combed, braided and wrapped her hair in a crown around her head; she hoped it would make her look older, serious, capable.

This was the day she intended to speak to Administrator Guida Erhard about her work and her future. Beate knew the importance of appearance and personal presentation. To get ahead, one must look the part, make the right impression, dress perfectly.

That afternoon, standing in the doorway to Frau Gerhard's office, Beate straightened her dark blue skirt, adjusted her starched white blouse and patted a few stray strands of hair into place before she strode into her meeting. Standing for several moments at Frau Gerhard's desk, waiting for Gerhard to acknowledge her presence, and finding neither acknowledgment nor an invitation to sit, Beate quietly and quickly sat down in the nearest chair.

Sitting stiffly, her ankles crossed, her hands properly resting in her lap, Beate began. "Frau Erhard, I have been here and working very hard for many months now and....."

"Ah yes," interrupted the Administrator, who finally looked up from her cluttered desk to face her visitor. "And your work here as been exemplary. Congratulations Beate. The children all love you and your co-workers all say wonderful things about you. You should be very proud of yourself."

Encouraged, a beaming Beate continued, " It is so good to hear this and very gratifying because I try very hard to do my best every day."

"And you have succeeded." said Erhard, "and that is why I'm glad you dropped in today. It's really quite a coincidence. I was about to call you in anyway." She hesitated as if to let her words sink in. "It's time for you to move on. There will be a change in your duties."

Up to then Beate had anticipated a difficult interview with her supervisor. But now, feeling certain that she was about to receive good news, she assumed a less formal manner. Shifting in her seat, she crossed her legs and placed a hand against her chest to quiet, if she could, her rising excitement. This is so much easier, she thought, than I ever imagined. She waited politely a few moments for Erhard to explain more, but impatience conquered prudence and she finally blurted, "A change, Frau Gerhard, what kind of change?"

Erhard carefully withdrew a folder from beneath a jumble of fly-a-way papers and placed it before her. Resting her folded hands on its top, she took a second glance at the name Beate Zinmann on its cover, and leaned forward in her seat. "You will now work downstairs in the Aktion T-4 section. It is still the Children's Shelter Program, only a different division. The children there are damaged, severely defective, most from birth, some from sickness or accidents. They need special attention. And since you work so well with children, I've decided to transfer you there. Either there or, if you prefer, to housekeeping, where there is always a shortage of kitchen help."

Appalled, Beate just barely contained her horror. Housekeeping! I have been considered for housekeeping! Her thoughts were racing. I must keep myself under control. Be calm, mustn't let my feelings show...but how could they even....? Forcing a smile, appearing unruffled she asked,

"What will be my new duties in the new appointment? Who will do my work here?"

Appearing anxious for the meeting to end, Gerhard quipped, "your replacement will arrive in a few days." Her attention then turned from Beate to a careful examination of her fingernails, then to pencils she placed into a pencil-cup alongside a box of rubber stamps, finally to the contents of a drawer from which she extracted a paper wrapper and which, assumed Beate, contained Gerhard's lunch.

Looking up and seeing Beate still in her chair, Gerhard seemed startled as suddenly remembering that she had more instructions to give.

"So you see how it is, Beate. Duties here are rotated. You are required to move on. As for your exact duties in Aktion T-4, my understanding is that your responsibilities will include keeping records as the children are processed. Also you will responsible for arranging their transportation. Clara Zander-mann will be your immediate supervisor and she will explain your new duties in more detail once your transfer is complete."

Frau Gerhard removed a thermos from a bottom drawer and placed it alongside the paper wrapper on her desk "Now, we have a few minutes before you go. Is there anything else you would like to ask?"

"Well yes," responded Beate. "Where are they going--these sick children?"

"I'm not exactly certain. I have been told that from here they are relocated to a special children's department, a clinic at Hadmar, a permanent placement. Here in this building we are unable to accommodate them, except to arrange their travel. Our function is to process, only process." She moved the paper wrapper nearer, unscrewed the top of the ther-mos then, her patience having apparently worn thin she boomed, "Now what else?"

Beate took a deep breath. She had come for a promotion and she would not easily be deterred. She cleared her throat, gripped the sides of her chair and resumed her earlier business-like posture. "Now this transfer," she began, "does it include a promotion; because the reason I asked for this meeting was to request a promotion, a higher position, a leadership position."

In the thick silence that followed an open-mouthed Guida Erhard, speechless and with raised eyebrows stared at her young employee. She sighed deeply, and shook her head from side to side, as she leaned back in her chair. "Well, Beate, I don't know what it is you expected from your assignment here." Her voice was crisp, her manner imperious. "But you were assigned here to work with children. This is your job."

"But I have worked so hard for so long in the BDM and done so well in every job I was given that I believe I have earned consideration for a promotion." Certain now that this meeting was heading for disappointment, Beate shifted nervously in her chair and patted her crown of braids to busy her trembling hands.

Erhard returned her wrapped lunch to the desk drawer and replaced the cap to the thermos. She opened the folder containing Beate's records and scanned the pages as if to refresh her memory of the contents. But before Gerhard could speak, Beate, almost shouting, pointed out, "My records will back up everything I've said. I've even been sent to Leadership School in Coburg...."

Erhard interrupted, "That was only for two weeks, Beate, to give you information about how to be a leader to the younger girls, if needed. It was never meant to school you for leadership. Those positions are reserved for the more educated young women. Their training is much more extensive than...."

"But I was given to believe that I had completed every-thing, and in record time....two weeks...I was assured...."

"Nein!" interrupted Erhard, "Your record clearly shows that you did not do well in school in Schoenbach. Your grades and attendance were poor. Your teachers liked you, but they all gave identical evaluations regarding your prog-ress. It was disappointing."

"But, but..." contradicted Beate in a loud voice.

"Nein!" shouted Gerhard even louder. You have still not moved from the Jew's house. You assured me that it was temporary; that you would make a change soon. I warned you from the beginning to move. And you did not!"

"But my work here took all my time. I didn't even have a minute to myself. When I asked for a little time you refused me. How was I supposed to....?"

"You did not keep your word!"

"But I...."

"YOU DID NOT!" screamed Erhard. She slammed the folder shut and swirled in her chair to face the window. With her back to Beate she shouted, "Go now. We are done here. Tomorrow you will report for work the same as usual and prepare yourself for your new duties! GO!"

Beate scrambled to her feet and rushed to the doorway. Even her father's screams did not terrify her as did those of Guida Erhard. She looked back and watched her supervi-sor bring out her lunch from the desk drawer, remove once again the thermos top, then calmly begin her mid-day meal. Beate, for a brief second, wished that God would strike her dead.

CHAPTER TWENTY- FOUR

Rhinehaus Lodge

Over the next few weeks Gerhard's words rolled over and over in Beate's head, like a song in rounds. She started her new job. Mechanically she tended to her duties, sorting the children's records, separating those with red check marks, then personally escorting them into waiting transportation.

She gave little thought to the destiny of the children. It saddened her that they were too sick to remain with their families. But she knew that they would be cared for at their new shelter. She supposed it was all for the best.

Beate was grateful for the work; it occupied her mind and hid her misery. But night after night she sobbed into her pillow, heartsick, unable to find comfort for herself. For Guida Erhard, determined, powerful, and impatient for her lunch struck a blow and struck hard; in the space of a few moments she drove from Beate's soul every expectation for which she had so single-mindedly struggled. Fearing that more consequences, not yet spoken, were sure to follow, she feared most of all that she would be released from the organization and sent home to Schoenbach.

Lying there in her darkened room, snuggling deeper into the comfort of Melly's eiderdown, her thoughts wandered back to Rhinehaus Lodge, a modest timber frame inn in the small village of Triberg. Overlooking the Middle Rhine

River, it was a special place where she and Franz enjoyed their time together. With no thoughts of anyone but each other, where simple, uncluttered, joyful pleasures captured every moment of their stay; and when not so very long ago her future, bright and vital, was a beautiful flower yet to be plucked.

Rhinehaus proprietor Horst Wagner offered his guests the best beds, the best schnitzel, and the romance of the Rhine River Valley. The welcoming sign over the door said so.

Franz, never certain when his tours would end took advantage of his official station and negotiated a long-term reservation with the amiable proprietor. Delighted that such a prominent guest as Herr Reich Leader Franz Westermeyer preferred his establishment above all others, Horst Wagner, in appreciation for the honor, donated his best Riesling, which he placed on the bedside table, filled the room with fresh wild flowers from surrounding meadows, and fluttered and fussed over the housekeeping details. He demanded nothing less than perfection from his staff before the expected arrival of these two special guests.

The first time Beate and Franz viewed the accommodations a delighted Franz joked, "This must be fairyland," as they stood spellbound at the window.

"Ach ja..." whispered Beate dreamily spanning the magnificent Rhine River Valley stretching below. Yet she worried about their first night together. She had never before been together with a man. Pregnancy was a real possibility. Her Catholic religion forbade taking measures to avoid pregnancy. Adolph Hitler openly declared procreating among his Aryan young men and maidens, a duty. Her thoughts raced with "what ifs," and with the dread of what her life would certainly become if such a calamity, a baby, came into her life. But she loved Franz. She wanted to keep him in her life. Their first night together was predictable, and their nights, yet to come, inevitable.

She turned to Franz, her eyes meeting his. Since, at that moment, there was no way she could think of to resolve this concern, she decided to trust in good luck. She would do nothing to spoil this time with him. She hooked her arm through his, nudged softy and asked, "Can we stay here?"

Instantly Franz turned to Horst. "I'll take it." Within minutes Rhinehaus Lodge became their home away from home, away from the eyes and wondering of the curious.

Their room, small and simply furnished, offered embellishments which added delight and amusement to their stay. They laughed, then swore never to undress before the small stone stove, overlaid with ornamental tiles bearing religious sayings and symbols. They stared in awe, grins planted on their faces, at the clothing cabinet, painted blue and decorated with pink and white angels on its doors and sides. But most endearing, centered above the mahogany four-poster, a mural like painting of cupid with harp smiled down on their heads, bringing gales of giggles that broke into waves of laughter. And when they stopped laughing long enough to wonder about the other guests and what they must be thinking, they laughed even harder.

Their first morning at Rhinehaus, dressed in hiking boots and sweaters, they strolled to the village to a quiet café, preferring to breakfast away from the lodge's dining room. They were hungry and ate heartily of boiled eggs, hard rolls with honey and tea. Franz lit his pipe and puffed the scented tobacco until it encircled his head. Upon leaving he suggested they investigate the countryside on bicycles.

"Besides," he said, "I believe it is necessary we have a talk... an understanding."

As they bicycled along the river path. Beate tried to anticipate what Franz had on his mind. But not able to imagine what it could be she decided not to worry. Whatever it is, she told herself, we can fix it.

After a few miles of pedaling and enjoying the fresh scent of morning grass, the sun broke through. Beate began to feel too warm. She parked her bicycle against a nearby tree and removed her sweater. While tying the sleeves around her waist she called out to Franz, busily removing ankle clamps from his trouser." So what is it you need to tell me.

Franz took her hands in his and began, "You know I love you. This is not the first time I said those words to you. You must never, never doubt my love for you."

"Ja...ja..I know... so...?"

"So...what I have to tell you is...as much as I love you with all my heart, that marriage is out of the question. Marriage is not in our future."

Astounded at his pronouncement, giving it time to sink in before answering she thought, he probably thinks that I want a husband, like all the girls. After all, that is what we were taught to strive for in the BDM; to be wives and mothers, especially mothers, the highest calling for German womanhood.

She released her hands and pushed her hair back behind her ears.

Leaning against a nearby tree she was about to speak when Franz broke in.

"No, Beate, say nothing. Just listen......"

"Franz...."

"Just listen, there is more. When I was a boy in the orphanage I became very ill for many weeks. Afterwards the doctors said that this illness caused...that it is unlikely for me to be a father. Do you understand what I am trying to say?"

Beate studied his face and realized that as much as he loved her, he didn't really know her; he had absolutely no idea of the overwhelming relief his words just brought.

Franz" she assured." I don't need to be married to love you, if that's your worry. I'll always love you, no matter what. And I'll tell you a secret that I have never said to anyone before." She paused, looked straight into his eyes. "I don't want to be married. If you were to propose marriage to me right now, I would decline." She saw the astonished look come over his face, but continued. "The truth is I need to be free Franz, to go ahead with my life, to be somebody.... But never doubt that I am committed to you, with all my heart, no matter what."

Franz raised her hands to his lips then placed them against his chest. "And I you," in a choking voice. "And I you." He climbed on his bicycle. Before taking off he called a light-hearted warning, "Remember, you promised to move away from the Jewish house. It might go against you some day."

"*Ja, Ja,* I will, as soon as I can," she called to his back, as he, and his bicycle, disappeared around a bend in the path.

But that was then. Now with months of Rhinehaus weekends and holidays behind them, months of long walks, long talks and long silences as they sat in fields of uncut grasses, Beate lay in her bed and thought about Franz's latest announcement.

"I will be returning from Berlin with special news. There is so much....I will tell you everything when I get back. We'll have a special celebration." he had said at their last meeting.

She recalled his voice filled with excitement, and his promise to tell her everything. But now, in her attic room, staring into the darkness, broken hearted about her work, and her future, she sank deeper into misery over her plight, whispering into the quiet night, "And I have so much to tell you...so very much.

CHAPTER TWENTY-FIVE

From The Highest Office

Whenever possible they brought a picnic and had their meals in their "Funny little room," as they called it. They had moved a bedside table to under the window, where they could view "Our magnificent river." They clinked glasses and toasted first, the river, then to successes in the years to come.

"You can't imagine," Franz began," the enthusiasm shown for my proposals. First off a new BDM school will begin in Bad Orb. My idea is to strengthen National Socialist ideas among the girls because I do not think they are serious about what is expected of them. And it is not their fault. They are not being taught correctly about what they have to know."

Suddenly remembering the luncheon spread, Franz wolfed down large bites of cheese and sausage and, without stopping for air, finished off a stein of his favorite beer.

"I am so hungry and excited I don't know what to do first. So, let me see...what was I saying....oh *ja*...the girls will hear talks on racial purity. They will be advised to avoid Jews and to teach that avoidance to their children. Also they will learn household skills and how to create a perfect German home; after all, it is up to them. They are the bearers of German culture. No young girl will ever question her value to the Reich."

Beate sat quietly, hearing, retaining his words, drinking in his exuberance. But then, slowly sinking inwardly at what had once been a girlish vision of her own future and the abrupt vanishing of that vision, she fell deeper into despair.

She nibbled on blackbread and liverwurst, sipped wine and fixed her gaze on him. I will not say anything about what has happened to me, she thought, not yet anyway. I will not spoil this moment for him.

"Also," continued Franz, "I have outlined a plan for BDM girls to have special evenings at home where they will gather and hear speakers. Prominent women leaders like Gertrude Scholtz-Klink and Elisabeth Zander are the two I have in mind to start."

Franz turned his attention back to the food before him, to the *gugelhopf,* fruitcake, his favorite. He broke off the first piece, offered it to Beate, then popped it into his mouth when she declined.

"But best of all," he continued, "I've saved the best for last...listen to this. I have been recommended to relocate to Vienna as youth Leader after the annexation of Austria... whenever that will be....But it will happen."

Franz clasped his hands behind his head and sat back in his chair. His eyes danced with excitement. His gaze never left Beate's face.

This man, she thought, her man, filled with aspirations, filled with strength of purpose, as if guided by escorts to wherever his sights were set, would one day leave....leave her. His brilliant future stretching before him like an endless sea to swim, would take him from her.

More from fear than upset, Beate's cheeks grew hot. Her insides tightened. At first she didn't trust herself to speak, didn't trust that her voice would not tremble, or that tears already close to the surface, even without this last bit of news, would not stream down her face. She waited, took a deep breath, then plunged in.

"Wonderful," she burst forth, her voice bordering on hysteria, "Your plan is wonderful and much needed I can tell you. This is just what the BDM lacked. Congratulations, Franz." She raised her wine glass, but as she did so her composure began to crumble. "But I guess this will mean even longer separations." Her voice weakened as the last few words stuck in her throat.

Franz, appearing bewildered at her reaction stammered, "Well yes...I guess it would," he said thoughtfully, "but I will always find a way...you must know...."

"*Ach,* Franz, I do know....Never mind me.... Pay no attention. It's only because I will miss you. I know that you must do this.... to go to Vienna. I truly do."

She was aware of his hands busily arranging and rearranging the tableware, of his eyes following his hands, wordless gestures telling her that he was troubled and deep in thought. When he finally spoke his voice was soft, his eyes still cast down. "So, you have something to tell me?"

"I do." With her hands folded in her lap, through a tear stained face, she told him of her meeting the Guida Erhard..."And she will never recommend me for advancement, never." Her words brought the misery in her soul to the surface. She could think only of her future, a future doomed to become everything from which she had struggled to escape.

"So," he said, "you did not do well in school. That does not sound so serious a drawback that you should be...."

"There's more," she interrupted. "She objects to my living arrangements. She is furious that I never moved from...."

"You still live with the Jews!" Franz shouted. "You were supposed to move out, find another place."

"I know, I know and I intended to do that but there was never the time. I worked at the shelter from early morning until dark, sometimes twelve hours a day. I worked many weekends when I was asked to do so, and then I put in extra weekends to accumulate extra time for us . There was no free time. No opportunity. Occasionally when I asked Erhard for an afternoon off, she always refused and then to punish me for asking, she ordered me to put in extra time. So I stopped asking. And now that I have been transferred and working in Aktion T-4, I don't know...."

Abruptly, Franz got to his feet and leaned across the table, his face almost touching hers. His eyes widened, his pallor blanched, and in a voice barely above a whisper asked, "Where? You're working where?"

"Aktion T-4, what's wrong? You're suddenly....what is it....?"

Franz slowly sat back in his chair, his elbows on the table, his hands cradling his face. "Beate," he asked, "has your work been explained to you? Do you know what your job is? Do you understand the fate of these Aktion T-4 children?"

"Well yes, of course I do. Why are you suddenly....what is wrong? These are very sick children, you know. I have been arranging for their relocation to special places for their care because the shelter is not able....So what is wrong with what I do?"

"Beate, these are not special care places! You have been sending them for euthanasia.....for extermination!"

"*Nein. Nein!* How can you say such a terrible thing to me?"

"Because it is true and you should know it."

"I was never told this!" a horrified Beate shouted. "Never!" She crossed her arms, grabbed her shoulders and rocked back and forth. "God will surely strike me dead for this," she wailed. "A sin against my church, against God, against everything".....and then the anguished cry, "Oh my God why?"

Franz then helped her to stand, took her in his arms, and tried to soften the shock of his words. Tenderly he pushed aside the hair that had fallen into her face and helped her back into her chair. He dipped his handkerchief into his wine and daubed her face. "This will make you feel better," he assured." If not better then at least cooler," he smiled at his weak joke.

They sat in silence. The only sound came from the hall-way, from the voices of guests returning to their rooms after their midday meal.

When Beate finally spoke, her voice was so low that Franz had to lean forward to hear. "Franz, how could you let this program happen. Children are your life...How could...?

It was not I, Beate. You must believe me. I was never, never brought into these plans. I raised my objections many times, and very loudly. I promised that I'd work out a solution for these children, rather than....this.

"But Franz, you...."

"They were adamant, committed to the program. They said that the children were damaged, irreparably; that their life was not worth living; that Aktion T-4 is for the good of the *volk*."

"But...."

"Do you not understand?" he shouted. "It came from higher-ups, from the highest office. I tried and tried but I was not able to prevent it, or stop it. From the highest office, Beate, it came. I was helpless to do anything."

Beate, broken, trembling and suddenly older than her eighteen years wailed, "I will not do that work any longer, *nein,* never.....never!"

Her voice whiny and sing-song rose and fell on her tumbling breath. "I don't care anymore what they do to me. It can't be any worse than what God will do. They cannot force me any longer to send children to be killed. That is what I will say to Supervisor Zandermann, first thing when I get back. After that I'll go to confession and do penance, and then they will probably send me home to Schoenbach."

Composed now, settled in her mind, she sipped her wine. "Thank you for the handkerchief with wine on my face." A small smile touched the corners of her mouth.

But Franz was not yet ready to put the seriousness of her situation to rest. "Beate, here's what you do." He took both her hands in his, held them tightly and rested them on the table between them. "Show up for work, same as usual, but say you are feeling ill, too sick to work. Say that you need to see a doctor. Tell the doctor whatever you must say to get his note or recommendation that you're sick, on the verge of something more serious, unless you are given leave time. What you must never say is that the work is too hard, or too wrong, or too much against your conscience. Never, never blame the work. And stall, stall, stall. After a while you will have used up all your leave time and you will be notified to return. Show up for work, but say nothing. Ask for nothing. Demand nothing. You will discover that you have been reassigned, that someone else is doing your job in Aktion T-4, that you were replaced. Then you do whatever job they assign. Whatever your new duties are, do them cheerfully. In the meantime I'll see what I can do to get you transferred to Berlin, however long that will take. But I will do my best to make it quick." Then he smiled a little smile, "and I'll transfer myself there also."

Franz rose from his chair. Pacing the room he continued, "also it is important not to call attention to yourself by going to confession. You already know that the government is at odds with the churches. It is a big mistake to ignore policy."

To herself Beate thought, I'll contact Erika. She may know a Priest who will do it secretly.

As if he could read her mind, Franz went to the window and without looking in her direction said, "There's something else. Everyone is under scrutiny. It is known that you and I are together. There is a good deal of eye-winking and back-slapping about it, but understand that everything you do reflects on me. If you put yourself in jeopardy, you put me there as well."

Franz resumed his seat and across the table once more took her hands in his. "Promise me, you must promise that you'll forget about confession."

The love in his eyes, the love in his voice for the moment overshadowed all the hurt and wrong done to her. "I promise you Franz, my solemn promise." To herself she thought, God surely knows I'm innocent; he will forgive me even without confession.

She studied the gold signet ring on Franz's little finger and touched it with her cheek. She lifted her eyes to his. If she could thank him in a million ways she would do so. But she could say only a simple, "Danke."

CHAPTER TWENTY-SIX

A Meeting With Deputy Director

"You are here to get married?" His jowls shook. His glasses clouded. "Well, right at this moment that is not possible." Herr Clerk Spengler in the Registrar's Office at City Hall, a white haired giant of a man, was adamant.

Ursula and Peter, side by side, heads tilted upwards stared into the face of this City Hall Official, astounded at his size, dumbstruck at his words.

"You must first go to the genetic counseling center before you can qualify to be married," he continued. "It's the law now. Everyone must go."

"But you see," began Ursula, who stepped closer to the counter ,"we...

"*Ach, ja, ja,*" he interrupted. "I know all about it. You're in love...lovebirds," he mocked, "want to be married...be together for always. Well none of that matters. What matters now are the laws for racial purity." He turned away, blew his nose into a crumpled handkerchief, then turned back to face them. "The laws are very strict. Jews and Aryans cannot marry each other."

Peter stepped up alongside Ursula, about to speak, but before he could begin Herr Clerk Spengler asked, "and your categories are....?"

Without hesitation, both at the same time answered, "Protestant."

Ursula then dug around in her bag and finally produced her Baptismal Certificate, which she waved at the startled official.

Again Herr Spengler's jowls shook. Again his glasses clouded. This time he snatched them from his face and dropped them into some mysterious place under the counter. His eyes narrowed, he rubbed his chin. It became clear to Ursula that he suspected something amiss.

"You see," Ursula began hurriedly explaining herself as Protestant, concluding with "I'm even officially registered in the Protestant Community. Their records will confirm everything." She carefully placed her Baptismal Certificate back into her bag and said, "and the designation *Geltungsjude* which was given me is a mistake because I'm not a full Jew as that designation implies. I'm not a Jew at all. I'm Protestant."

As she spoke Clerk Spengler began stacking folders into two high, wobbly piles until he successfully blocked their faces from his. And Ursula and Peter, holding hands and staring into that deliberately erected wall of paper, not knowing what to do, did nothing.

Several minutes passed. Upon pushing one pile aside and seeing them both standing there, Clerk Spengler exploded. "You are still here?" In a high pitched voice he screamed. "Go, Go! Do you not understand that I cannot marry you now?

They glanced quickly at each other and scrambled to leave, when Clerk Spengler called after them. "Wait, wait, you Fraulein, don't go yet. Here is a name and address where to go." He scrawled quickly on a pad, tore off the sheet of paper and handed it to Ursula. "Here. You go here. See this Official, Beate Zinmann. Fraulein Zinmann is in a positon to help you get a reclassification that may allow you to marry after all. She can tell you more about it when you see her. I urge you to go and go quickly before the laws change again."

Hesitantly, Ursula accepted the paper held out to her and glanced at the writing. She exchanged looks with Peter and saw a mixture of confusion and fear come over his face. In the many months to come, whenever her thoughts turned to Peter, it was his face at this moment that she envisioned.

They walked from the dank, static corridors of City Hall into the sunshine, into a gentle stir of air, into the animated street sounds of Berlin. Leaning against the building, heads together, they studied the paper in Ursula's hand: Deputy Director Beate Zinmann, Women's Social Welfare and Service, Schillertrasse 16a....

The day was still early. Too early for midday meal but not to late to investigate Clerk Spengler's recommendation.

"I don't know about this," a doubtful, troubled Peter stared at the paper. "I don't trust...."

"Ja," said Ursula in a slow, thoughtful voice. " But maybe it's what I have to do. Maybe there is a procedure in place for reclassification after all. We must find out."

Schillerstrasse 16-a, converted from an abandoned tavern, was sandwiched between a rundown hotel with an overhead sign that read simply "Hotel," and an apartment building that appeared deserted. Once inside, a narrow hallway led them to a back, airless room. Above the open door a sign read: "Beate Zinmann, Deputy Director, Women's Social Welfare and Service."

Ursula and Peter, with clasped hands stood in the doorway uncertain about how to proceed. Timidly, Ursula tapped on the door frame. "Please," she called in the smallest voice to the woman behind the desk.

Beate, startled at first, looked up from her work, rose from her seat, and walked around the desk to Ursula. Smiling broadly she held out her hand. "Welcome *Fraulein*. Please do come in." Then to Peter she said, "This is a women's center. I'm sorry but you must wait outside. And don't look concerned. Nothing terrible will happen to her. I promise."

Shown to her seat, Ursula took in her surroundings. A sagging, black leather sofa missing one cushion stood opposite rows of crates holding files, folders and various sized ledgers; a black and white checkered coat, which Ursula assumed belonged to the Deputy Director hung carelessly on a hook over the front of the lavatory doorway; a short stack of books under a corner of the desk replaced its missing leg; a lopsided ashtray, a struggling Jade plant reaching for a bit of light from its place under the widow, and one other chair at the side of the desk, into which Ursula was now sitting,, comprised the furnishings of the room.

In Ursula's opinion, the room seemed surprisingly shabby for the office of a Deputy Director, a radical departure from the plush, comfortable office she had envisioned earlier while on the way. She wondered briefly about the black and white checkerboard coat hanging over the lavatory doorway and why there was no coat room.

But then, impatient to begin her reason for the meeting and hardly waiting for her interviewer to settle herself behind her desk, Ursula poured out her story. The words came fast and tumbling, at times babbling, other times through shouts of indignation. She sat at the edge of her chair and leaned on the desk, her arms outstretched, hands folded into tight fists.

Deputy Director cleared her throat. "And you ....?"

And Herr Spengler at City Hall," continued Ursula, "said that you could help me. He said....maybe with a special exception, or even a reclassification."

She withdrew a handkerchief tucked inside her sleeve, blotted the dampness from her face and sighed deeply, as she studied the impact of her words upon Deputy Director Zinmann, a woman who held the power to decide her future with an act as simple as a stroke of the pen.

And Beate, whose eyes never left Ursula's for an instant, stared in silence, then rose and pulled her chair to where Ursula sat. Face to face, her voice barely above a whisper she said, "Listen carefully to me. Do not interrupt or ask questions. Tell no one what I am about to tell you because I will deny everything and you will be in worse trouble than you are already." She reached out and took hold of Ursula's hands. "You were sent here to be sterilized. This is my job here. I evaluate women for sterilization. As a Jew, you qualify."

Ursula gasped and tried to pull her hands away. But Beate's tight grip held Ursula in her seat. She wanted to run, to scream to Peter for help. She remembered the same feeling of horror seconds before collapsing in Herr Loeber's office in school two years before.

"No. No. Listen to me. Listen...stay calm...do not say anything." Beate tightened her grip on Ursula's hands even more. "Herr Spengler probably thought that if you consented to sterilization, then based on your not being able to have children, Jewish children that is, and taking into consideration your conversion as a baby, a reclassification might be possible so that you could be married."

Once again Ursula tried to pull away. She opened her mouth to speak, but Beate interrupted.

"No, say nothing. Just listen. You are absolutely not a candidate for sterilization. My conscience would never let me rest if I made such a recommendation." Beate paused for a few seconds, then released Ursula's hands. She resumed her place behind her desk and faced her visitor.

"Rather than marriage, another solution would be to find work in another country, perhaps England. For an umarried girl, it's a real possibility. I hear the English love nannies from Germany," Beate lowered her head to the papers on her desk. "Now, as far as I'm concerned we never had this talk."

Danke," whispered Ursula to the lowered head. She understood, indeed, that this meeting could have turned out very differently. She felt relieved, even grateful to this stranger. Yet the grinding hurt in her stomach reminded her of the disappointment, the frustration and the outrage at being sent on this potentially harmful errand. As she turned to leave, she noticed for the first time two photographs on either side of the doorway. She supposed they were of the Deputy Director's family, and paused to study them.

On the left an older couple, he, smiling broadly, proudly held out a line of fish; she, wearing a floral apron hugged a pan against her chest, presumably in which to cook the fish. Back in the distance three boys stood ankle deep in a lake. Each held a fishing pole. While two girls, looking very serious, stood side by side in the forefront. Ursula immediately recognized Beate and surmised that the other girl was her sister. "Your family?" asked Ursula suddenly

"Oh, *ja,"* called Beate, looking up. 'That is my family. I'm standing with my sister Erika. She is older and married now. And that other photograph, the one on the opposite side, they are also my family....in a way."

And there they were. Melly and Inge smiling and starring into Ursula's face, just as Ursula remembered them from years ago when they stayed the night at her home. There was no mistaking them. Melly, plump and proud, held tightly to the hand of a little girl with golden Shirley Temple curls... Inge's hand.

Pivoting on her heels Ursula scowled at her interviewer. Filled with the shock of not only seeing the picture, but the words claiming them as family spoken from the mouth of a Nazi official, combined with all the wretchedness of the day, was more than Ursula could tolerate. She exploded.

"Who are these people to you?" she screamed. "How do you know them?" What are they doing here...on your wall? They are not your family! They are not...."

Ursula strode to where Beate sat. She leaned across the desk into the stunned face of the woman who had just moments before claimed kinship...."in a way."

"They are *my* family," hissed Ursula. "*Mine!*"

She forgot the kindness just shown her by this Nazi Official who, with wide-eyed astonishment, appeared stunned by Ursula's words. As for Ursula, long and deeply held resentments over the growing turmoil in her life rushed to the surface. With an ugliness from a place in her soul, a dark place even she never knew she possessed, Ursula growled, "We don't have Nazis in our family. In our family Nazis are not welcome."

As Ursula spoke, Beate grew pale. "Please sit," said Beate, indicating the chair which moments before Ursula had vacated. And Ursula, shaking, resumed her seat and stared into Beate's strained face. In a low voice, almost a whisper, Beate explained her relationship with the Wallerstein family. She spoke in detail, of how she came to live in their attic, of their kindnesses, of how Melly took care of her when she became sick and depressed over her work at the childrens' shelter. "They were friends to me when I needed friends and understanding. They were my parents when I needed parents, and I will always be grateful to them, and I will always keep them in my life. They are my family. And" Beate added even more softly "we keep in touch regularly, Melly and I. When I have some time off, I go to Frankfurt to see them, and when I can manage I bring something special for Inge. And my room in the attic is exactly as I left it. For me it's coming home. They are my family."

The long silence that followed was broken when Beate said, "You never told me your name . But I ask now."

Ursula, whose wrangled emotions could not endure another minute in that room, whose eyes never left those of Deputy Director Beate Zinmann, only wanted only to escape. Standing now in the open doorway, she stole one last look at the desk, at the stack of books holding up its corner, at the black and white checkered coat over the lavatory doorway, and wondered if she would ever see Beate again. Her eyes came to rest on the window sill behind the desk, to the Jade plant straining toward the sun, striving to survive in its otherwise dingy world.

She called across the room, "My name...my name is Ursula Steinhard-Wallerstein," Her defiant tone suddenly softened. " You have been kind to me. I'll never forget...." She turned and exited Schillerstrasse 16-a to where Peter waited, to the comfort of the familiar.

Berlin
1937

CHAPTER TWENTY-SEVEN

The British Love German Nannies

Outside Schillerstrasse 16-a, Ursula and Peter linked arms. Wordlessly they walked to a nearby café. Over coffee, Ursula, not knowing the best way to tell Peter about her interview, finally blurted, "I think you should go to Holland without me. I'll join you there as soon as I'm able, but I don't believe it will be soon."

"*Nein, nein!* I'll wait. I'll...."

"Peter, please listen." She leaned toward him and whispered, "There was no help for me at that Women's Welfare Office. I can't say anything more about it, except to tell you that marriage right now is not possible."

"I will not hear of it. No! I will not leave without you. I'll wait while you make arrangements for leaving, and when they are made we will go together. Once we are in Holland, we will marry there."

The next morning, at the Passport Office, Ursula was told that she needed to wait her turn. She was directed to the passport line that snaked around desks and filing cabinets then outside and around to the back of the building where Ursula took her place at the end, behind a young mother holding a crying infant. She felt confident that when she explained her reason for a passport, one, certainly, would be granted. So even though standing in line wore on her nerves and strained her stamina, nevertheless, she remained resolute. It was what she needed to do. She would get her passport and move ahead with her life. After four hours she was guided to a seat behind the desk of a Passport Clerk.

"Jews are not allowed passports for foreign travel." He smiled graciously, but shook his head from side to side, as he handed Ursula's application back to her.

Ursula pasted the sweetest smile she could manage on her face. "I simply cannot seem to make anyone understand that I am not a Jew. It's all such a big mistake." She reached into her bag, withdrew her Baptismal Certificate, and offered it to the clerk, who ignored the gesture and instead consulted his watch.

"And besides," Ursula continued as if nothing unusual had just taken place, " I'm not applying simply for travel, or for vacation. I have serious reasons. I want to leave Germany and live in Holland. I will be married there. I will make my life there." As she spoke her eyes never left the eyes of the clerk. Now that I have explained everything, she thought, now surely he will reconsider my application.

"I'm sorry *Fraulein,* it's the law. I can do nothing unless you have a visa....But I suggest before anything else, that you attend to that mistaken classification as a Jew. Have it corrected. You need to do that."

She rolled up the Baptismal Certificate and slowly, carefully placed it back into her bag. "But where.....?" she asked.

"The Ministry of the Interior," he replied. "Start there. They can tell you how to proceed, what to do." He collected his papers and, as Ursula was leaving, yet within her hearing, said to his co-worker, "*Ach,* another Jew looking for a miracle. They will keep her very busy at the Ministry Office."

As the days passed into weeks, Ursusla, acting on the advice of the Passport Clerk pleaded her circumstances before one Ministry official after another. And Peter, upon

Ursula's urgings, slowly began accepting the likelihood that her leaving would be delayed. He decided to go ahead of her.

"It breaks my heart to go without you" he explained. "But I can't wait any longer. Each day is worse than the day before. I'm afraid of the streets, of being continually stopped and questioned by the Gestapo. And the gangs of Brownshirts, they race through the streets screaming and terrorizing and pushing people over. It's terrible, terrible. I have two choices. Either I go into hiding, or I leave."

He held her face between his hands, tenderly drew her hair back, then pulled her into his arms. "Promise me, Ursula, promise that you will keep trying; that as soon as your passport is approved, that very second, that you will pack your bags and come to me. Promise."

"I promise," as she grinned into his face. "But I will need more than a few seconds to pack bags and arrange travel," she teased. Secretly though she felt relieved that the marriage would be delayed. In the back of her mind, hope lingered that another way for her would open.

Two weeks later Peter sent word that he had arrived safely, resumed his studies at the University of Amsterdam, and had comfortably settled himself into living quarters near the school. Once again he expressed gratitude to Ilse and Simon and said that he was impatient for Ursula to arrive and that he longed for her beyond words.

Months passed. Neither her application to correct her status from Jew to Protestant, nor her request for a passport had been forthcoming. Deputy Director Beate Zinmann's words, "Make your life elsewhere...the British love nannies from Germany," had entered her thoughts every so often. But she quickly put the idea out of her mind. After all, she thought, I don't know anything about taking care of children.

But she also remembered her promise to Peter never to give up trying. And because Beate's words opened another door to try, she asked her parents for advice. "Maybe the British would have a way to expedite my passport. All I need is to get there. Once I'm there I'll look for a way to go to Holland; or if that doesn't work out then I'll find a way to continue my studies in England. But one way or another....."

"*Ach, ja,*" encouraged Simon, "England has fine schools. And as a nanny you would be in a fine home."

"You will need to learn the language fast," urged Ilse. "But that would not be difficult for you, I'm certain. So *ja, ja,* Uli, you go. Try. I think it's a fine idea. We are still waiting for clearance to leave. I applied for clearance for the three of us and, it shouldn't be much longer But in the meantime, Uli, you do what you can."

With renewed hope Ursula joined a long, slow moving line of hopeful would-be nannies at the British Consulate in Berlin. After several days of waiting she was finally called in for an interview.

"So," said the British Official, "you want to work in England, as a nanny."

"Or a housemaid also would be fine," she interrupted eagerly. "Anything..."

The British Official chuckled. "Oh yes, I'm sure....but you see all those other young ladies there?" He pointed to the waiting room that she had just left, "All here for the same reason as you."

He plucked a pen from his shirt pocket, unscrewed the cap and drew a line through a name on a list in front of him. Assuming that it was probably her name and that the British Official was on the verge of dismissing her, Ursula remained in her seat anyway. She needed to explain her circumstances. She needed to keep trying." But you see, I.....".

"So you see how it is," he interrupted, I have to tell each one," indicating again with a finger pointing to the waiting room, " the same thing I have to tell you. And that is, while we would be most pleased if you came to England, the truth of the matter is that right now there are no jobs. Not at the moment. But don't be discouraged. Positions do open from time to time. When your turn comes, and when you have your passport ready, proper arrangements can be made. So thank you for coming in, *Fraulein*. Next Please."

Still seated, Ursula assumed her most engaging manner "But I thought you would be the one to expedite my passport as part of those arrangements."

"Oh no, miss. We can't do that. We have no authority over passports for German Nationals. You must take care of that yourself. And I urge you to do it straight away. Next, please."

With those words, with no avenues remaining, Ursula lost all hope. I'm going home, she told herself. And I'm staying home. It was never my idea to leave anyway. I'm exhausted. I'm not even an adult yet. It's all too much for me and I'm not doing this anymore.

She walked through the streets of Berlin, her progress delayed as marching soldiers carrying Nazi flags, and gathering crowds filled the streets. Loudspeakers, blaring praises of "Our Fuhrer," hundreds of arms raised in the Nazi salute drove her to forge ahead without caring who, or what, she pushed aside. Suddenly thoughts of Peter flooded her mind. I will send word to him soon, first thing. I don't know if we will ever marry. It seems less and less possible. She paused to study the ring she had so solemnly accepted with Peter's proposal. I cannot wear this any longer. She drew it from her finger and let it drop into her bag. Maybe another time.. maybe someday, but for now I'm going home.

Frankfurt
1938

CHAPTER TWENTY-EIGHT

A ride on the Streetcar

November 10, 1938. As far back as Melly could remember, every 10th of November was reserved for rededicating the Goldschmidt building in Dusseldorf. It was among the many justifications invented by the family for celebrating. But it took on even more significance when she learned that November 10th was also Kurt's birthday.

From her kitchen window in Frankfurt, Melly watched the autumn leaves, caught in sudden gusts, swoop and scatter in giant swirls of gold and red. And the sun, strong, insistent and golden, its glow, like a warm kiss, touched her face.

Lured by the season she so dearly loved Melly decided to take Inge for a day out. Maybe take her to the park to run through leaves. Or maybe even go to the movies.

With the zoo day months into the past, Inge's spirit had healed. Kurt, who had devoted weeks of watchful attentions to Inge, pronounced her "Recovered from her misadventure," and "Just fine," and "The same little girl as always."

Now, as Melly washed and dried and placed the last of the breakfast plates into the cupboard, she turned to Inge, still at the table, selecting only perfectly round raisins from the bowl, and one by one lining them along her arm like railroad tracks.

"Inge, Melly began, " I think today we go to the movies. Shirley Temple is playing."

Inge looked up and Melly saw a spark light up in Inge's eyes

"We can go right this minute," said Melly, hoping to keep that spark from fading. Without stopping for a breath she continued, "And since it's early we can also go to the park first. And this time, for a special treat at intermission, we can have lunch from the sandwich man. And I heard there's a puppet man with a Shirley Temple Doll who sings the songs in the movies."

As she spoke, Inge, whose eyes brightened even more, scrambled from the table, overturning the last of her milk. Her carefully constructed raisin tracks scattered to the floor as she ran to Melly, hugged her legs, and jumping up and down chanted, "*Ja, ja, ja, ja....*" to the tune of "*du, du....*"

Melly laughed and thought, I think, after all, that I may never tell her that Shirley Temple is from America.

After boarding the streetcar Melly inched to the rear, passing chattering, bustling riders, scolding and coaxing children, holding out handkerchiefs under runny noses with orders to "*schnupfen!*" Selecting a window seat, Melly sat down to watch the streets go by with one eye always on Inge, who loved to swing around and around the trolley pole.

Not long into the ride, as though a curtain had parted, a surreal stage setting opened before her eyes, Melly viewed with mounting alarm the scene from her window.

Along the street small fires were smoldering from what appeared to be burnings of religious Jewish artifacts; sacred prayer books, blackened Menorahs. Torahs and prayer shawls littered the sidewalks. The synagogue, which sometimes she, but always Kurt, attended every Saturday morning, was burned out. Pews and stained glass windows were smashed. Everything was destroyed. Everything, that is, except the

massive synagogue door; a showpiece of brass ornamentation said to have survived ancient times. In time to come
Melly would learn that the Nazi's had confiscated that door;
that it had become one of hundreds of priceless treasures
stolen from Jews and Jewish Institutions throughout Europe.

Gradually, the stirs and and prattles of fellow passengers
had ceased. All eyes were fixed on the havoc outside. At
first, not understanding how such destruction could have
happened, Melly's mind was numb. But as the streetcar continued and more and more wreckage came into view, she
realized that only the Jews were targeted. That it was not a
natural disaster, but deliberate. At that moment, trembling
with fear, she looked ahead through the motorman's window.
As though rained from the skies, shattered glass covered the
thoroughfare as far as the eye could see. Except for a strag-
gler or two the streets were deserted, while the trolley, in
its quietness, seemed to glide through a dead world.

Melly felt a small hand on her shoulder.

"Mutti?"

Without looking up Melly patted the seat alongside for
Inge to sit. Pale and stone-faced, as though chiseled from
marble, Melly kept her eyes on the back of the motorman's
head, not bearing to see the welling tears she knew were
already in Inge's eyes, or see the color rising in her face, or
attend to the swallowed cries so deeply submerged they
could not surface. She grieved for her precious Inge, for the
toll on her spirit. And she grieved for herself, for her own
anguish over her words and deeds that, moments before, had
brought joyful expectations to her child; because no matter
how well meaning, Melly brought instead this moment of
profound disappointment and sorrow..

The streetcar ground to a halt. Wordless passengers
disembarked. Holding tightly to Inge's hand Melly, began the

walk home, wending around piles of smoking debris, stinking from smoke and urine, feeling the crunch of shattered glass under her feet. Strauss's Bakery, where she bought challah Friday mornings, in ruins. Wasserman's Butcher store that carried the best *wurst*, burned out.

Ahead, an old woman in a long, black, man's coat, and on her head a black babushka, stood over a mound of smoldering Torahs and religious books and wailed and rocked back and forth on her heels and talked to God all at the same time.

Trembling at the sight of this mourning woman, her eyes wide with fear, Inge stood transfixed, unable to continue the walk with her mother. And Melly, knowing that this moment would stay in Inge's memory for her lifetime, could only lift Inge in her arms, carry her home and try to say comforting words which Melly, herself, did not believe.

.As Melly turned the corner, Kurt, waiting outside, rushed to her, his face a mixture of fear and confusion. They spoke no words; their faces spoke for them. He took Inge from Melly's arms, carried her inside to bed, where Melly knew he would lie down beside her, hold her, and speak soothing words of his own until she drifted off to sleep.

Melly had just filled the kettle to boil for tea when Kurt sat down at the table. "She hasn't spoken since we left the trolley," she said. Sitting opposite Kurt and not knowing what else to do, she could only stare into his face. One hand covered her mouth as she rocked in her seat. The other nervously rubbed the back of her neck, until the kettle boiled and she brought tea to the table.

"We have to help her, Kurt." Melly's voice was soft, calm. "She needs this from us, to be helped." She expected Kurt's reaction to be the usual argumentative display always sure to follow whenever the subject of Inge arose.

"*Ja*," he said simply. "*Ja*," as he nodded.

While Kurt's response surprised her, at the same time Melly felt encouraged. He's changed, she thought. He'll listen. She cleared her throat for a few moments before going on.

"Kurt," she began. "I've spoken to neighbors whose children went to England.

"*Ja?*"

"*Ja*. The Rabbi places them. He makes the arrangements. Inge could go. Live with a Jewish family. Go to school. Be with other children. Have a normal childhood."

"*Ja.*"

"Be safe."

"*Ja.*" The sob in Kurt's voice was unmistakable. He bent forward, covered his face with both hands and cried out, the cry of a broken heart.

Melly rose abruptly from her chair She knelt at his side, cradled his head to her bosom, and wept, Their cries filled the house, and reached into Beate's room in the attic, where Beate, now on her bed, wide-eyed and mute, stared at the ceiling.

CHAPTER TWENTY-NINE

The Aftermath

Melly's routine never changed on Saturday afternoons, not even after *Kristallnacht*, the night of broken glass. Standing before her grand Biedermeier cabinet where, behind its slender lead-glass doors, the family Dresden dinnerware was displayed, Melly's thoughts drifted to earlier times, happier times.

She shifted the contents, making space, cups here, dessert plates there, recalling when the cabinet stood in Dusseldorf, in the home above Goldschmidt's. She smiled to herself as she lingered over memories of family gatherings when any playful excuse resulted in a party. But these days when Melly opened the cabinet to arrange and re-arrange, it was mostly to touch, to visit a time when life was predictable and safe and filled with the warmth of family. Someday, she thought, all these beautiful pieces will belong to Inge. But her memories, what will they be?

Kristallnacht terrified her. If she had any doubts about leaving Germany before that night, those doubts all dissolved in light of what had become became crystal clear the morning after. Jews were in serious danger, conditions were insufferable and worsening. "We must get out and do it soon," she declared to herself. " No matter what anyone says, no matter what Kurt says, or thinks, or wants. We must go!"

Frightened and worried, nevertheless, Melly felt a strong sense of relief and calm since she and Kurt made the decision about Inge. To send a child away was the worst anguish Melly could imagine. And she, who could never even bear to leave the room without Inge's hand in hers, or envision anything or any place as distant as the other side of the sea, felt the heartbreak just at the thought of it. She glanced at Inge sitting contentedly, near the stove, quietly turning pages in a picture book, a gift from Kurt for her sixth birthday. For a single brief moment panic claimed Melly. What if she never saw her little girl again? What if Inge would be lost to her forever? What if all the assurances from the Jewish Agencies against such a possibility proved wrong? No! No! her thoughts screamed. I cannot do this!

Then suddenly, as though a switch had been turned on, rational thinking returned. Keeping Inge at home had already taken its toll on her little girl. And as hard as it would be to let Inge go, Melly comforted herself with the thought that making Inge safe would be the first step for saving her family. Standing before her heirloom cabinet, fragile teacup in her hand, her thoughts flew to Otto Hoffmann and his promise to sponsor their move to America. Maybe if.......

Suddenly the door burst open. Inge's screams, "Mutti, Mutti," the crashing of Melly's cup as it fell from her hands to the floor, as she spun to face two men in the doorway in black SS uniforms. They stormed into the room, waving clubs and shouting, "Where is he, where is your husband?"

Melly felt the room spin. Frenzied impulses to run, scream, strike, all collided in her mind, wiping away any coherent thought. The taller of the two men pushed his face into hers, "Where is he?" he screamed.

"What are you doing here?" she shouted. What do you want?" A hammer pounded inside her skull. A tightening gripped her chest. In the next few seconds of silence the aroma of chicory floated into the room, and the sound of a spoon being stirred inside a cup, clanged like a fire bell, it seemed, announcing Kurt's whereabouts.

"We want your husband," the man screamed again into her terror stricken face, "To take to the police station with all the Jews. Where is he?" He raised his club and moved to smash the Biedermeier!

Melly threw herself in his path, her arms outstretched to shield the glass doors. "No, no!" Panic wiped out her terror. With both hands against his chest, using all her strength, she pushed him away and watched his look of surprise as he stumbled backwards. "Get out, get out," she shrieked Get out!"

Just then, Kurt, a terrified expression on his face, stood in the doorway. In one hand he held a cup, in the other a spoon poised above the cup. He was about to speak when the two SS men rushed and grabbed him. One pushed, the other pulled a stumbling Kurt outside to the street. Melly, frantic, could think only that Kurt needed a coat. She turned to snatch it from a hook in the hallway when she saw Beate, standing at the bottom of her attic stairway. Her hands were covering her mouth. Her eyes were wide with horror.

Terrified, Melly screamed. "When will he be back?. Where are you taking him?" She ran after them, pushing Kurt's coat over his back and shoulders, where it promptly fell into the street, as the two men dragged him into a waiting van. Sobbing, blubbering incoherently, and not knowing where to turn, frantic Melly ran inside to Inge. There she discovered Beate sitting with her Inge, one arm holding her close, in the other, Inge's favorite storybook. Beate stopped reading. She raised her eyes to Melly. "I think you should go to the police station. Find out as much as you can."

Her voice was calm, controlled, business-like. " I will be here with Inge until you are back...whenever....She'll be fine with me. Later we'll have some supper." Then looking into Inge's expressionless face asked, "Would you like that Inge? First a story, then supper, then maybe another story or a game." Inge's response was to drop her eyes down to the book.

Melly stared at her little girl. Except for Kurt, she had never left Inge with anyone, not even her sisters. Even now that same fear of separation surfaced.

But how could she take her along...the way she is? How much more can she tolerate before....

Beate pulled Inge closer and looked into Melly's over-wrought face. "I promise you, Melly, she'll be fine with me. I won't leave her side for a moment." Then, as if she read Melly's mind, "The police station is not a good place for a child."

Melly nodded, kissed the top of Inge's head, then tenderly took Beate's hand in hers, "*Danke...danke schon*," in a trembling voice. Assured that Inge was protected, Melly rushed from the room and into the deserted streets, running the blocks to the police station. Standing outside, other women had gathered in small clusters, pale forms in stoic silence.

Inside the station Melly cried out, "Where is he? Where have you taken him? When is he coming back?"

"Don't worry, lady," a Gestapo agent said. "Don't worry."

Melly sat in the station all night, waiting for news of Kurt. At dawn when no word had come, exhausted, and not knowing what more to do, Melly walked home. For a few moments she watched Inge and Beate as they slept soundly in each other's arms. Then, carefully, she lay down alongside them and surrendered to sleep.

Days passed, then weeks. If asked how long it had been since Kurt was taken, Melly's troubled answer would have been a simple– I don't know. Every morning she walked to the police station, carrying Inge most of the way, hoping for news of her husband. And every afternoon, just as all the preceding afternoons, when still no word came, she returned home to soothe her tired, cranky child.

Several weeks later, on a Monday morning, Inge, hand in hand with Rabbi Wiesengrund, walked out of Melly's life to go to England. With eyes, fixed on their backs, Melly watched them become far away dots until, by turning a corner, they disappeared entirely from her view and from her life. That was the instant when all the hours of careful preparation did nothing to relieve the anguish of the final goodbye; when the last bit of light in her soul went dark, and when, on leaden legs, she stumbled through the rooms to bed.

Briefly, Melly recalled the evening before when Inge asked, "But why *Mutti,* why do I have to go so far away?" She remembered saying, "*Ach* , it's not so very far. It's a vacation. You'll have a good time. And our Rabbi will come for you, and a nice lady from the Jewish Agency will take you........" But now, a sobbing Melly fell into a fetal curl, neither eating nor bathing, for how many days, she did know, or care.

Dimly she heard Beate's voice urging soup, saying over and over "Melly, you must get up. You must eat something." She was aware of Beate dabbing her face with a cool washcloth and brushing her hair and saying words of comfort that did not comfort her. Nothing could reach her until she received word that Inge had arrived safely.

Word first came in a letter from a family in England. It was brought by the Rabbi who translated it to German as he read it to Melly. The family wrote that they had a little girl the same age as Inge, and the girls became instant playmates and walked each day to school together. Inge was learning English so quickly, the wrote; they thought it was remarkable. Letters from England came frequently,, assuring Melly that Inge was well, and adjusting to her new life, and ending with Inge writing her name in giant script, followed by three xxx's and a red heart surrounding the word "mum" at the bottom of all the letters.

One Saturday morning, the following month, Melly and Beate sat over tea. Beate came to Frankfurt from Berlin each weekend to be with Melly. With Kurt and Inge gone, Melly was quite alone. Even her sisters had left Germany and were now settled in New York..

This particular morning Melly watched Beate search in her bag, extract a scrap of paper, then glance at it quickly before tearing it into confetti. "I know where Kurt is."

Carefully Melly placed her cup in its saucer. Her hand flew to her heart. Her eyes riveted on Beate's face. She said nothing, waiting for whatever was to come.

"He is in Buchenwald, a concentration camp near Weimar. He has not been harmed."

"Danken Gott, danken Gott," Melly broke into sobs of relief as she thanked God over and over, until her voice gave out and she could only mouth the words. She dabbed at her face with her napkin. then feeling confused at where to put it, finally sat on it. For the first time in weeks Melly smiled, even if it was just a smile of embarrassment.

Beate, leaning toward Melly across the table, said, "I have more to tell you, but first you must promise that you never speak of it to anyone, never, never. It will go very bad for me, very bad, and bring terrible consequences to my friend if it is discovered that he had a hand in this." Her voice was intense, barely above a whisper. She grasped Melly's hand and squeezed. "Swear Melly. You must swear."

"I do. I swear. I promise you. I swear. Now tell me. Tell me"

Beate withdrew her hand and placed her cup in its saucer.

"I have a friend in a high position in the Nazi Organization. I pleaded with him for Kurt's release. On his own, you understand, he has no authority to do this, but he knows many officials who have this authority, and who owe him favors. Well, at first he refused. He said that it's against policy; that he could fall under suspicion and his loyalty would be questioned. He said it's too risky."

Beate put down her cup and reached for the blackbread and Liederkrantz cheese that Melly held out to her in an automatic gesture.

"I pleaded and pleaded with him. I told him how you are like parents to me. How you took me in, gave me a home even sometimes when I didn't' have the rent because there was no money to pay me. And I told him how you cared for me when I was so sick that time—remember? I said how much I loved you, like a mother and father."

Tears came into her eyes as she continued. "But you see, Melly, he never had parents. He can't understand or feel that kind of love. But then seeing how miserably upset I had become over this, he agreed to see what he could do. He couldn't promise anything, but he said he would try."

Beate stood and pushed her chair back under the table. "Kurt was given a job in the camp's office, taking care of records. They told him that he was given special consideration because he was a war hero. That was a lie, of course, a cover-up, something for the record. But Kurt believed it.

"He will be released, but I don't know when that will be. It's a matter of when his work there is completed and then a question of transportation.

But be assured that he is well, unharmed and eventually he will be released."

Melly dissolved into tears again, tears of relief and gratitude as she embraced Beate whispering words of appreciation over and over. They clung together, one a German woman who embraced Nazism with national pride and a dream of personal betterment. The other, a Jewish woman who experienced Nazism as the worst evil of her existence. Yet, there in Melly's kitchen, neither Jew or German, were just two women, swaying and weeping as one.

"Oh, one last thing." Beate turned and stepped into the hallway on the way upstairs to her room. Her voice trembled." I am so sorry, Melly, but I can't come here anymore. My superiors have warned me that my trips here to Frankfurt are too many. They said that I should use my spare time to better advantage by staying in Berlin, where there are many new programs and not enough hands to work them.

Melly lowered herself into her chair. *"Ach, nein."* she pleaded, you can't mean never....."

"I don't know anything more, Melly,....I will miss you more than I can say. And I will miss my room with its comforts that you so kindly furnished. But I will always keep in touch, no matter where I go."

Melly locked eyes with Beate's. "I will miss you also, very much. But my heart tells me that it won't be forever....so...... *Auf Wiedersehen*....for now."

As she climbed the stairs to her attic room Beate called, " I need to pack my bag. I'll be leaving for the station later today."

Melly cleared the table, rinsed the cups and plates, a small grin on her face. Beate's words, that Kurt "Will be released" played in her mind like the chanting of a lighthearted child. She was unaware of her tapping toe, caught up in the rhythm, or of the slight swaying of her hips, keeping time, as she shifted from leg to leg.

Pausing in her silent celebrations to dry her hands, her thoughts moved from Kurt in Buchenwald, to Inge in England, then to Beate, whose life was mostly a mystery to her. But she marveled, all the same, that she was blessed with two daughters: one from Kurt. The other, surely, from God.

She moved into the next room, a spring in her steps, to the top drawer in Kurt's bureau, where he kept pen and paper. Then seated at the kitchen table, not conscious of the grin still on her face, or that she was gently humming the melody to *"Du, du,"* she began her letter, the first of many, to Otto Hoffmann, in New York, America.

CHAPTER THIRTY

Nowhere is Safe

On the morning of November 10, 1938, Frau Miller raced home, never having reached the market place, her customary Friday practice. Between screams, sobs and fitful trembles she described to her family the destruction of synagogues and Jewish owned shops on the streets of Berlin, the aftermath of *Kristallnacht,* the night of broken glass.

Many months had passed since either Ursula or her parents ventured outside the house. "There is no reason to leave," they said. Ilse had no committee or board meetings. Simon had no work. Ursula had no school. "One could not even enjoy a walk in the fresh air,"without encountering anti-Semitic signs and slogans posted along the way." Inside the house was best," they agreed. Dependable, capable Frau Miller took care of everything.

And, indeed, Frau Miller, as always efficient and uncomplaining tended to the house and household. Even though visits to the market, once an enjoyable and looked-forward-to excursion, became a dreaded chore as she wrestled with food shortages, long lines and cranky merchants. But with never a grumble, meals were on the table, served on time and elegantly so, no matter how sparse the menu or how scarce the funds, since the Wallerstein-Steinhardt fortunes were no longer secure. The Nazis froze their assets, seized their property, and made it impossible for them to earn a living. To buy food, they resorted to selling their personal possessions: Ilse her gowns, Simon his books. Frau Miller, with nothing to sell, accepted charity from her Church

The house itself, being old, needed constant repair. Military conscription created a shortage of workmen, and Frau Miller, frequently challenged with leaking pipes, intruding mice and blocked drains, found solutions with pails, rags, and wires. She saw no reason to trouble the family with the difficulties of everyday life.

But the havoc, the wreckage, she had encountered that *Kristallnacht* morning, was beyond anything her stoic nature could endure. Horror had reached into her soul, a permanent lodger. In the many months that followed, regardless of how she seemed to rally, regardless of how composed she appeared, Frau Miller was a different woman from the one that left the house that morning. For the first time in her life, her spirit collapsed. For the first time in her life, she took to her bed in the middle of the day. For the first time in her life, she questioned God.

Kristallnacht brought despair to the family. All those many months waiting for clearance to leave brought no results. Later that same day, huddled in the sitting room they spoke in hushed tones of their many late night talks and optimistic plans for the future in a new land, future plans now crushed, beyond hope. Their utterances were now expressions of disappointment, and the painful realizations that their connections to high level officials, who had given their assurances, and upon whom they had depended to expedite their emigration, had been of no value. The process had been started too late. They would never get out. They sat stonily, frightened and confused, passing a single handkerchief one to the other, clinging to their resolve that inside the house was safe. Their home, their fortress inviolate, would keep all harm away.

Ursula, seeking comfort in her room, settled herself into her favorite window seat, a copy of Thomas Mann's "Magic Mountain," in her lap. Once immersed in her book and carried into another realm, she knew that all her inner trembling would be calmed.

Suddenly, the downstairs front door crashed in. Male voices, unfamiliar voices shouted and screamed for the "Jewman." Breaking glass, Frau Miller's terrified shrieks again and again, all reached into Ursula in her room.

She scrambled to her feet. The book dropped to the floor. Frozen in mounting fear she heard the sounds of boots thumping up the staircase, and then the ultimate act of terror played out before her eyes: two SS men broke into her room swinging clubs, smashing photographs, their crystal frames reduced to splinters flying about the room. They screamed again and again for the "Jewman! Where is the Jewman?" Their eyes swept the room, passed over Ursula, and came to rest on the dollhouse. Before her horrfied eyes the two SS men exchanged glances. Then with their clubs they smashed the dollhouse into a pile of debris. "We want the Jewman!"

A fury rose from her throat like the roar of a crazed animal. Every injustice, every disappointment, every ounce of misery heaped upon her culminated in a ferocious rage. With one swift, herculean movement she lifted and hurled her drawing table across the room and knocked one SS invader to the floor. She pummeled the chest of the other with eyes shut tight and screamed for her mother until the SS man on the floor, got up and pulled her off then flung her across the room.

Even with Ilse's protective arms around her, Ursula's screams continued. Even as she saw Simon race into the room, wild eyed, arms outstretched towards her, Ursula's screaming continued to fill every corner of the house.

Only when the SS men grabbed her father amid his out-cries "What do you want? What......," and pulled him from the room, and when his screams rose above hers as he tumbled down the stairs, and her knowing that he had been pushed, only then did she become mute. Her shaking legs gave way and she dropped like a marionette cut loose from its strings

She had no idea how long she, her mother, and Frau Miller were together on the floor. Ursula glanced about the room, at the broken drawing table, at the dollhouse in shambles ten feet from where she sat. Filled with such profound sorrow she pointed to the ruins, to the violent death of her dream and wailed a plaintive, " Why, why, *mutti,* why....?"

That night, three figures huddled around the fireplace in Simon's study, their ears trained to the radio, desperate, but unable to clearly hear the broadcaster through the cracking and static coming over the airwaves.

"Ach, du lieber Gott!," for God's sake, Frau Miller's voice shook with exasperation as she reached over and snapped off the radio. She folded her arms across her chest then stared into the cup of tea perched on her lap.

Ilse, never before needing to cultivate skills for surviving, who all her life unabashedly relied upon financial bullying to rule her domain, now stared at the troubled Frau Miler. " Where can we go? What do we do now?" Like an impatient child waiting for answers, she leaned back and drummed on the arms of her chair. She glanced at Ursula sitting beside her, a wounded, limp, shell who met her eyes, then looked away. "Uli....Uli...look at me, please....Uli."

But Ursula barely heard her mother's voice. She stoked the fire, unable to hold onto a thought for more than a few seconds. The events of the day flitted in and out of Ursula's mind like glimpses of schooldays' cue cards asking questions. Only now there were no answers. Every few moments she cried softly, hugged her knees and rocked back and forth. Every few moments she paused in her attentions to the fireplace and thought about being only eighteen, hardly past childhood, and surrounded by the wretched conditions that had overtaken her life. Every few moments she drifted back to school, when she won medals and glowing reports, when she was chosen to read her poetry to the entire school assembly, when she and Peter designed and constructed the dollhouse.... the dollhouse......Her stomach tightened. A soft moan escaped her lips and brought her back to the present. She resumed her self-imposed task of tending to the embers, fast becoming ash, stoking until the last bit of glow died. Placing the fire iron against the wall nearby, and with her hands pressed between her knees, Ursula leaned against her mother, feeling her warmth yet missing Ilse's once comforting plump softness. Then, as though following a scene in a play, she watched Frau Miller draw her shawl closer around her shoulders and heard her words. "There is something I must say to you both."

Ilse shifted in her seat. Her voice was hoarse, hardly above a whisper.

"So, say it."

"Before I called you Madame, I called you Ilse. I brought you up from a baby. You are as much my child as Ursula. So now I will tell you what you must do."

"What is it you think I should do? What is there to do?" In shrill tones Ilse cried out, "I can't solve this...I have nothing....nothing...."

"Ilse, tomorrow morning, first thing, you must go out. You must find out where your husband is and what you need to do to bring him home."

'Go out!" Ilse shouted. She jumped to her feet. "Go out into the streets? Never! How can you even suggest such a thing...to put me in such danger."

A stern Frau Miller rose and confronted Ilse, now red faced and shaking. "If we learned nothing else from today, Ilse, we learned that nowhere is safe" She paused to place her cup and saucer on the mantle, then covered Ilse's hands with hers. "Now listen to me," she continued. I know you are frightened but you must trust me. They took only your man. Why not you? Why not both of you?"

"Well, I don't know...."

"Think about it, Ilse... It's because they want money. They need you to bring money to get him out."

"But I have no money....nothing..."

"Tomorrow, early, go to the Gestapo. Find out how much. I have some money saved." She reclaimed her cup from the mantle, grumbled that her tea "cot cold," and ordered, "Ilse, you must do this. Do not rest until he is finally home".

For several intense seconds, Ilse stared into Frau Miller's set face, then without looking away she hunched over, brought Ursula to her feet, but gently seated her back down, unable to keep Ursula steady on her legs. "But what about my Uli. Before anything or anyone we must find a way to make her safe....First Uli...."

"*Nein, nein!* Ursula is not in danger right now. But your poor husband...." Frau Miller shuddered, wrapped a second shawl around her legs, and dropped into her seat. "I have an idea about Ursula, but first you must promise that you will go to free your husband."

"But...."

"Promise me!"

"*Ja,*" Ilse replied in a low voice. " *Ja,* I make you a promise. Yet in a smaller voice asked, "and Uli....?"

Ursula looked up from toying with a button on her dress, her heart racing, her head throbbing, a baffled expression on her face. If only my heart didn't pound so. she thought. If only....She looked from her mother to Frau Miller. "I feel so sick," she said aloud, not knowing or even caring if she had been heard.

"You are going to be all right, Ursula," Frau Miller promised. She cradled Ursula's face between her hands. "But you will have to leave here, leave Berlin. Don't shake your head. No, don't pull away. Listen to me. Listen! The church has ways....I can arrange through the Church for new identification papers for you. When the time comes and you leave Berlin, you will live in the countryside with clergy. When that will be or where, I don't exactly know yet. But wherever, you will be protected, not all the time living in fear."

Ursula remained silent. One consideration after another crossed her mind. Leaving parents...for how long... and her home she so dearly loved, and her city....She had never been away from Berlin except for short trips to the lake... and Peter, how will he ever find her when he returns. She turned to her mother.

Ilse embraced her daughter. In a trembling voice she urged, "Go, go, Uli. You must go, leave here. Frau Miller believes it is he best thing, and so do I. I hoped it would be to Holland with Peter, but.... And don't look so worried. Families find each other all the time. It's a strange fact of life, but it seems to be true."

At the end of a long sigh, Ilse turned to her housekeeper. With tears and a shaking voice Ilse offered to repay her devoted Frau Miller in the only way she could.

"There are no words to thank you enough for all you have done for this family. I have nothing to give you. I have only my blessing to give you if you choose to leave us, to relieve yourself of the burdens put upon you because of all that is happening to us. You could be spared all this....live with your sister's family...have some peace, a normal life."

A slow smile lingered on Frau Miller's face. With shoulders raised, palms out, and nodding her head *"nein,"*, she replied softly, "You, the Steinhardts, your parents, your husband, Ursula, you are my family. This is my home where I have lived most of my life, and this is where I will stay, whatever happens." She reached out and clasped Ursula's wrists. Looking straight into Ursula's eyes she said, "And you will always know where I will be, where you can always find me, right here like always. waiting for my family to come home."

Ursula did not know the exact moment when her sick, troubled soul calmed, when a sense of peace opened her spirit , when soft and deliberate, the words of Jeremiah given her at confirmation spoke to her:

> *Say not I am a child for thou shall go to all*
> *that I send thee, and whatsoever I command*
> *thee thou shall speak. Be not afraid of their faces:*
> *for I am with thee to deliver thee....*

Looking into Frau Miller's eyes, it seemed to Ursula that those words were shared between them. "Well," said Ursula with gentle wonder, "God knows where to send me after all. And it's not Holland, or England..it's to live in the countryside....imagine...."

At bedtime, unable to bear the sight of her dollhouse in ruins, Ursula slept that night beside her mother. She breathed deeply in the dark, quiet room finding comfort in the rose-scented fragrance rising from the bedcovers. The pillow beneath her held the faint smell of cigar and brought soft, tender thoughts of Simon; the way he called her *Liebling* as if it were her name; his gleeful chuckles when she stood awestruck at the exhibition of Queen Victoria's doll house on loan to the museum in Berlin; and Peter, he brought Peter into her life.... Sweet, endearing memories which were suddenly stolen by the horrors of the day. Each time they arose, she pushed them away, but it was never far enough from the brutality of Kristallnacht, from her father's screams, from the destruction of her proudest achievement: the dollhouse.

The thought of leaving her home frightened her. But even more frightening was the idea of living with strangers. She wondered about that family. They would be Church people and that relieved some of her anxiety. She imagined her life in the countryside. Would she be growing food in a garden, she wondered, or collecting eggs from a hen house rather than going to a market place like Frau Miller? Or instead of streets she might have to walk through fields from place to place. Then she wondered about what those places might be. At that point her imaginings ceased. I just have no idea...no idea at all.

Just thinking about it made her feel homesick.. And she would always miss *Mutti* and *Vati* terribly, that would be the hardest part.

She inched further into the eiderdown, moved closer to her mother, and to the comfort of Ilse's snoring. How mortified her mother would be to learn that she snored. Even a well-bred, genteel snore: Unthinkable!

CHAPTER THIRTY-ONE

The Need For Home

After helping with the childrens' breakfasts and tidying the rooms, Ursula informed Pastor Wagener and his wife that she would be away for several days–to Berlin.

It was her 20th birthday that day, but she had also acquired a second birthday when she became Helga Calmann from Hamburg. Ursula remembered the events of two years ago, as if it were yesterday.

"She is my niece, my oldest sister's child," Frau Miler had explained as she handed Helga's identification papers to Ursula. "Helga was sent to America, to live in New York. You are both about the same age."

To Ursula's questioning gaze Frau Miller said, "Ask me nothing. This is all you need to know. If you are questioned, make up a good story because it doesn't matter what you tell them. Just always be consistent. So, now, pack your bags. Tomorrow morning, first thing you will go to the countryside outside Elmshorn, in the North country. All the arrangements are made."

Suddenly faced with the reality of leaving home, Ursula blanched and slumped into a nearby chair. Her heart began racing. Dear Lord," she whispered, "please don't let me collapse."

"I promise you," assured Frau Miller gently, "you will be in good hands. "They are good people and they look forward to your coming." She paused for several seconds, drew Ursula close and lovingly stroked her hair and face. "And I'll be coming with you tomorrow to help you settle in. But then I must return to be with your mother. You understand that your mother needs me, *ja,?*"

"*Ja,* I do," said Ursula with a weak smile.

But now this morning, the morning of her 20th birthday, it was almost two years since she last saw her parents. While her life in Elmshorn with the Pastor's family remained safe and constant, the world beyond had been thrown into chaos. Germany went to war. Bombs dropped on Berlin. The worry for her parents was constant. And she feared for Peter. His messages suddenly ceased after Hitler invaded Holland.

When she had first arrived in the Pastor's home, Ursula, in guarded language sent word to Peter. With a troubled conscience she broke her promise to marry saying that because of life's circumstances, she did not believe their marriage would ever take place. She wrote that she would always love him, her mentor and best friend, but life was uncertain and planning a future, futile.

Further, she wrote, that before leaving Berlin she removed his ring and gave it to Frau Miller to keep safe for him. She wished for him the best and would always keep him in her prayers.

Promptly responding, Peter said that he would always love her and promised faithfully that some day, some way he would find her and they would be together. Then to her surprise he relinquished the ring, saying that it really belonged to Ursula's mother. She gave it to him to present to Ursula when he proposed, since he had no funds to buy a ring and Ilse wanted her daughter to be properly engaged.

Ursula smiled when he ended the letter by saying that she was never supposed to know the truth about the ring and that...well, there goes another future plan.

Living in the Pastor's home with his family, Ursula's shattered nerves healed. She learned that caring for children, and there were six of them, was not beyond her capabilities. There was work and there was worship and then there was laughter as she, not very far from her own childhood, romped and roughhoused with her charges.

If Ursula could have chosen a new life for herself it would not have been this one. The house, a ramshackle, rambling clapboard cottage ,showed traces of having once been whitewashed. But mostly it showed a weakened structure with feeble attempts, here and there, to rescue its decline.

Inside, surrounding the kitchen, the largest room, where the family congregated for meals and prayer, were several alcoves for beds and belongings. Sharing a bed with the two youngest girls at first seemed intolerable to Ursula. But she was mindful that her presence in their already space-starved home, likewise caused them inconvenience, even though they had never voiced it..

Settling into her new life, Ursula embraced all manner of rural life, except for the outhouse; especially the outhouse in winter, which she privately condemned as barbaric.

The two suitcases she brought with her contained some clothing and shoes, but mostly books and writing paper. Neighboring families observed that Helga, the nanny, the Pastor's new *Kindermadchen,* was not adequately prepared with outerwear for their severe winters and sent over sweaters and coats and heavy woolen socks for inside her boots.

Promising her mother, through tearful goodbyes, that she would write often, Ursula kept that promise as faithfully as keeping a journal. Her letters, relayed through the Church, were noncommittal, filled with chatter of everyday trivia. But matters of importance were relayed, back and forth, by word of mouth messages through Church channels. In this way she learned that her mother had joined with Gentile women to protest the confinement of their Jewish husbands and to demand their release. Sometime later she was relieved to learn that her father had been released for a sum of money; Frau Miler provided the funds.

Daily life with the Pastor's family was structured and orderly. Each knew his or her place, each knew and attended to certain chores, and each knew that their presence at every meal was a strict requirement.

On weekdays, meals were simple, but aways sufficient in spite of food shortages throughout the land. Usually there was soup, frequently some cheese, but always bread baked by the Pastor's wife, who baked extra to barter for asparagus, onion, flour and, when available, a bit of chicory for the Pastor's breakfast.

Saturday, the family prepared for Sunday. The cottage was scrubbed and polished. Produce was gathered from the garden and made ready for the next day's meal, which usually included a chicken from the hen house and always a sweet pastry. Occasionally a fresh fruit in season ended the meal.

But Sunday, the Lord's day, was special. All nine, in their Sunday best walked two miles to Church and settled into a single front pew, except for Pastor Wagener who took his place behind the podium. Under his watchful eye the children dared not doze or fidget or neglect to participate fully in the service. And it was Ursula's job "To see to it," ordered the Pastor, and then to remain with them afterwards for their Sunday School lessons.

Afterwards, with high spirited banter and boisterous play, they tramped through fields of tall grasses, disappearing suddenly, popping up unexpectedly, yodeling and mooing into each other's faces, until the house came into view. Then abruptly they assumed serious, dignified Sunday manners. In size order they walked single file into the house to their places at the table, and took turns saying grace from behind their most theatrical, angelic, and holiest Sunday manners.

For Ursula, Sundays were always the most beautiful day of the week, the same as in Berlin. Except, except, of course, for Saturday and the Saturday walks with her mother. When she had pangs of homesickness, they were quickly dispelled by the comfort of her Church and the church people around her. This is who I am, she told herself. This is my place now. My home in Berlin, my parents, my studies, all of these have been stolen. But not my faith, Never my faith. Never!

Yet on this day, the day of her 20th birthday, Ursula, longing to be in the house she so loved in Berlin, to be with her parents, to sleep once again in her room, put aside her worry about traveling with Helga Calmann's papers and prayed for an easy journey. For while on the outside Helga was a courageous woman, a timid, vulnerable child quaked inside Ursula.

" Helga is who I am," she scolded her image in the mirror. "And today brave, bold Helga is going to Berlin."

CHAPTER THIRTY-TWO

The Visit

Ursula walked with rapid strides, her shoes making clackety sounds on the cobblestones. She congratulated herself on her good sense to travel light with only an overnight bag, less to pack and carry. But, more importantly, it was to avoid calling attention to herself. Uppermost in her mind was Frau Miler's instructions to have a good, consistent story ready, in the event she was ever stopped.

Moments before when she disembarked at the Berlin Station, she avoided the crowded terminal by taking a short cut and exiting a side door directly to the street. Luckily her trip ended without incident,. At least not yet, she thought, as she hurried toward her destination several blocks away, a surprise visit home.

But her progress slowed as she approached roadways and walkways obstructed by piles of rubble, the aftermath of recent bombings. Poking her way over and around obstacles in the streets, she was thankful for the daylight. For these same streets that once carried the promise of home and all good things, now were less familiar, less promising.

In one dreadful moment, she wondered if her home was still standing. Turning the corner at Steinstrasse she stopped and peered into the road. With a deep sigh of relief and a quick "Thank you Lord," she saw that her home, the entire neighborhood of homes for that matter, had survived. Except when she looked closer she saw that not all the homes escaped damage. The bombings had caused some destruction, after all. In home after home, alabaster statuaries, marble fountains and majolica bird-basins were toppled and lay like rigid corpses.

Standing midway between the ruins of a fallen street lamp and the entrance to her home, she noticed the brass plate, etched with the house number "6," had fallen from its place over the front door, and was now face down in a withered iris bed. And the moon-globe that once lighted the walkway and welcomed all who approached with its soft glow, lay in shattered ruins, a jumble of glass, wire and scraps of ornamentation.

Shocked at the sight before her, at the shabby neglect, at the accumulated litter, Ursula's heart sank. From somewhere the stink of fecal waste sickened her and she raised her scarf to cover her nose. But most abominable, most unbearable was the realization that the wrought iron surround, those magnificent gates and railings that had dignified and set this beloved home apart for decades, had been removed. Months back she had heard that the Nazis were confiscating iron throughout the country to melt into armaments. She supposed that was the fate of the Steinhardt iron as well.

For a brief moment she wondered about her decision to make this visit. Maybe it's a bad idea, she thought. Maybe I should have stayed in Elmshorn, with the Pastor's family. This is too hard....too hard.

But standing amid this chaos and having come this far, she told herself, almost like a wish, that once inside all would be different. Inside was family. Inside was home. She reached down and reclaimed the brass address plate. Hugging it to her chest as one would a precious gem, she turned the doorknob and stepped over the threshold into the center hallway where she was met, not with the serenity and comfort of home, but instead with more calamity. Bedlam beyond anything she could have imagined had claimed the house.

Shrieking children encircled her in a game of tag, running around and around, holding her stupefied and frozen in her place. Voices from the kitchen, new, strange sounding voices cried out and argued over tasks and space. Pots clanged. Plates clattered. Babies wailed. Doors slammed. The toilet flushed again and again....

She stood transfixed, watching a short, plump man trotting behind a shorter, plumper woman, his fist raised and shaking while shouting into her fleeing back to wait, to stop running away. While she, over her shoulder, screamed back "Nyet Nyet!" over and over, as if there were not enough "nos" in the Russian language to hurl at him. Then suddenly the woman halted, whirled, spit and marched away. He stopped short, turned and stomped in the opposite direction, continuing his tirade to no one in particular.

In that instant, every hope that Ursula held for a bit of the old life, even for just one day, just one hour, evaporated. A slovenly rabble from only God knows where had invaded her home and turned it into a madhouse.

Heartsick and needing her parents more than ever, Ursula placed her travel bag in a corner near the stairway and dropped her coat over the banister. Noticing a crack of light from under the closed sitting room door, she headed for its promise of escape from the surrounding chaos. Putting her ear against the door she hoped to hear her mother's voice from behind it. But hearing no sounds at all, Ursula opened it just a crack and peeked inside.

There across the room before a fireless fireplace, sat Ilse, Simon, and surprisingly, Melly. All three were conversing in hushed tones over tea.

"Mutti!" screamed Ursula, as she ran to her mother.

"Ursula? Uli!" shouted Ilse, scrambling to her feet and rushing to her daughter. *"Ach du lieber, Gott,* why are you.... why have you come....are you sick, is something wrong?" She locked her trembling child in her arms. "Oh my darling Uli," Ilse crooned, "my Uli," while Ursula, safe in her mother's arms, poured out her anguish over the havoc inside the house.

"Who are they?" she shouted. "Why are they here? Throw them out, out! Throw them out!" Exhausted, she dropped into the sofa, into her father's embrace, hearing her father's voice shushing, and cooing and assuring that "Everything will be just fine, *Liebling,* just fine...you'll see...." And for that moment Ursula once again became her father's little girl, protected, comforted and feeling, for the first time that day, hungry. She helped herself to ginger cookies and tea, settled back into the sofa, and studied the faces of her parents. They have aged so much, she thought, since I last saw them. So old.....

Ilse, had become thin and pale. Dark shadows under her hollow eyes showed the strain of unrelieved misery and of nights with little or no sleep. Her hair, now grey, worn pulled back in a single braid, swayed like a pendulum when she moved. She became round shouldered and, Ursula noticed upon first entering the room, severely stooped and noticeably shorter. So much so that her skirt, now too long, puddled around her feet and onto the floor where sat.

But more than the change in her mother, was that of her father. Simon, frail and unkempt wore a woolen moth-eaten Dutch cap. "I need it to keep my head warm...with no hair...."

he explained to Ursula with a smile. His monocle, once the family joke, dangled from his neck on a string and rested on scraggly white whiskers,. She was about to remark that he reminded her of pictures she once saw of Leo Tolstoy, the Russian novelist, but then thought better of it. Suddenly, Simon pointed to his monocle, "The Nazis took my glasses, *Liebling,*" he said gently. "This helps me read."

Ursula reached for his hand and covered it with her own. "*Ja, Vati,* it's a good thing you kept it." She tried to keep her voice light in spite of her sadness. She wondered if she succeeded.

She brushed the last of the cookie crumbs from her lap, placed the teacup onto the serving tray. And looked across at her mother, sitting with folded hands as though she was waiting for a signal to begin talking. Then catching Ursula's eyes, Ilse began.

"Uli," what I am about to tell you is disturbing news. But you must stay calm. Promise me that you will be strong because there is nothing we can do to change it, or fix it, or make it right. Promise?"

"*Ja.*" Ursula replied softly, "*Ja,* I promise."

"Uli, the Nazis have taken the house. They have turned it into a Jew House, or what they call *Judenhaus.* Jews from all over the city, maybe even from outside the city were expelled from where they lived and forced to come here, to this house."

"But why? For what reason?"

"I'm really not certain, Uli. I have heard that it has something to do with relocating the Jews. It's all rumors, of course. No one really knows for certain what the Nazi are doing. Just one day the government came here and told us that our home was selected as a central distribution place. They said it was a honor to be chosen. Can you imagine....?"

"But how long do you think....?"

"I don't know, Uli. All this started several days ago. Every day more and more people come here. It gets worse each day. And the Nazis, you know, don't tell the truth anyway, so there's no use asking anything. So, all we could do was to take over this room for ourselves and wait it out. We eat and sleep in this room and pray that the plumbing doesn't break down from over-use. Why, we can't even put up Melly for the night before her train leaves in the morning. And it's especially troubling because....."

As if by signal, all eyes turned to Melly, whose quiet presence, until then, had been overlooked by Ursula. Sitting silently, hands in lap, Melly's head was tilted to one side as if to turn the good hearing ear towards the conversation.

" *Ach, ja,* well, I don't want to talk about this morning anymore," said Melly. "But, Ursula, it is so good to see you again. The last time I saw you, a long time ago, in this house, you were still a child, a very delightful child."

"Oh, Melly, I'm so very sorry. I was so upset when I came in I forgot my manners to say hello. Please, please forgive me." Ursula rushed to Melly and took her hand. I'm truly, truly sorry. And I am so glad to see you again. And *Ja,* I remember when you visited.. You came with your baby. But why are here? What is .....?"

"I'll tell you why," interrupted Melly. I came here to say goodbye because I'm taking the train tomorrow morning to the boat that goes to America. *Ja,* America. I thought I might stay the night, but I see there is no place. So, I'll stay in the station until my train comes. I'll be fine there."

All at once Ursula remembered the photograph of Melly's family in the office of Beate Zinmann at the Women's Service Agency. "I know your good friend Beate," Ursula blurted out with exuberance, and excitedly continued to explain in detail their meeting that day, and the photograph of the Wallerstein family.... and then stopped to catch her breath as her eyes spanned the room.

"But where is Inge, your little girl. Is she not with you?"

"Inge is now in England." Without going into detail Melly explained the circumstances that compelled the decision to send her to England, "Where she is safe, and according to all her letters, happy. But, oh, I miss my little one so much." Melly's voice cracked and tears welled up. "But we always do the best we can."

"And Kurt?" asked Ilse gently. "Where is....?"

"Kurt is in Frankfurt. He does not wish to leave Germany." Her voice was strained, grainy. Melly reached for a napkin on which she placed several sections of dried fruit. She dropped her eyes, began eating, and clearly indicated by her manner that the subject was closed.

The awkward silence that followed was broken when Ursula jumped to her feet and exclaimed, "But where is Frau Miller? Is she gone? Did she leave?" Where is she? You must tell me. I have to see her." Blood rushed to her head. Her face felt hot. "Where is she?"

"She's here, Ursula, here with us. Don't upset yourself," as Ilse gently lowered her daughter into a chair. " But she has not been well lately. She stays in her room behind the kitchen almost all the time. And now with all these people in the house and all this commotion going on....well...she's just not herself. We look in, make sure she is eating and getting what she needs, but she stays in bed all day. She probably doesn't even know that you're here."

Ursula studied her mother, now sitting with her chin in her hands, a worried frown between her brows. "But will she be all right? I mean, what does the doctor say?"

"There is no doctor, Uli. She refuses to see one.. She won't leave her room. I don't know what to do."…. She drew a deep sigh and locked eyes with Simon, as if asking for help.

"*Ach, Liebling,*" shouted Simon as if rudely awakened from a nap. Then with softened voice continued, "Of course, of course, we will take good care of her. She just needs time to adjust….all these changes…coming so fast…. She'll be just fine…." He jumped to his feet, snatched a cookie from the tea table and hastily tucked in his shirt, as if he were intending to leave the room. "But what about you? Why have you come…….the reason for the visit? Are you having some trouble?"

"Oh, no," assured Ursula. "No trouble. But I was worried about the bombings the last several weeks. I became frantic. I had to see for myself…." She paused briefly to quiet her quivering, voice."And I thought that maybe I would stay for a day, but I see that's not possible."

With those words the front door banged open. Stamping feet and excited voices announced the arrival of more displaced intruders.

"When, when will it end?," cried Ilse."When?" she buried her face in her lap and looked up imploringly at Simon, who shrugged, then seated himself at the far end of the room. With the"The Biography of Friedrich Nietzsche" in his hand and with the back of his chair facing his family, Simon, in his way, said a goodnight to Ilse and a goodbye to his daughter and Melly.

I need to leave here, thought Ursula. All this is too awful, too hard. I wish I could take my family with me. If only… She rose from her seat and looked into Ilse's stricken face. "*Mutti,* forgive me. I'm leaving now. I'll go along with Melly and stay the night in the station. In the morning I'll leave for Elmshorn."

She lingered, wondering how long it would be until she saw her mother again, her beloved *Mutti*, and her *Vati*, who, she so adored...to hear his gentle voice calling her *Liebling*. She pushed her thoughts aside and turned to Melly. "Whenever you're ready to leave you can find me with Frau Miller." For a few seconds she rested her hand on Ilse's shoulder, then kissed her cheek. "*Auf Wiedersehen*," she said in a low voice.

"*Ja, auf Wiedersehen,* Uli, ...my Uli...." Ilse did not look up.

Ursula stepped into the hallway and closed the sitting room door, leaving the old life she could not resurrect, the heartbreak of her parents she could not heal, and the despair of Frau Miller, yet to visit, for whom Ursula had no hope to give.

Suddenly, impulsively, in one last act before leaving, Ursula bounded upstairs to her to her room, ignoring the strange inhabitants who had taken it over. She crammed as many of her charts and drawings that could fit into an enormous, blue canvas bag, once belonging to Peter.

Later, on the way to the Berlin Train Station, Melly said, "I have a really big surprise to tell you, Ursula. A big surprise is waiting at the train station." Into Ursula's questioning expression, she continued, "And if you stop for a minute, I'll tell you."

Leaning into Ursula's ear Melly whispered her news. And for the only time since coming to Berlin that day, Ursula smiled. At first, just a small smile. Then gradually as the news unfolded a big broad smile washed over Ursula's face, and her eyes shone with excitement.

"Really, Melly, really?"

'Oh *Ja,*" laughed Melly, "come, *schnell,* let's hurry while there's still some daylight." They tried linking arms, but they had too much baggage and they tripped over their bundles and their own feet. Still they arrived at their destination before dark.

But once inside the Railroad Terminal, their steps slowed, then halted, as they gazed in horror at the sight confronting them.

CHAPTER THIRTY-THREE

The Blind Man Hears

First it was the glass roof. Gone. Blasted out, Melly supposed, by the shock of the bombings. Only jagged shards, like shark's teeth, remained along the iron grids overhead. Then it was the stench of urine rising from giant stains, a myriad of map-like configurations covering the stone floor beneath her feet. Then it was the silence.

It was a very different station from the one in which Melly had arrived this morning. Then it teemed with travelers, a place alive and swarming with bristling, nervous busyness; people hurriedly bumping across the vast expanse of the terminal burdened with bags and boxes; others shouting excited commands over their shoulders to hurry, *schnell, schnell*," in high pitched voices, passing family clusters lumpily sitting in pew-like rows, thermos bottles and bags wedged between them, relieving their boredom with sausage and handfuls of dried fruit. Perched on suitcases, the impatient, oblivious to the commotion around them, sat with eyes riveted to timetables; others stood in the depot's center, their faces skyward, their attention fixed to resounding, garbled announcements sailing from overhead loudspeakers, listening for the one call that would prompt them from their places to their seats on the train.

She recalled that she stood this morning in the midst of the commotion, her bags on the floor near her feet, wondering how to manage her way through the chaos. When suddenly from nowhere a tall, lanky man, wearing a grey knitted hat pulled down over his ears, grabbed her bags and began pushing through the crowded station.

"Stop! Stop!" Melly screamed. "What are you doing? *Gott in Himmel,* he's stealing my bags! Stop!" rushing after him, lumbering on short legs and swollen ankles, pushing people aside with her elbows, catching glimpses of his grey knitted hat as he dodged about the terminal and exited to the street. Melly, in close pursuit, screamed "Stop.!" Then with all her might, and the flat of her hands she slammed into him from behind. He stumbled forward and fell face down on the pavement, surrounded by Melly's bags. He seemed to be unconscious. Melly waited to catch her breath. A crowd began to gather mumbling about "thieves... everywhere you go these days...." As he began to stir, Melly quickly gathered her bags. Someone from the crowd placed her bags, then helped her, into a cab. Before she could ask his name and thank him properly, the cab took off. From the back window she saw the police helping the thief from the sidewalk; his chin was scraped raw and blood ran from his nose and mouth.

Now, although she was still feeling some distress over the events of this morning, she was able to brush those thoughts aside, feeling safe now that she was not traveling alone. Yet, she wondered about the quiet, compared to the din of voices when she first arrived earlier; then a continuous, swollen, earsplitting roar of human sound, was now, gone. Only the sporadic cough of a blind man as he crossed Melly's and Ursula's path, hitting his cane along the stone floor, and the clump of their shoes echoing through that mausoleum-like terminal were all the sounds they heard that evening.

Melly put her bags down and took in the strangeness of the place. It seemed incredible that it was so silent, so deserted. "What happened, Ursula, that it is so empty? No trains tonight?" .

It seemed as though Ursula did not hear. Rather, she appeared to be fixed on the destruction overhead. She turned to Melly, her face was pale and strained. Her voice was filled with awe. "I never saw this, Melly. When my train came in I left by one of the side doors. I didn't come through the terminal. Did you see this, Melly when you came?"

"*Nein,* I was chasing a thief running away with my bags.... But I see now this damage. *Ach ja, it's* terrible."

"Oh, such a pity......a shame....." Once again Ursula scanned the wreckage peering from one overhead corner to the other. "I remember seeing the original plans." She pointed to the blue canvas bag. "They might even be here in this collection of charts and papers I brought with me." Once again they walked side by side.

"*Ja,*" agreed Melly, half listening, less concerned with Ursula's interest in her charts and plans and more with her own feelings of uneasiness.. So it's quiet, she thought. Quiet doesn't have to mean trouble. Quiet is quiet, nothing more..

Suddenly Ursula's voice broke into her thoughts. Her gloom apparently cast off, she called out, "There she is Melly," and pointed diagonally across the floor toward the back, near the tracks. "She's over there." Ursula gripped the rope around her oversized, bulging, blue canvas bag. Outwardly energized by her excitement at seeing Beate, she dragged and bumped the bag sideways along the station floor and called over her shoulder, "This way Melly, come, I'll show you."

Melly hoisted her huge valises, feeling the pull in her shoulders and arms and the familiar ache in her knees. She thought how comical she must look, elbows out, hat askew, her home-made black felt-like coat, sewn from the only fabric available and jokingly called "Hitler Cloth," by everyone, hiked above the hemline of her dress. She lumbered on short, thick legs, bowed from the thrust of run down heels. Her eyes were fixed on the back of Ursula's tan Chesterfield coat. *"Ach du lieber, Gott,"* she called, Don't go so fast....I can't keep up...."

Melly stopped and put down her bags. Her heart was racing and she was out of breath. She watched Ursula hurry across the empty terminal, calling ahead to Beate, "Over here Beate, we're over here," her calls filling the quiet terminal with eerie echos.

Just then a figure, lean and leggy, wearing a black and white checkerboard coat, emerged, but just barely, from a shadowy corner. One arm cradled a large black handbag against her chest. The other, stretched outwards towards the sound of Ursula's voice, her fingers clasping and unclasping in quick nervous movements as if to hurriedly draw her in. They stood, at first, timidly at arms length, each one examining the face of the other. Speechless, their eyes locked and held them in their places until finally they embraced, then clung, while teary wet babbles filled the next few moments.

Barely able to make out their muffled prattle Melly wished for them to finish up so she could find a place to sit. Her legs hurt and now her back began to ache. Finally, thankfully at last her two companions broke into embarrassed giggles, unabashed nose blowing, and ended their emotional reunion. A relieved Melly picked up her baggage and trudged toward the far end of the terminal. Beate and Ursula, side by side, followed behind.

It was dusk. Daylight from the open roof was fast disappearing. A creeping darkness infused the deserted station with a queer, spookish quality. Melly seated herself between her two companions. The long wooden bench, backless on uneven legs, wobbled and swayed and gave way to sudden, jerky movements as the three settled and resettled themselves for the long night ahead.

Melly shoved her bags underneath the bench near her feet after first examining the contents to assure herself, one last time, that her family photographs, her generations old good luck Mezuza from "Goldschmidt's" and her mother's sterling carving knife and holiday Menorah were safely packed and on their way to America with her. She removed her hat, taking care to thread the two hat pins back into its crown, then balanced both hat and purse gingerly on her lap.

A jostling against her right shoulder drew her attention to Ursula making short grunting sounds while she struggled to push her huge canvas bag up the wall behind the bench, and then into a deep, recessed ledge overhead.

"Oh, I'm sorry, Melly, if I'm bumping you. It's my bag. It's too big. It won't fit under the bench like yours." Then stretching as far as she could, with one final drawn out grunt, she pushed the bag onto the ledge where it rolled to the back and out of sight.

Shivering and muttering about the dampness in the station, Ursula drew her scarf closer to her chin, buried her hands into her coat pockets and dropped onto the bench beside Melly. She sat numbly, her eyes cast downward, a posture of sadness reflecting the remnants of recent goodbyes to her family, to the only home she had ever known, and to the city she so dearly loved.

Ach, such a pity, thought Melly, to be so young and so troubled....She scooped up a mixture of dried pears and raisins, hastily crammed into her handbag the night before. Folding them into a nakpin she placed them in Ursula's lap.

"Here, Ursula, have a little something. It will make you feel better." But Ursula made, no motion toward the contents on her lap, and slumped further into her seat.

Melly turned to Beate, busily drawing a comb through her long hair, tawny and fly-away, reminding Melly, even in this fading light, of swaying autumn grasses. She knew so little about Beate; only that her short and mysterious presence in her life must have been directed by God. She could think of no explanation other than His doing..

"Danke, nein," said Beate, shaking her head, no, as she tapped away Melly's dried fruit offering. "Maybe later." Her hair made crackling snaps into the air as she combed and patted and finally swept it into one long curl, nervously positioning it first over one shoulder, and then the other.

Retrieving her comb, which clattered to the floor from shaking hands, she placed it across the crevice in her lap, and looked directly into Melly's eyes." I asked to meet you here tonight, Melly, because I have something to tell you."

"Ja?"

"Ja." She hesitated for a short moment as if reconsidering her intended words, then blurted, "I'm not ever coming back to Berlin, not ever." Her voice sounded grave and strained and trembled from her throat. "I'm going home, to Schoenbach. I'm sick with worry for my parents. I haven't heard from them since...I can't even remember, it's been so long. And now with the bombings and everything else, I don't even know if they're alive anymore."

"So you can just leave, just like that?" asked Melly slyly, the same way she had probed Inge about her secrets. "No papers, nothing, you just go, just like that?"

"And my brothers," Beate continued, "I have no news of my brothers. What is happening to them I can't even imagine." She reached into her purse, withdrew a handkerchief and patted the dampness on her forehead and upper lip. "And Goering!" she shouted before her voice fell into a whisper, "What did he say? Didn't he promise and swear we would never be bombed, that no bombs would ever fall on Berlin. He promised! Now we have bombs on our heads... the worst kind of hell."

"So," Melly persisted, her voice now registering alarm, "it's all right for you to do this?" To leave Berlin where you have been working...to leave your job and just go... no permission...nothing?"

"My job, my job," Beate, agitated and overcome with resentment, poured out her disappointment and unhappiness over her work, "I'll tell about my work. First they had me send children to be killed, then they had me send women for sterilization....They made me into a criminal. I acted against my conscience, against my religious beliefs. I betrayed my parents. I betrayed myself. I believed their lies. But no more, no more."

Beate turned in her seat and scanned the still deserted station. Turning back, she placed her hand on Melly's forearm. "I know what I am about to do is a risk, but I've made my mind up. I was given permission to take two days for myself, and I didn't tell anyone that I'm not returning....except my dear Franz, my special friend, and he would never betray me. But I had to tell him, to say goodbye, otherwise I'd disappear and he'd be frantic with worry." To Melly's questioning stare she assured, "I know my secret is safe with him, as surely as I know there is a God."

For the first time Melly noticed that Beate was pale and fidgety and casting abrupt glances about the station, to where the blind man was stretched out and snoring, then over her shoulder to the entrance doors at the far end of the terminal. Sensing Beate's nervousness, as though contagious,

251

a slow dread began creeping into Melly's thoughts. When just a few moments before she was filled with optimism and calm, now fear claimed her spirit. And in this mostly dark railroad station, in this her only chance at flight, she begged to God in silent prayer. Please *Gott,* please let it end. Her stomach began to knot, and her chest felt tight like a balloon pumped to bursting. Please, please no trouble. Not after I've come this far. Not tonight. Not tonight.

Just then Ursula reached across Melly and grasped Beate's wrist. "Come with me Beate," she said, her voice eager, urging. "I know where to go where you'll be safe."

"Go? With you? But where?"

"Away from here. I can't tell you any more about it; only that if you come with me you'll be in safe hands."

"I don't know," sighed Beate, as she leaned back against the wall, "I don't know. I want to see my parents. I must. I can't think of anything else right now." Still clutching her comb, she stuffed it back into her purse. "There, now I don't have to worry about dropping that thing again," as she snapped her bag shut. Appearing more calm than she had been all evening, she shifted towards Melly, as if sensing something amiss. "But why is Kurt not with you"? she asked softly, a tinge of fear in her voice. "Where is he?"

"Kurt is staying,"

"Staying? In Germany? You mean you wil come back for him?" Her nervous fingers began separating and stroking her hair. "*Ach,* no," she corrected herself. "What am I saying. That will not be possible. You must mean that you will send for him later on, when you are settled in America."

"Kurt is staying." It was Melly's turn to lean back against the wall. She smoothed the front of her coat with the palms of her hands before crossing her arms across her chest. She remembered Kurt's voice, his stricken face, his pleading for her not to go. "Don't go Melly," he had begged. "Don't go. Stay here with me. You'll see, all this will change one day. If you leave, who knows if we'll find each other when this is over. Someday Inge will come back to us and it wil be the three of us again, like always. This is our home. This is where we belong, here in Germany. Here I know my enemies. Somewhere else...who knows...."

"No," she whispered aloud as though he was standing before her. Then "No!" she shouted, her voice resounding and filling the station.

She pictured him as he had been their last night together. Shrunk, ashen, he sat in his familiar way: legs crossed, body pitched forward, a lit cigarette between his fingers. She remembered how he had held her face in his hands...and the look in his eyes, piercing and filled with agony. "Haven't I been a good husband, and father to Inge? Hasn't our life been good, more than good?"

She remembered that she had pulled back and stood over him. "Come with me, Kurt," she sobbed. "You can come with me right now. I have papers for you, everything. It's not good here anymore. They can come back for you any day, any minute. Why can't you believe that, know that?"

"Know? I'll tell you what I know!" his voice rose in anger. I know that I am a war hero. I know that the government promised to take care of its heroes. I know that I was released from Buchenwald because of that promise. And I know that no harm will come to me because I am a war hero. Why can't you believe that!"

"Because it's a lie! It's all lies!" She shouted back. For a brief moment she was on the verge of explaining Beate's intervention in his release, but then she remembered her vow to Beate, her promise not to reveal her involvement. She held back, said nothing. It wouldn't matter anyway.

He would not believe anything she told him, only what he wanted to believe..

Now, sitting on a bench in the Berlin Station, Melly was unaware that her knuckles were rubbing her eyes, or that she was smearing their salty wetness against her cheeks. She she fought back the impulse to give way and scream aloud one last time, YOU MUST COME WITH ME!

A scampering from some indeterminate place, like the noise of animal, caught Melly's attention. A sheet of news-paper propelled by a draft of air skimmed across the floor near her feet, and Melly emerged from her memories.

"It's a long story, Beate," she said shakily. "Right now the way I feel, the way I am, I can't talk about it, except to say that as much as Kurt loves me, he loves Germany more. It's that simple."

For the next few moments, the station was still. Then in one sudden, swift motion Beate twisted in her seat toward the direction of the entranceway. "Oh God, oh God" she said as she clutched Melly's arm. Her voice was strained, choking. "There he is. He just came in. You see, way down there near the doors. "Oh God."

Melly spun in her seat and peered down the length of the station. She could see, but just barely, a man's form in a uniform of some kind. "He's probably only a soldier," she whispered hoarsely even though every instinct she pos-sessed told her otherwise.

"No!" Beate protested, fear and panic rising in her voice. "I can see he's SS....Gestapo. Oh my God, Melly, it must have been Franz...no one else knew anything. Franz reported me. He swore to protect me...oh God...that SS man is looking for me and he knows where I am going...I have to hide, Melly, someplace...oh God, what should I do, oh God."

"Shush," murmured Melly. "Shush. Maybe he'll just look fast around and leave." Suddenly the bench wobbled and vibrated and she heard tip-toeing steps on the floor. She glanced sideways in time to see Ursula inch backward and wedge herself into a dark corner between the wall and the bench.

"My papers are false papers." Ursula's whisperings were low pitched, her tone, desperate. "He may want to see my papers. He may suspect something...please, oh please don't let them...they'll maybe take me away...oh God."

Melly straightened, her heart feeling about to burst in her chest as she watched the stranger walk to where the blind man slept and poke him awake. No, she thought, that fellow is not going to leave so easily. She heard muffled sounds of conversation and then the sounds of his boots, deliberate and resonant, as he walked the perimeter of the station. Every instinct told her that they were in terrible danger. Except maybe not her. Maybe the others, but not her.

After all, she reasoned, I'm not being hunted. My papers are all in order. All I have to do is pick myself up and walk away. He would stop me, of course and ask my name and where I was going and why I was in the station when no trains were running. And I would say that I would be taking the train in the morning and then make up some story about wanting to be safe from the bombings...just in case...because the overnight shelter is close by. And then he would ask for my papers and maybe he would be so distracted that Ursula and Beate could hide someplace. But no matter because after seeing my papers he would let me go. There would be no reason to hold me. *Ja,* I could get away right this minute.

Blood rushed to her head, pulsing and pounding like a fast beating drum, walk away, walk away, walk away ,walk away, and her dead father's warnings bursting into her mind, commanding over and over for her to leave, Melly leave. And then her sister's voices urging, intermingling and pleading for her to leave, protect yourself, leave...all surging in her head like a mighty choral symphony.

All at once the voices stopped. Before her towered a black-uniformed man, silently commanding her attention with narrow, steely eyes. Slowly, Melly rose to her feet taking in his Nazi insignia and then his face. Their eyes met and held. In the next second the worst fear of all seized her. He was SS.

A slow smirk touched the corners of his mouth. He pivoted on his heel and stood before Ursula. She emerged from the shadowy corner, faced him squarely and presented a calmness that concealed her inner terror. In time to come, whenever she spoke about this incident and the courage she had shown, she said she got through it because she kept telling herself over and over that she was Helga Calmann, and that the SS had no interest in Helga.

Which proved to be the case because he then turned, faced Beate and stared down at her. She remained seated, her back straight. Beate returned his stare with a practiced, cultivated brazenness.

"You, Beate Zinmann, come with me," he ordered. He loomed over her, a dark massive presence, and extended his arm to clamp on her shoulder.

"No!" she screamed, and struck his arm away. Her composure strained to breaking, all the hidden terrors, now no longer carefully concealed, rose to the surface. She went white and shrank back against the wall. Her eyes were wild, darting from side to side. "No," she screamed over and over, "No! No! " and again struck his arm away. She was not aware that she had jumped to her feet, or that a stream of urine trickled down the inside of her thighs and calves onto her ankles and shoes and into a puddle around her feet. "No! No! No!" Her screams filled the empty station with her horrors.

Melly did not know the point at which Beate's screaming ceased. All conscious thought had been driven from her mind. Never taking her eyes from the SS man's back, Melly withdrew her mother's sterling carving knife from her bag, and drove it into him. Only after he fell soaked with his blood, his choking and writhing ended, his last breath gasped and the knife removed, did Melly notice that Beate had stopped screaming.

Melly held the knife loosely from her wrist, stepped backwards, and collapsed onto the bench. Blood had spattered her coat. Soaked with sweat she felt suddenly cold. From somewhere a loud cry wailed through the air, and she realized, with a shock, that it came from her. In the thick silence that followed nothing sounded except the blind man's cane, its taps becoming fainter, then suddenly silent as he and his cane exited from the station.

When her head cleared Melly noticed that she had placed the blood smeared knife across her lap, while Ursula and Beate stood on either side of the body, shock still, staring down at it.

Despair swept over Melly. She would never be free. She thought. Never get away. Everything for which she had struggled would never be realized, all of it gone because of this one, terrible, unspeakable act.

She closed her eyes and went back over it....remembering the SS man, his smirking arrogance, his cold callous eyes, and then Beate's screams. She could not recall removing the knife from her bag. But she did remember, all too well, the details of plunging the knife and making certain it went in all the way to the hilt.

A sickness rose in her throat. She shuddered. The knife... put it away. Put it away! She wiped the blade against her blood splotched coat, slipped it back into its silver holder and returned it to her bag.

"You must help me." Melly's voice was hoarse, barely audible "You must help me hide him. Then we go on."

"Hide him? Hide him?" Beate's voice was shrill, rising to hysteria. "Where, where can we hide him?"

"Shush, sha sha" said Melly. "We must keep calm so we can think. I don't know yet where to put this fellow....maybe under the station someplace, or maybe where coal is kept to bury him under. But we got to do it soon or...."

All at once Ursula looked up towards the ledge where her bag was stowed. "Someone, help me get my bag down. I have some blueprints and plans for government buildings in there, maybe even for this station."

She climbed onto the bench and tried scaling the wall. "It's no use. I can't reach it. It's too far back."

"Here, let me try. I'm taller," said Beate. Standing on tip-toe she stretched until her fingers touched the corner of the bag. "I have it, I have it," she whispered excitedly to Melly, who stood just below the ledge ready to catch the bag on its way down.

Ursula went through the dumped out contents, but returned one rejected document after the other to the bag. "No, there's nothing here." At first her voice was flat, then panic. "Nothing! Oh my God Melly, what are we going to do?"

They stood over the dead man and stared into each other's terror stricken faces. Then, in one shared telepathic thought, three pairs of eyes turned upward to the ledge that had held Ursula's bag.

"Ach du lieber" said Melly, "I know what to do". Excitement rose in her voice, as she covered the dead man with her coat. "Help me, quick, quick. We roll him up in this and hide him way in the back. He won't be found up there.... for a long time. We'll be far away by then. Safe."

"We'll never get away with it, Melly, never." Ursula's high pitched sobs caught in her throat. She could barely speak as she pointed to the floor. "There's blood here...and here... and over there."

"Never mind, never mind, that's nothing. It's not much," said Melly. We wipe it up good, the best we can. No one will see that it's blood. They'll think a spilled thermos, or an accident happened in someone's pants. Come, *schnell, hurry,* let's do it!"

Patchy, moving clouds cast dappled patterns of sun and grey around the terminal, as the first morning light came through the open roof. Early travelers began filling the terminal forming groups, becoming crowds, then throngs. Three woman emerged from their places, separated, and one by one mingled with the rapidly growing multitudes. Before parting they had said their goodbyes and their promises to find each other when the war ended.

"You know where I'll be...in New York City...always in New York City living with Kurt's sister, Hanchen, in the beginning, anyway.. But you will be able to find me easy. After all, how many Wallersteins can there be in New York City. You must both swear!"

"I swear," promised Beate and Ursula in unison.

"Well," said Beate, unsure of where to go, "I can't go home now. I'll get picked up for sure. That fellow we're leaving up there on the ledge, wasn't the only one looking for me. I'm certain of that." Then, as though a light had been turned on she said, "I know, I'm going underground. I know how to find my sister Erika, in the underground." Excitement mingled with relief shone in her face. "But first I have to get rid of this checkerboard coat. I can be seen in it from a mile away." She quickly removed he coat, then not knowing where to hide it, turned it inside out where only the grey lining showed, and put it back on her body. She smiled, a victorious smile.

Ursula consumed by her own worries, barely heard anything after making the promise to Melly. She thought, I have to talk to the Pastor as soon as I arrive. Maybe through the Church he can send me to England...get some work there,.. a maid...., anything at all...start a new life for myself....because what if the house is destroyed from bombs....what will be there to come home to afterwards....and what if I have to spend the rest of my life living in the country....what if...what if......

Three blocks from the station the blind man, who had tapped his way into the station, and that same night, out of the station back into the street, awoke from the dark entranceway of a shut down tavern where he had spent the night. "My God... my God," he muttered. He picked up his cane and made his way along the street, tapping from side to side. The familiar barking of a neighbor's dog, and the sound of a canopy being cranked open, signaled the opening of the café where he went every morning for coffee. He took his usual seat, at his usual table and was brought his usual morning fare. *"Gott in Himmel,"* he whispered to God in heaven. He sipped his coffee. He shook his head from side to side. *"Gott in Himmel.*

+++++++

EPILOGUE

At war's end, Melly was settled into a small apartment in New York City's upper west side. She worked cleaning houses and offices and sometimes cooked for private households. She and Kurt had corresponded regularly until 1942 when his letters stopped. Years later she learned that Kurt had been deported to Auschwitz, an extermination camp in Poland, where he, along with hundreds of thousands, was gassed to death.

In 1946 Inge, reunited with Melly in New York City, completed High School and in 1955, at age 23, she married. She had one child, a girl she named Mellyanne in memory of her mother; Melly, died four months before the birth.

Beate connected with her sister Erika and went underground. She joined in rescuing children in peril by moving them to France where they were hidden by nuns. She married an American G.I., came to the United States as a war bride and established a home in upstate New York, near her husband's work and family. Once each year she returned to Schoenbach, to her parents, who were debilitated from years of hunger and from sorrow over the loss of their sons, all of whom died as soldiers. Beate went one last time to Germany to bury her parents in the church's cemetery, and to say a final goodbye to the house where she was born. She never saw Franz again.

Franz, immediately after Beate said "goodbye," reported her to his superiors, knowing that if he did not, he would be suspected of conspiracy once her desertion was discovered. In 1940, two years after Germany invaded Austria, Franz was dispatched to Vienna with the mission to create an extension of the Hitler Youth Program. But, tormented by unrelenting guilt over his betrayal of Beate, he drank heavily, brawled constantly, and became less and less able to function at his work. His mission failed. Upon removal from his duties and stripped of his title, Franz Westermeyer put a gun to his head and ended his life.

At war's end, in the summer 1945, Ursula returned to the house in Berlin, partially in ruins, totally uninhabitable. But there, in her room behind the remains of the kitchen, Frau Miller, true to her promise, waited for her family to return.

After several months of waiting for her parents, the possibility of Ilse and Simon returning to Berlin became unlikely. When all hope died, Frau Miller and Ursula separated: Frau Miller to her sister's family, Ursula to Elmshorn to make her life with, and remain connected to her church community. She taught Sunday School, headed the Ladies Circle for Charitable Works, and immersed herself in bible studies and theological texts. At the same time, frantic to find her parents she wrote constantly to the Red Cross.

Finally, after almost two years, Ilse and Simon were located. They were living in Israel after four years of forced labor in Theresienstadt, a concentration camp in Czechoslovakia, and months afterward in a Displaced Persons Camp. Ursula visited them several times a year in Tel Aviv, where they eventually settled and remained for the rest of their lives.

But Ursula was not successful at locating Peter. After years with no word or information regarding his whereabouts, she presumed that he did not survive Germany's invasion of Holland in 1940.

But Peter did survive. Soon after the invasion, he was arrested one morning in Amsterdam as he was leaving his apartment. He, along with thousands of Dutch citizens, was deported to Lubeck, Germany into forced labor. At war's end, he returned to Hamburg and discovered his parents living behind a pile of rubble, once the apartment building they had called home. The next years were devoted to his parents helping them secure housing, food and medical attention. His search for Ursula ended even before it started with the construction of the Berlin Wall, which situated the Steinhardt home in the Soviet sector of Berlin. It was rumored that once inside the Russian zone, visitors were detained from returning to the American side, sometimes for months. Peter chose not to take that risk.

He lived out his life in Hamburg. At first working for the Americans in rebuilding the city, then as a school teacher. By arrangement he married Alma Winkler, a war widow. They had one child, a son he named Simon.

Made in United States
North Haven, CT
29 April 2022

18739946R00150